TWO MEN, BOTH WITNESSES TO A SHADOW WAR. ONLY ONE COULD ESCAPE ITS BRUTAL CONSEQUENCES. THE OTHER WOULD HAVE TO SURVIVE THEM.

Sydney Schanberg and Dith Pran. One was a seasoned American reporter who made his living covering other nations' nightmares. The other was a courageous Cambodian who tried to convey his people's agony in the language of the daily headlines.

As journalists covering America's secret war in Southeast Asia, they were partners. As two men sharing common danger, they were friends. But when Cambodia fell to the fanatical Khmer Rouge, Schanberg was able to escape while Dith Pran was trapped in a nation that had turned into a slaughterhouse.

It would take all Schanberg's efforts to bring Dith Pran's story—and Cambodia's—to the world. It would take all Dith Pran's valor and endurance to escape to tell it.

THE KILLING FIELDS

Christopher Hudson

A DELL BOOK

Published by
Dell Publishing Co., Inc.
1 Dag Hammarskjold Plaza
New York, New York 10017

Dell ® TM 681510, Dell Publishing Co., Inc.

ISBN: 0-440-14459-0

Printed in the United States of America

First printing—October 1984

For Rowley

Christopher Hudson was educated at King's School Canterbury and Cambridge where he gained a double first in English. He was also the editor of *Granta*. After Cambridge, he was a commissioning editor at Faber and Faber for two years, working on poetry and drama. In 1971, he became Literary Editor of the *Spectator*, also writing a film column.

In 1973 he turned free-lance, writing with the director Stuart Cooper the screenplay for *Overlord*, a film about the D-Day landings, which won a Silver Bear Award at the 1975 Berlin Film Festival and the *Evening News* Special Award in 1976. *Overlord* was published by Panther in 1975.

For the next two years, under a Harkness Fellowship, Christopher Hudson traveled throughout the U.S. and studied under Saul Bellow at the University of Chicago. His research thesis was on ideas of Paradise in Western Civilization, and his completed study will be published by Constable. On his return to the U.K. in 1977, he wrote editorials and reviews for the London *Standard*, for which he now edits the Books Pages. His first novel, *The Final Act*, was published in 1980 by Michael Joseph in the U.K. and Holt, Rinehart and Winston in the U.S. In 1982, his second novel, *Insider Out*, was published and acclaimed by Ted Allbeury as "A first-class spy thriller belonging in the top league."

Christopher Hudson lives in Bayswater, London, with his wife, the writer Kirsty McLeod, and their baby son.

This book is inspired by the true story of Sydney Schanberg and Dith Pran at the time of the collapse of the Cambodian Government in 1975 and the subsequent ordeal of Dith Pran under the brutal Khmer Rouge regime. To convey the atmosphere of the time, numerous incidents have been embellished or invented, and many fictitious characters have been introduced. It is not intended that these fictitious characters should be identified with any actual persons living or dead, or that all incidents depicted herein should be regarded as having actually occurred.

Author's Note

"This is a story of war and friendship, of the anguish of a ruined country and of one man's will to live." With these words, the American journalist Sydney Schanberg began one of the most extraordinary documents to have come out of the war in Indochina.

It opened in war-torn Cambodia in August 1973. Since as long ago as 1968, there had been thousands of American B-52 bombing raids over Cambodian territory—an attempt to dislodge the Vietcong who had established forward bases in the jungle from which to strike across the border at Saigon. Despite blanket bombing and the replacement of Prince Sihanouk by the U.S.-backed government of Marshal Lon Nol, the Communists were making headway. Aided by North Vietnamese troops, the fanatical Khmer Rouge had beaten back Lon Nol's army to the Mekong River.

It was at this stage of the war that Sydney Schanberg persuaded the foreign desk of his newspaper, *The New York Times,* to take on an official stringer—his Cambodian assistant, Dith Pran. What happened to Schanberg and Pran when the Khmer Rouge rebels overran the Cambodian capital Phnom Penh and instituted a reign of terror, was the true story Schanberg had to tell. Published in 1980, in *The New York Times Magazine,* it became the basis of David Puttnam's film, *The Killing Fields,* directed by Roland Joffé. This book is inspired by Schanberg's document and by Bruce Robinson's screenplay for the film.

My chief debts, naturally, are to Bruce Robinson and Sydney Schanberg. I should also like to acknowledge the help given me by John A. Nicol, who generously allowed me to use his collection of books and newspaper articles on Kampuchea, and by William Shawcross, author of *Sideshow,* the best book that will ever be written on the war in Cambodia, who kindly read the manuscript and proffered suggestions.

PART ONE

Cambodia, Summer 1973

A sudden crack. Sydney Schanberg flinched, like the other newsmen at the table. Strung between the sugar palms, one of the colored bulbs had burst. A velvet-footed waiter knelt and picked a sliver of red from the grass.

It was a hot, fragrant night. The tables around the Hotel Phnom pool were crowded. An embassy diplomat was on his fifth double whiskey at the next table, slurring his words in front of two high-ranking Cambodians who smiled and nodded and sipped pineapple juice. Farther along, a French banker finished a story that brought ripples of laughter from two of Madame Butterfly's hookers, dressed like schoolgirls in white blouses and long, narrow skirts of black silk.

Schanberg glanced up again at the hotel window. The curtains were still drawn. He forced his attention back to his own table where Barry Morgan was wiping flecks of beer off his three-day beard.

"*Plus ça change, plus c'est la* same bloody thing." Years as a Fleet Street journalist hadn't softened Morgan's South African twang. "I've been coming here since the summer of sixty-nine—that's four years—and each bloody time the band is playing 'Moon River,' the beer tastes of warm piss, and the chef at the Café de Paris is on his bloody *vacances*."

"There's a war on," said Al Rockoff. "Or so I'm told." Schanberg grinned. One of the best war photographers in the business, Al sat huddled behind dark glasses, gazing at the colored lights flickering tracer bullets across the hotel swimming pool. "There's a war on," he muttered again.

"There's a war on." Morgan imitated. "So what do we all do? We chase rumors nobody confirms about battles none of us can get to. That's what we do. Right, Des?"

"What do you want? A Khmer Rouge press coach?" The fourth pressman at the table, Desmond France, had a bald domed head and distinguished features on which perched a small, unconvincing mustache. He was trying to attract the waiter's attention and spoke without turning around. "Like Nixon said about the illegal bombings in sixty-nine, there are times when, to mislead the enemy, you can't afford to level with your friends."

Schanberg didn't react to the provocation. He disliked Desmond France. A Fleet Street colleague of Morgan's, he talked GI slang in a drawling English voice. He was the kind of journalist the U.S. authorities approved of, the kind that grows plump on spoon-feeding. They were in the majority out here, newsmen who toed the Pentagon line. It was damned hard getting at the truth about this war; harder still to write it and face the constant official hostility. If he,

Schanberg, wasn't the local bureau chief of *The New York Times*, they'd have found a reason for expelling him months ago. He lit a cigarette and glanced up at the curtained window.

"Mind if I join you?"

The speaker, Jon Swain, was a lanky, casually elegant figure, younger than the rest of them, with a long, pale, intelligent face and a mess of blond hair which he brushed back now in faint embarrassment.

"Jon, what are you doing here?" Schanberg clapped his hands, and this time the waiter paid attention. "I thought you were in Saigon?"

"Had a problem with a plane." He looked around with a wry smile. "Nice to see all the regulars. Barry. Desmond."

"The day Desmond leaves the pool side," declared Schanberg, "the staff will go into shock."

"Cut it out, Schanberg. It's been a very difficult day."

There was an uncomfortable silence. Swain sat down. "What's been happening?" he asked. "Sydney, you look like you haven't slept in weeks."

"The usual stuff. You heard about our ambassador?"

"Paul Kirby? Is he still chief of mission?"

"Not much longer." Schanberg tapped ash on the grass. "He's been ousted. Seems Kissinger wasn't getting the right kind of gung-ho reports about the inspiring achievements of Marshal Lon Nol and his brilliant troops. So he's recalling him and appointing him to some advisory job stateside."

"Who takes over?"

"Bob Wilbur, his deputy, Henry's favorite son. Six

feet eight inches of hostility toward anyone seen carrying a notebook or a camera.'' Schanberg mimicked Wilbur's patrician accents: ''Gentlemen, my task is to keep this show on the road and out of the press. Good day.''

Desmond France cut in. ''Sour grapes, Schanberg. Just because Wilbur treats *The New York Times* like any other journal. I've found him most obliging.''

Al Rockoff gave a wheezing laugh. ''There speaks one of the world's great journalists.''

''That's right.'' Schanberg glanced up at the blank window and took out his frustration on France instead. ''Remember reading one of their editorials once. Someone decides to get frank about Northern Ireland . . .''

Jon Swain was grinning. Even Rockoff had the beginnings of a leer. ''. . . By the end of it, I'm searching through Pravda in the hope of a little less bias!''

Desmond France got up without a word and stalked away. Barry Morgan reddened with anger and pointed a finger across the table. ''The problem with you, Schanberg, is you've got an inflated opinion of yourself and your newspaper. It's about time you woke up to the fact that this entire war isn't an exclusive for *The New York Times*, run for your sole benefit.''

Swain and the others waited expectantly. New Yorkers tend to win a shouting match; it's what passes for polite conversation in Manhattan. But Schanberg seemed oddly distracted. He fell silent and looked into his glass. Morgan smiled. He threw a handful of notes on the table and strolled off to greet the drunken diplomat, whose two Cambodian guests had departed.

The band had moved on into an uncertain rendition of

"Tie a Yellow Ribbon Round the Old Oak Tree." A huge, moon-faced U.S. Army colonel stood up and began a lurching dance, dangerously near the swimming pool, with a distinctive Cambodian girl, bearhugging her to his beer belly.

"I think another drink, don't you?" said Swain awkwardly.

Schanberg shook his head. He had barely heard Morgan's last remark. He left the rest of his whiskey and got to his feet, fishing in his pockets for the money. Al Rockoff frowned. He took off his dark glasses to reveal innocent, pale blue eyes and an expression that was no longer sinister but trusting and good-natured.

"You're not upset about that, are you, Syd? You could assassinate that fucker any day of the week. As for Desmond, he's only bald because the embassy staff has patted his head so often."

Schanberg smiled. "I'll buy you a drink for that, Al," he said, adding some notes to the ones Barry Morgan had left. He walked away with his back to them and looked up again, discreetly, just to make sure. The curtain had been drawn back. A dim room light was flashing on and off, on and off. As he hurried through the garden doors of the Hotel Phnom, he checked his watch. Just past midnight. There probably wasn't that much time.

What stopped him in his tracks was the sight of the tall, bony, sad-faced man in a dinner jacket standing at the hotel reception desk—a diplomat from the embassy, James Lincoln.

"James . . ."

"I can't talk to you."

"You can."

17

Lincoln had turned tail the moment he saw the newsman approaching. Schanberg caught up with him at the hotel entrance and drew him into the shadows. "You know what I'm going to ask you. Neak Luong."

"I've got nothing to give you."

"Yes, you have. The entire area closed down for strategic reasons? Back here, the Preah Keth Mealea Hospital out of bounds to reporters?"

Lincoln refused to meet his eyes. "The embassy's jittery as hell. You want information? Get it from our press officer."

Schanberg clamped his arm around Lincoln's shoulder. His smile was menacing.

"Let's not start insulting each other," he suggested mildly.

"Okay." Lincoln looked around and lowered his voice. "This is off the record. There was a computer malfunction at the base. It put out a junk set of coordinates—and there happens to be a B-52 homing beacon right in the middle of Neak Luong."

"How many?"

"You'll be briefed tomorrow. We're estimating around fifty-five military, and probably go for thirty-five civilians."

"*How many?*"

"Okay. I hear two hundred. Don't quote me. Just tell me one thing. Who was your source on this?"

But Schanberg was halfway down the hotel steps before Lincoln had finished. Sarun's gray Mercedes was parked across the street. Dith Pran was sitting with the door open, trying hard not to look anxious. They had maybe twelve hours' start.

Pran was the source, as he was for most things. Pran

had been at Pochentong Airport that morning; he'd heard the 3700-horsepower Lycoming jets of the big Huey transport helicopters as they'd thundered down, one after the other, to the airport's off-limits military zone; he'd raced up to the balcony and seen the ambulances sprint across the tarmac and around the back of the hangars. Since then, they'd been trying to break through the smokescreen the embassy had sent up even more thickly than it did over its normal operations in the Cambodian war. Lincoln had been the first of them prepared to open his mouth. A B-52 computer error. Neak Luong closed to visitors. Schanberg could see the story right there in front of him. Jesus, he could see it over three columns with a picture if they could patch it together. He banged on the car roof. "Well?"

"Nobody gets through on the roads," announced Pran from the front seat. "No planes taking any passengers, even Khmers. I try patrol boats, but they won't take us."

"So what the fuck did you call me out for? Unless the Martians are kindly lending us a flying saucer."

Pran turned around. He was trying to preserve a modest nonchalance, but there was a gleam in his eyes. Schanberg knew the expression well. "Monsieur Oscar say he will take us. For one hundred fifty dollars he will take us. He is leaving the jetty at one A.M."

Schanberg frowned at his Rolex. "Sarun, let's step on it," he said.

Sarun, the driver, let out a high-pitched giggle, and the car shot forward. Out of the rear window Schanberg saw Lincoln on the steps, gazing up at the hotel roof. Maybe he was thinking of getting a B-52 homing beacon up there, above the journalists, and then praying for another computer error. Schanberg smiled. Sarun, noticing it in the mirror, nodded joyfully.

Even at midnight there was traffic on the roads—cycle drivers, trucks filled with military spares, cabs taking high-ranking Cambodian officers home to their mistresses in the big white villas on the hill. Farther south, behind the native stores and gas stations, huddled whole new town-ships of wretched shanties, built of cardboard and thatch and a few sought-after pieces of corrugated iron. The refugees had been trailing into the capital ever since 1970, when the American bombing of the borders had driven the Vietcong farther into Cambodia and taken the war to the villages. Phnom Penh had been a peaceful, spacious city of 600,000 souls in Sihanouk's day. Now it was a million and growing, with refugees from the war.

Without warning, Sarun swung left down a narrow, uneven road. It quickly engulfed them in the jungle that had always been somewhere around them and now pressed close to the sides of the car. They were in a narrow, black tunnel lined with brilliant green where the headlights dipped and swerved at the trees. Pran whispered instructions. Sarun showed his teeth and said nothing.

The trees thinned out. They emerged into a clearing of rough bamboo huts, people asleep on matting on the ground. The refugees were here, too. Sarun stopped and switched off the lights. At once, the night pressed in on them with soft, humming, rustling noises. Schanberg looked at Pran, who pointed silently. Across the clearing was the Mekong River, glinting in the moonlight.

Schanberg and Pran got out. Little boys appeared from nowhere; Sarun reversed into the jungle before they could start picking at the hubcaps. Schanberg checked his watch and ran down to the wooden landing stage. Pran followed, carrying the camera cases.

There was nothing in sight. Nothing moved on the water, except for a couple of fishing yawls nosing quietly at the quay. As Schanberg looked around, a brown hand came up from nowhere and knocked politely on the toe of his suede shoe. A candle flickered, and he saw the row-boat beneath the wooden jetty. Pran had his finger to his lips. Cambodian navy vessels could not be far away. Cautiously, he lowered himself into the boat and helped Pran down, and they swung out on a long rope to wait in the river current.

The noise, when it came, was like a very old boiler being dismantled and broken up for scrap. With a clattering and banging and groaning of steel plates, a dumpy black silhouette of a freighter suddenly blocked out their sky. Hands reached down, dollars were passed up, and Schanberg and Pran were pulled on board.

Schanberg had been on this rusty old tub before, on the run up the Mekong from Saigon to Phnom Penh. He stepped over sacks and crates roped none too securely to the deck, and he made his way to the wheelhouse. Gazing through binoculars over a solid six-foot wall of sandbags stood a huge bush-bearded figure in overalls and an oil-stained baseball cap.

"Hallo, Oscar," said Schanberg without enthusiasm.

"When I tell you," rumbled the Australian, "hit the deck."

They were rounding a bend in the river. Schanberg could see nothing. When the Khmer voice came through the loud hailer from what seemed feet away, he made for the floor without waiting for Oscar's command. The voice from the patrol boat hailed them again, this time in English.

"Please identify yourself. State your identity and your destination."

This time Oscar answered without the aid of a megaphone. "*Delta Queen*," he bellowed in flat Aussie accents. "Making for Neak Luong with urgent medical supplies!" Lowering his voice, he added, "Stupid pinhead bastards. If the Khmer Rouge are on the bank, they'll blow us both to purgatory."

A searchlight played over them briefly, and the patrol boat churned on upriver. Schanberg got to his feet. "What did they tell you about Neak Luong?" he asked.

"Don't ask me. You're the reporter. I'm running up mainly sanitation equipment. Seems they've got an urgent problem with their drains."

Schanberg nodded. Leaning back against a sandbag, he felt the tension unravel from him for the first time that day. The air smelled of kerosene and something stronger. The night sky was full of shooting stars, which turned into yellow parachute flares as they sank toward the horizon. The hum of a mosquito became the drone of unseen helicopters overhead.

When he opened his eyes again, the sky was tinged gunmetal with the early dawn. Oscar hadn't stirred from his place at the wheel. Schanberg went below deck into a confusion of cardboard boxes packed with tinned fruit and crates of chickens who set up a squawking and flapping as he edged past. In a cleared space at the back, a group of dark-skinned natives squatted around an elderly Chinaman who was sitting bolt upright on a reproduction Louis Quinze

22

chair. Still half-asleep, Schanberg saw Pran among them and went over.

Pran stood up hurriedly. "I think we are in Neak Luong very soon," he announced.

"What does the Chinaman say?"

Pran looked at him. The Chinaman stared straight ahead, impassively. "He has heard there are many dead. He is going to see his family."

"How did he hear?" Schanberg scowled. "God damn, *we* only just heard."

Pran shrugged.

"Well, ask him!"

Pran bent his head. There was a muttered exchange. When he looked up, there was the hint of a smile on his face.

"Well?"

"He says, 'Dead men tell tales.' "

Schanberg left them there, among the gossiping hens, and went back to the wheelhouse. Colors had seeped into the landscape: violent green for the jungle undergrowth, chocolate for the water buffalo who stood up to his knees in the dirty Mekong and jutted his head as they went by.

Oscar beckoned Schanberg over and pointed to a column of smoke rising from the jungle on their left. "A village on fire. The Khmer Rouge burn everything. It scares the shit out of people in the next village, takes the fight out of them." He half-turned; Schanberg saw the foot-long knife in the belt of his dungarees. "Don't worry. It's going north that's tricky. The commies have got the Mekong less than twenty kilometers from Phnom Penh. All I hope is, they don't win too quick. I got taken short like that in Bangledesh." He frowned.

"What's the matter?"

"Over that clump of trees ahead. There should be the top of a pagoda. I don't see it."

Flakes of ash were beginning to float around them. The ash settled on the sandbags, on Oscar's ginger beard, and laid a gray scum on Schanberg's cotton jacket. That, and the haze of brick dust Schanberg had taken for early-morning mist, and a dry bitter smell of burning that tasted acrid on the tongue, were the way they knew they had arrived at Neak Luong.

The dust is in their throats. Pran puts away the camera and takes a notebook and pencil out of his shirt pocket. That is what he is here for. A journalist first, then a human being. The other way around is of no use to Sydney. No use at all.

He has taken many pictures, some for Sydney, some for himself. The midday sun has been getting stronger through the haze, and he has been careful to alter the exposure dial. He has pressed the shutter button on two people carrying a stretcher-load of black meat ending in a head of hair; on a bloodstained pillow crushed under the ruins of a house, its doorway, still intact, decorated with Chinese characters for good luck; on a circular iron stairway spiraling up to nowhere in the middle of a wasteland of rubble; on a small boy being pried from the wreckage of his home and the blood-soaked fruit he'd been eating when his head was crushed; and on a large bomb crater with a bus sunk nose first in it, its side opened up like a tuna-fish can by the explosion. On Sydney's instruction he went up close on that one to snap a gaping window, its edges matted with flies and caked with dried blood.

Now Pran has his notebook out. This is a scoop. It is an important exclusive. It's not his fault if the people standing around watching him don't understand that. "Devastation," he writes in a neat hand. "Power lines down. Many dead, many wounded. Standing in the Place National, there is nothing but ruins." This is not right. What is Sydney's word? *Waffle*. But Sydney has not taken him on as his official stringer this very month, in order he should waffle. He starts again. "Survivors estimate attack came yesterday at dawn, from B-52 bomber. From size of bomb craters we estimate five-hundred pound bombs, dropped down the main street as far as to the Mekong. American B-52 carries thirty tons of bombs."

He looks at Schanberg. A man has grabbed the hem of his jacket and is explaining in broken English, with great, excited sweeps of his arm, how the plane was so high nobody could see it, how people and houses had flown through the air and landed on the other side of the street, how the earth had quaked at the impact of this mighty weapon and had brought down houses many meters away, which were not constructed according to the proper methods that had been handed down in his family for generations. Sydney has such an intent face, so sharp and pointed even for a Westerner; he is interrupting the man, scribbling notes and barking questions, his whole body concentrated on the facts. His motto: *Nobody gets the drop on* The New York Times.

Pran sighs. A small truck has slowly navigated the shattered street and now unloads two latticed baskets of squealing pigs. He writes, "Life blossoms even at the mouth of the grave," and puts his notebook away.

*   *   *

A man of Pran's age, in his mid-thirties, was bumping toward them on a Honda motorcycle. On the back was a girl with a full mouth and enormous, dark eyes; beautiful even with her long hair tied back in a scarf, especially beautiful in this scene of desolation. The man shouted across at them. Pran translated for Schanberg.

"He says his name is Sahn. The girl's name is Rosa. They were going to be married. Yes. His father was killed. Now they will wait till the end of the war."

Schanberg nodded. "Has anyone told them why it happened?"

Pran put the question back. This time it was the girl who answered, in a high, tearful voice, not looking at them.

"It doesn't matter," she says. "Nobody cares why. Only when. Only when the war will stop. Everybody wants the fighting to stop."

A little girl with a walleye was plucking at Pran's sleeve and waving a shiny Mercedes badge. "Buy! Buy!" she cried in a shrill voice. Sahn repeated his question.

"He wants to know, did the American Government arrest the pilot?"

There was no answer from Schanberg, who was busy searching his pockets for a few coins to give the little girl.

"They have no home to go to now. All the houses at the edge of town are destroyed. He will show us—"

"No. Not yet. Tell him we'll come later. I want to get to the hospital."

Pran translated. "There is no hospital."

"I know. The hospital's been destroyed, I know. Can he tell us where the hospital was?"

Pran relayed the question and answer. The Honda skidded away, Rosa with her head buried in Sahn's shoulder.

Schanberg started after them; Pran shouted a warning. Two Cambodian Army jeeps were jolting toward them across the Place National.

Schanberg smiled. He kept the smile on his face while he spoke to Pran. "It's all right. Let's keep it casual. We walk toward them with a big grin, and while we do it, you're going to take the film out of the camera and stick it in your socks. Casual. Keep it casual."

Pran dropped the camera bag and hastily knelt to make the transfer as the jeeps skidded to a halt. Soldiers leapt out with a clatter of boots, shouting in shrill voices. In the back of the first truck they had two prisoners, trussed behind the elbows like chickens. Hardly more than young boys, they stared with black, terrified eyes at Pran and Schanberg.

The soldiers shoved them out the back of the truck, and they lay on the muddy ground kicking feebly, their eyes still fixed upon the newsmen. Schanberg raised his camera and lowered it again. The soldiers spat at the two youths and taunted them, goaded on by two young girl soldiers in the second jeep, who were giggling behind their hands.

Pran translated. "They say they kill many villagers . . . execute old people with bayonets . . . and pregnant women . . . also kill two men with rags, soaked in gasoline . . . pushed down their throats and made on fire."

One of the girl soldiers was listening to Elton John's "Rocket Man" on a Japanese transistor radio. The two Khmer Rouge boys in the mud looked innocent of any crime more shocking than breaking a mother's heart. A Cambodian officer pushed into the circle of soldiers and gave an order. To renewed taunts and curses, the two prisoners were dragged in front of a refrigerator, which stood upright and unscathed, on a mattress in the ruins of a flattened house. Pran whispered to Schanberg again, his voice hoarse.

"They are going . . . they say that when they are dead, they are going to cut them up and freeze them until they are ready to eat."

Children had gathered to watch the spectacle. The soldiers lazily checked their rifles. The little girl with the Mercedes badge scampered between their legs, looking for other shiny objects in the mud. As the rifle bolts snapped back, a tear formed in the younger prisoner's eye and rolled down his cheek. He lowered his head in shame.

It was too much for Schanberg to resist. Scrambling to a better vantage point, he raised his camera and focused on the executioners. The Cambodian officer, smartly dressed in khaki trousers and an American-issue flak jacket, gave a howl of rage. He had been prepared to stage the execution in front of the whole of Neak Luong to advertise the peril of associating with the KR. The camera lens of a foreign journalist was a different proposition. Angrily, he waved the firing squad to wait, and sent two soldiers to fetch Pran and Schanberg over at the point of their guns.

The two newsmen raised their hands. Schanberg spoke out of the side of his mouth. "Keep smiling. Ask what we can do to help him."

Pran cleared his throat and spoke to the officer, his voice a pitch higher than usual. The Cambodian officer gave a terse reply and nodded to the soldiers who lowered their M-16s. Pran dropped his hands, smiling in relief. "He says we are under arrest."

"What? Why?"

"I'm sorry, Sydney."

Before Schanberg could protest, they were herded away down the street. Behind them, they heard the snap of rifle bolts and a fusillade of shots. Neither man looked back. The little girl, who had been dogging their steps, suddenly ran forward and pushed the Mercedes badge into Pran's hand, closing his fingers over it. Then she scampered off down the mangled street, skipping over the broken drains, the shattered pots, and the unidentifiable scraps of what yesterday might have been living flesh.

It must have been a schoolhouse before it was commandeered by the Army. A scattering of exercise books lay on the floor in between the ammunition boxes. In one, a childish hand had penciled in round, careful letters *"J'aime, tu aimes, il aime, nous aimons, vous aimez, ils aiment."* A picture of Lon Nol smiling his fat smile had been stuck on the wall over a colored map of Indochina. Dirty muslin was pinned up over the windows where the bombing had blown the glass in. Shards of glass had been swept casually under a desk, along with the usual littering of shell cases.

Schanberg, groggy with tiredness and Nytol, raised himself on the mattress in the corner and scratched the bristle on his cheek. His legs ached; his cotton jacket was limed with chicken shit from the hens who had been dislodged from the mattress to make room for him. The dawn light filtering through the muslin meant that he must have let the whole night slip past his consciousness. His story could have been on the New York presses by now. He punched his fist on the mattress and swore aloud.

Their guard, who had been sitting dozing on top of a stack of ammunition cases, woke with a start. His rifle

29

clattered to the floor, and he went after it in a panic as hens flew in all directions. A skinny figure dressed in green U.S. Army surplus several sizes too big for him, he hugged his gun to him as if it were the only covering he had. Schanberg rubbed his aching eyes and groaned.

"Listen, you asshole. I'm a United States citizen. I'm on your side, okay? I'm here to tell people about the bombs, okay? About the bombing?" He glanced at Pran, who was squatting quietly in the shadows. "Tell him, Pran. For fuck's sake. We've got to get out of here."

Pran shook his head but translated, anyway. The soldier's only response was to wave his rifle at them like a watering can. Schanberg got to his feet and stomped to the window.

Their prison was close to the pagoda Oscar Dougal had missed seeing from the *Delta Queen*. The reason was clear enough. The shock waves from the bomb load had toppled its bulbous spire and shattered it on the ground. Nearby, a row of stilt houses that had looked across a wide fish market to the quayside had collapsed in a tangle of splintered wood and bamboo. Women were poking in the wreckage, watched by a saffron-robed Buddhist monk who occasionally prodded at the ruins with his black umbrella.

Pran joined him at the window. Schanberg felt a stab of embarrassment and anger. "This is what they meant in the briefings," he said. "The one about our bombs falling in near-uninhabited areas, causing minimum loss of life to civilians but inflicting substantial damage on enemy positions. This is what it means."

Pran turned away silently. The anger Schanberg was feeling found its escape in furious exasperation at his assistant's politeness. Shit, it was like trying to explain natural human emotions of aggression and hatred to a child who didn't understand. He wanted Pran to shout at him or make some bitter, sarcastic remark. Saying nothing made Schanberg feel guiltier than before, and lonelier. If Cambodia had been defending the U.S. and had accidentally bombed Buffalo flat, by Christ, he'd have had something to say about it.

They were footsteps on the stairs outside. About time, too. But when the door opened, it wasn't the officer Schanberg had been expecting. A little boy in an outsize helmet walked in, holding two bowls of noodles. He couldn't have been more than thirteen, but a couple of hand grenades dangled from his Army belt; he was puffing a cigarette and squinting as the smoke got in his eyes.

He dumped the two bowls of noodles on the desk and sat next to them, his bare feet dangling some inches from the floor. Schanberg let some of his feelings out. "How much longer are they gonna keep us here? Go on. Tell him I demand to see an officer. I *demand* to see an officer."

The soldier clutched at his gun. Schanberg shrugged; he scowled at Pran. "Go ahead, eat," he ordered, gesturing at the food. "Eat! Eat!"

Pran shook his head. His eyes were wide with fear. "I'm worried, Sydney," he said.

"Why?"

"I'm the guy who brought you here. They can accuse me. They can arrest me—"

"How can they arrest you? You're already arrested. Eat."

The schoolroom door opened again, and another soldier appeared, holding the M-16 as if he knew how to use it. Gratefully, the night guard stumbled down from the ammo crates and headed off for a sleep. Schanberg shouted.

"Hey, you! Pran, tell him I need some cigarettes and a piss."

Pran was muttering. "They phone Phnom Penh about me."

"Will you tell him I need a piss."

Pran translated. "He says, no piss."

"What does he mean, no piss? A piss is a piss. I demand a piss."

Pran translated again. "He says, piss out of window. Americans are used to pissing from a height."

"What is he? A fucking comedian? There are *people* out there." Schanberg fumbled at a packet of the local Bastos cigarettes, found it empty, and hurled it down among the shellcases. "I've had enough of this bullshit! I'm getting out of here. I've got a story to get to New York."

He made for the door, pushing aside the guard. Pran froze in horror.

"Don't leave me, Sydney!"

A bolt snapped back on a rifle. There was another soldier at the foot of the stairs. His gun was aimed; his finger was on the trigger. Schanberg's hands flew up. Slowly he turned. "I'm not going to leave you, Pran," he said.

The hours passed. Schanberg paced between the mattress and the window. Outside, more people had gathered to scrabble in the ruins. A couple of hospital workers had managed to lift away a sheet of corrugated iron. Schanberg averted his eyes from what lay under it. Directly below the window, a refugee family was sitting in a bullock cart. The man and his wife had square, brown, peasant faces, lined with hunger and tiredness. The man held the reins in one hand and with the other kept rubbing his eyes as though they were infected. His wife was twisting and tugging at strands of her dusty black hair but continued staring calmly in front of her as if she couldn't feel the pain. Their little daughter sat in the back, in a jumble of cooking pots, blankets, a sack of grain, a heap of clothes wrapped inside a rolled-up mattress.

Wedged between a mattock and a hoe was a shiny transistor radio. What use had it ever been to them? It could not have given them any warning of the B-52 bombing raids. It would not have reported the successes of the Khmer Rouge, advancing slowly across the country like an acid destroying what it could not transform. Nor was it powerful enough to pick up the speeches of President Nixon in Washington D.C., reminding people in bullock carts everywhere that small nations were finding themselves under attack, and that if, when the chips were down, they couldn't control their own destiny, the United States of America would step in and save them from "the forces of totalitarianism and anarchy, which threatened free nations and free institutions throughout the world." No. If the radio told them anything, it was that in Phnom Penh, to which they were surely heading in the morning, the weather was hot and sticky with the chance of a little thunder later on.

"Mister!"

It was the small boy with the hand grenades. Swinging his legs, he grinned shyly at Schanberg and babbled in Khmer.

"What's he say?"

Pran translated, smiling. "He says he is twelve. And he likes America."

"He does? What does he like about it?"

This time the boy plucked up courage. "Cars," he said

in English after a long pause. "America very good car. *Everybody everywhere* got good car."

"Where'd he learn his English?"

"American adviser with his unit . . . teached him," translated Pran. "He asks what car you drive in America."

Schanberg thought of the clogged canyons of Manhattan. "I don't have a car. Just the Mercedes."

The boy's face lit up. He wiped his arm across his nose and grinned. "Mercedes. Good one. Very good one."

Schanberg studied the boy. He was too small to hold an M-16. Perhaps that was why he'd been given hand grenades instead. "Pran, ask him why he has no boots."

Pran spoke, listened, translated. "They have no shoes because they have no pay. They have no pay because the generals need houses. . . ."

The new guard shut him up with a few terse words in Khmer. The boy got up to leave, bowing politely to Schanberg as he did so. On an impulse, Pran held out the Mercedes badge the little girl had given him. The boy took it and, with another delighted bow, padded out of the door. The guard scowled and spoke again to Pran, who shook his head.

"He says the reason he has no shoes is not enough American money."

Schanberg shrugged and turned back to the window. The reason was too much American money, not too little—especially since January's Paris Agreement to stop bombing Vietnam had made Cambodia the only game in town. It had turned the army commanders greedy. It had bought them luxurious villas, fast cars, and a succession of mistresses—not to mention a foreign bank account and a quick flight out of the country if the going got tough.

When the flow of greenbacks sent inflation rocketing, they found other ways to keep rich. Via middlemen, they sold U.S. Army guns and mortars to the Khmer Rouge, their enemies. They created whole battalions and brigades of phantom soldiers and pocketed their pay packets; one-third of all military salaries went to soldiers who did not exist. Many commanders refused to pay even those soldiers who did exist their pitiful thirteen dollars a month and charged them for the rice they were supposed to hand out as rations.

The result was predictable. Troops who were meant to be fighting the Khmer Rouge and Vietnamese had to spend half their time scavenging in the local countryside, stealing chickens, fishing, gathering firewood. Right now, the only thing plentiful in Cambodia was American ammunition. With a limitless supply of it, nobody was too bothered about aiming straight—least of all these sons of farmers and water carriers who had never properly been trained how to use their guns.

This, of course, was the kind of thing he tried to write about and got hammered for. The embassy in Phnom Penh, backed by the Pentagon in Washington, regarded it as subversive. The United States of America was involved in a war against the creeping menace of Communism. It was bad for morale to suggest that this war was being lost from within the country as much as from without.

A stretcher was being carried down to a patrol boat tied up at the quay. Schanberg remembered the Chinaman, very upright on his antique chair, and looked round at Pran. His assistant was sitting patiently on the floor, in his white shirt and gray trousers, amid the shell cases and the chicken shit, like a bank clerk waiting for the doors to open. A very hungry bank clerk. Pran looked up and caught his eye, and Schanberg almost smiled. They were in this together. He went over to the desk and picked up the two bowls of noodles. Now that the Nytol had worn off, he realized he was as hungry as hell. He sat down beside Pran and positioned the two bowls between them.

"You know what always amazes me?" he told Pran. "The way these people just get on with their lives in the middle of so much death and destruction."

"They suffer just the same," said Pran after a pause. "The only difference, maybe, is that with Cambodians, the grief leaves the face quickly. But it goes inside and stays there for a long time."

Another hour passed, maybe two. They lay half-asleep in a coma of thick, stifling heat. Even the flies seemed drugged with it as they buzzed slowly around the food bowls. Pran had his eyes closed; Schanberg was on the verge, looking through half-closed eyes at the sun glinting on the guard's rifle barrel.

A sudden bellow in Khmer startled him awake. A loud-speaker announcement. Pran started to translate almost before he was awake.

"The Cambodian Government joins with the United States in its sympathy to the citizens of Neak Luong. . . . The United States Government will award generous compensation . . . four hundred dollars for any dead, twenty dollars for each person injured . . . forms will be distributed . . ."

The outrage of this drove sleep from Schanberg's brain. He scribbled in his notebook and made a further note to check what punishment had been handed out to the crew of the B-52. He didn't hear the noise of the helicopter until it was almost overhead.

"Huey," said Pran at the window.

Schanberg scrambled to his feet. The big-bellied American helicopter was settling gingerly in the fish market ground next to the pagoda. If there had been glass in the window, Schanberg would have smashed it with his fist. "They brought in a pool of us," he said in hoarse disbelief. Then bellowed it, furious: *"They brought in a fucking pool!"*

Over Pran's shoulder Schanberg watched the bright uniforms step down into the rubble: two Marines casually toting machine guns in case the inhabitants had something to say to them. A couple of Cambodian military chiefs followed along with General Hemans, and Major Slade of the U.S. military staff. Lincoln, whom Schanberg had last seen on the steps of the Hotel Phnom Penh; Barry Morgan; Desmond France; a couple of women reporters for American magazines; an Indian journalist . . ."Jesus, look at them," said Schanberg, smiling without humor, "hand-picked ass-lickers to do the fucking laundry."

He swung around toward the guard, so furious he could hardly focus on him. "I wanna tell you something," he shouted. "I'm walking out of here. *Now.*"

The guard shook his head. Another soldier ran up the stairs. Schanberg took out his passport and waved it in their faces, stabbing his finger at his photograph. "What are you gonna do, blow my fucking head off? We got the Marines and the general over there. And this is a U.S. passport. And this is me. And I'm walking out of here."

Pran translated urgently beside him. "He must get Officer—"

"Then get him! *Get him!*"

By the time Schanberg and Pran got down to the fish market, the scene had, in some strange way, been Americanized. Everywhere there were friendly faces. Hands were shaken. Backs were slapped. Apathy and despair had vanished in the face of a feverish energy, which infused the townspeople with the hope that things weren't as bad as they were. Some of the Marines even gave a hand with the stretchers.

On a raised dais formed spontaneously by the flattened ruins of a fisherman's home, a senior U.S. embassy official, flanked by an assortment of Cambodian army officers and Buddhist priests, was bringing his speech to a conclusion. "In war, one learns to suffer. But, I think you will agree, it is especially disheartening to receive death and destruction from your friends. All I can say to you, from the bottom of my heart—"

The rotors of a second descending Huey blew away the rest of his words, but the assembled townspeople and journalists clapped enthusiastically when they saw him hand over the microphone. Barry Morgan, meanwhile, had persuaded a stretcher party to pause in front of the pagoda. He took the picture when the hand flapping feebly on the bloodstained sheet had fallen still. "Mercy dash across a fabled landscape," he murmured, and waved the stretcher party on.

Schanberg was in no mood to join the spirit of amity. On the other side of the Mekong, a noisy firefight was in progress, by accident or design. Across the wide stretch of water, heavy-caliber guns sent out vibrations he could feel on his face. F-111s screamed overhead; Huey helicopter gunships sent orange napalm blossoming high over the distant sugar palms. Slade, in green khaki, was *compère*ing the battle for a group of journalists. Schanberg made for him, trailing Pran, who was scribbling furiously, sucking his cheeks with concentration.

"That Huey's gonna make a second run using the thick smoke as cover," Slade was saying. A beefy, pink-complexioned man, built like an American footballer, he had enormous muscular hands that could rip a prayer book in two. "Those little black rats keep comin', but every yard the KR take costs them a score of lives."

"Can't you dump a bigger load on 'em?" asked Desmond France.

Slade sighed. "I wish we could, sir," he said. "Right now the Seventh Air Force is running eighty sorties a day over Cambodia. That's twenty more than the maximum per day over Vietnam and, frankly, we've got problems of air traffic control. There are so many damn bombers up there, we can't process the air strike warnings quick enough. It's like playin' pinball with eight lights flashin' up at ya—I guess that's not a game you play much, Mr. France!"

There was a titter of laughter at this sally. Schanberg intervened, breathing heavily. "Unlicensed pinball, Slade, seeing as how both Houses voted all the bombing should stop six weeks ago."

Slade glared at him. "Don't preach to me about breaking the rules, Schanberg."

Somebody tapped Schanberg on the shoulder. It was Lincoln, smiling at him grimly. "Still in one piece, Sydney?"

"Fuck you." Schanberg strode off. It was vital to get

back to Phnom Penh before the cable office shut down for the night. A TV correspondent in spotless fatigues and snakeskin boots had just disembarked from a patrol boat with his crew and was setting up a shot that would take in the pagoda and the firefight across the Mekong. A P.A. was at his heels, reading his lines to him: "From the age-old verities of Buddhism to the high technology of modern warfare has been a tragically short step for this beautiful, doomed land."

Schanberg stopped to let a stretcher go by. It was from a barge, unloading the wounded from the battle over the water—a girl soldier with a yellow flower in her helmet, half her stomach blown away, still dazedly clutching her transceiver and moaning gently. As he looked at her in horror and pity, Lincoln caught up with him.

"You were being unfair back there, Sydney. After that Congressional vote, they gave the administration a seven-week extension on the bombing to try to force a cease-fire. You know that. *We've got to negotiate from strength*."

"What was it Tip O'Neill said? The bombing should stop because 'Cambodia is not worth one American life.' His phrase. Look around you, James. What *is* all this agony worth? What is it to America?" He shook his head. "Excuse me, I've got a story to send."

He signaled to Pran, and they made their way toward the Huey past the muslin tents of wounded. Slade saw them and bellowed across.

"You go back to the *boat*, Mr. Schanberg."

Schanberg stared at him, too choked with rage to speak. He'd been in Neak Luong for twenty-four hours getting this story in detail. Now preference was being given to a pool who had come in for twenty minutes and would go

40

out with pictures of a few bandaged casualties. Lincoln tried conciliation.

"Listen, Sydney, you're the reason for all this. If you weren't down here, I wouldn't be down here. I don't want to be down here. What good has this done?"

Something that had been waiting to explode in Schanberg all day finally hit surface. "It'll throw up a few breakfasts in New York!" he yelled. "And maybe teach a few people what this war's about!"

The light was already fading as the patrol boat with Pran and Schanberg set off upriver. Across the Mekong on the jungle horizon, a Huey spread artificial sunlight, as if there was no yesterday and no tomorrow.

PART TWO

Cambodia, Spring 1975

Al Rockoff had swapped his blue jeans for a flowered shirt and pressed trousers, for this was a respectable, nay, a distinguished, occasion. New Year's Eve in Phnom Penh, and a senior diplomat, Howard Best, was throwing a party. The last few minutes of 1974 were being celebrated with champagne and Sinatra and dancing on the lawn— ladies in long dresses being advised to steer clear of the barbecue where the spare ribs were merrily spitting hot fat onto the grass. It was a soberer version of one of Prince Sihanouk's parties in the old days, which went on until dawn unless the exhausted diplomats in their white, wine-stained court uniforms were given early leave to retire. Not that many people present could remember Sihanouk and the old days. That was a different Cambodia, a provincial place, something of a backwater in most Westerners' view.

Not any longer. The diplomats at the party could carry

themselves with a sense of importance. Cambodia, after all, had been given a key geopolitical role to play. It was possible to stand on the balcony and look across the colored lights and the garden dance floor to the Mekong and to know with a small thrill of sober pride that somewhere out in that darkness the red tide of Communism was being contained. Here on this very spot, among the fancy hats, the free world was making a stand against tyranny. A refill of champagne, and one could drink a toast to freedom.

It was a decent Krug champagne, and Al Rockoff had drunk several toasts already. If this was democracy, he went for it. Shuffling up to the buffet, he filled his plate with caviar and mayonnaise and began to circulate. In his pink paper hat and his shades, he was beginning to feel invisible. Straight ahead of him, a broad expanse of green and blue organdy was filled to bursting by a large, pink lady wearing three strings of pearls and teardrop diamonds in her fleshy ears. Beside her, Major Slade, bulging out of his dress shirt, was holding his champagne glass between two fingers and nodding sympathetically.

"That's true, Mrs. Shaw-Stewart. I mean, how do you explain Communism to a Doberman?"

"Of course. It breaks my heart," replied Mrs. Shaw-Stewart in a cut-glass English voice. "I suppose in war one has to make sacrifices. But I don't know how I look Geoffrey in the face if we have to put him to sleep. I mean, what does one say?"

"The answer is, one doesn't," said her husband in decisive tones. He was a man clearly used to making painful decisions. "If the worse comes to the worst, I'll have to have him put down quickly and efficiently. No nonsense.''

Al Rockoff was about to step forward and suggest a very good vet for poor Geoffrey when there was a rustle of medals behind him, and Howard Best joined the group with a brace of generals in tow. Although Best clearly had more serious things on his mind than party-going, fulfilling his duties, he dealt out the introductions briskly.

''General and Mrs. Green, I'd like you to meet the Mr. and Mrs. Shaw-Stewart. General—uh—Colonel Kem Kosal, who's our new minister for communications here, and Madame Kosal. Graham Slade, I think you know. And this is . . . this is—''

''Alan D. Rockoff,'' said Rockoff politely, balancing his plate on his glass and offering a hand. Slade narrowed his eyes.

With British aplomb, Mrs. Shaw-Stewart managed to speak over the heads of the diminutive Cambodian minister and his wife without appearing to exclude them from the conversation. ''You're the ones with that marvelous bougainvillaea?'' she asked Mrs. Green.

''I told them about the Sheerings,'' Slade interposed.

''Rosemary has a passion for flowers,'' said Mr. Shaw-Stewart. ''In fact, she's terribly worried about what will happen to our garden if we have to leave at short notice. There's absolutely no indication that the Khmer Rouge has any interest in horticulture or landscaping. The whole thing could be uprooted.''

The signals Rockoff was getting were unmistakable. He beat a retreat back to the buffet, through strains of Frank

Sinatra singing "My Way" and snatches of bibulous conversation.

"If things get really bad, we're moving back to Saigon."

"I wish you could have got to Angkor Wat. Marvelous architecture. Makes you see the Cambodians in a different light."

"Regrets, I've had a few, but then again, too few to mention . . ."

"On peut manger des escargots absolument frais!"

There were strawberries and cream, and profiteroles in chocolate sauce. Rockoff shoved them both on his plate and turned to the ice cream. He was topping the lot with crushed pistachio when Slade caught up with him.

"What are you doing here, Rockoff?"

"Celebrating. We must have won something."

"The host wants you to leave."

"Oh. Okay."

"Now."

"Okay." Rockoff handed his brimming plate to Slade and sauntered toward the door. Slade looked around for somewhere to dump the food. A plump, bronzed bureaucrat from an international health organization, with gold-rimmed glasses on a gold safety chain wagged his finger reproachfully.

"They'll kill you."

"What?"

"The carbohydrates. On your plate."

"Ah. Doctor Horrle, right? We've got a couple of the Red Cross team here. Might be nice for you to meet?"

Sinatra had been replaced by Elvis singing "Heartbreak Hotel," and the specially laid dance floor was crowded with couples moving slowly, cheek to cheek—Americans and Cambodians, French and Chinese, Australians and Germans, English and other English—it was extraordinary how a war could bring so many nationalities together in harmony, cement so many friendships and business acquaintances and love affairs. Desmond France was there, dancing on spindly legs with a mustard blonde; Lincoln moved fiercely smiling through the throng, wearing a Napoleonic tricorn and a luminous bow tie.

A wolf whistle from the public address system was followed by a crackling voice.

"Should auld acquaintance be forgot . . ."

Music and conversation stopped. Lincoln, standing on a small platform by the illuminated Christmas tree, smiled sheepishly. "Just testing your reflexes, ladies and gentlemen. False alarm. We are twenty-three minutes and counting."

An auld acquaintance of Rockoff's, the one with hands that could tear a prayer book in two, appeared on the steps leading down to the garden. A roundabout route took him up to the balcony where Mrs. Shaw-Stewart and General Green's wife were still sparring. At the bar, Horrle had waylaid the doctor from the Red Cross, Gordon McIntyre. An abrupt Aberdonion, McIntyre was scowling into his glass as Horrle expounded.

"What we're going to do is a cell analysis. Take a cross-section of the kids, put the whole thing through a computer, and find out scientifically at what point hunger starts having a debilitating effect on the mental and physical processes. It's the kind of thing our people like to know."

"Mr. Horrle. Dr. Horrle, I'm sorry. How long have you been in Cambodia?"

Horrle consulted his Swiss watch. "Eight hours."

"How long do you intend to stay, may I ask?"

Horrle winked at the Cambodian girl beside him, who was pretending an interest in the conversation. "That kind of depends on the planes," he said with a chuckle.

McIntyre turned away in disgust. But whiskey and anger overcame his party manners. He jabbed in the direction of Horrle's gold spectacles. "When a child with a belly bigger than yours dies in my arms, I don't need a cell analysis to tell me the reason was starvation. And when I see mothers in every street and alleyway of this city who can't afford to eat properly, and so can't produce milk, and have to wean their babies on the water they boil the family rice in, I don't need a research program to tell me aid is needed. This city is dying, my friend. You can't see it from this balcony, but you'll smell it tomorrow if the wind's in the right direction." He stopped. Horrle was nodding gravely, humoring him, probably thinking that out of all these two hundred fun-loving people it was just his luck to have run into a doom merchant. McIntyre had committed the sin of pessimism, of course, forgetting, as a Brit, that out here optimism was more than a state of mind; optimism was a philosophy.

He left the balcony bar and wandered downstairs. By the Christmas tree, he was pumped full of holes by someone pretending to shoot him.

"You're dead!" screamed a boy with a band around his teeth.

"I'll get drunk first," McIntyre promised, "then I'll fall down."

The party had reached the balloon-bursting stage. On the dance floor, couples played softball with balloons and cigarettes, greeting each loud pop with shrill sounds of glee. The space was packed, and an obese Indonesian *chanteuse*, hired for the night from the Moulin d'Or, was keening into the microphone by the tree.

> Yesterday-ii
> Love was such an easy game to play-ii
> Now I need a place to hide away-ii
> Oh, I believe in yesterday-ii . . .

Standing directly above on the balcony, Rockoff squinted thoughtfully. There was something calculated about those lyrics. Maybe she'd been infiltrated by the KR to spread black propaganda. If he tipped his reclaimed plate of ice cream on her, it might blow her cover and help the war effort.

"I thought I requested you to leave, Mr. Rockoff?"

Rockoff spun around. Redder in the face than ever, Slade was standing over him. Close enough to make it impossible for him to inflict physical violence were Thibaut the French vice-consul, General Green, and a little knot of Cambodian top brass including the minister for communications, Kem Kosal. They stopped talking and glanced around.

Rockoff shrugged. "I couldn't find the stairs to the helicopter pad," he declared. The Cambodians looked shocked. Nobody joked about evacuation. "Notice one's been installed on the roof," Rockoff went on, enjoying himself.

Slade controlled himself with an effort. "There's no helicopter pad on the roof."

Rockoff swallowed a mouthful of ice cream and looked

critically at his plate. "I thought maybe we were all going upstairs to America?"

Down below, Lincoln had edged aside the Indonesian crooner and was counting out the last seconds of 1974 over the PA.

"Four, three, two, one—twelve o'clock, everybody! It's midnight, twelve o'clock! Happy 1975!"

A flock of black and white balloons went up, and the party erupted into cheers and applause. Lincoln hugged what he could reach of the *chanteuse*. Desmond France kissed the mustard blonde and got powder on his mustache. Lincoln launched into "Auld Lang Syne," and the guests joined hands in an enormous linked chain that spilled out of the reception rooms into the garden, as far as the ashes of the barbecue . . .

> Should auld acquaintance be forgot
> And never brought to mind?

The Cambodians smiled faintly, as if pleased to discover that Westerners, too, had meaningless rituals. The chain split into two circles that expanded and contracted as they danced to the old drinking song in the tropical night. Rockoff and Slade found themselves almost face-to-face, and Slade bellowed as he was dragged backward.

"You're just a vulture, Rockoff. And I'm going to personally see that the Cambodians put you on the first plane out of this country!"

Around they went, and in and out; the Cambodians and other Asians doing their best to join in . . . .

> For auld lang syne, my dear,
> For auld lang syne . . .

Flushed faces swung toward each other again. Rockoff pushed his shades back over his nose and yelled at Slade.

"Smoking section! And a vegetarian meal!"

There was the crump and roar of a massive explosion. All the lights went out. The circles broke in confusion. Each person, alone in the darkness, waited for a long moment before the huge fireball rose slowly into the sky on the other side of the Mekong.

Another explosion, and screams, but the lights had come on, and Lincoln was appealing for calm over the PA. Nothing to worry about, ladies and gentlemen. This building is reinforced concrete through and through. Until electricity is restored, the emergency generator is providing the light—and it's keeping the champagne cold for you, too.

The Cambodian high-rankers were murmuring among themselves. The two Marines who had quickly moved to the side of the party's host accompanied him to a small study on the ground floor. A CIA staffer came in.

"Mr. Best, the insurgents appear to have begun a major assault on government positions north, east, and west of the city."

"Are they holding?"

"First reports say the North is slipping back, sir. They've come under very heavy Communist artillery and rocket fire. We think the gasometer across the river might have been an inside job."

The Ambassador thanked him bleakly and went back to the party. He listened to a wry little joke about the expense of firework displays; but it was not hard for his better-informed guests to surmise what he was thinking. The mission in Phnom Penh was under firm instructions from Dr. Kissinger: to *negotiate from strength*! But Lon Nol's troops were growing weaker, and the Communists stronger, with every month that passed. Now that the dry season offensive had begun, only the Khmer Rouge running short of ammunition, as had happened in '73 and '74, could save them.

Most of the remaining guests had congregated on the balcony, where they could get a better view of the whizbangs. Below, McIntyre had taken the microphone from Lincoln to give Burns his proper due.

> We twa hae run about the braes,
> And pou'd the gowans fine;
> But we've wandered mony a weary foot
> Sin' auld lang syne . . .

As the flares soared and the shelling grew louder, McIntyre sang all the choruses himself in a reedy bagpipe of a voice. Then another KR shell hit the gasworks, and a light brighter than any yet flared from across the Mekong. It froze the partygoers in a battery flash of whiteness, a freeze-frame silhouette.

It froze the hands of the Swiss watch on Dr. Horrle's plump wrist; it froze white balloons and white shirtfronts and white champagne in white glasses and the white hair of the blonde to whom Desmond France was murmuring a witticism about *son et lumière*, and the wide, white eyes of the Chinese waitress picking up bleached rib bones off the lawn.

> We twa hae paddled i' the burn,
> Frae mornin' sun till dine;

54

But seas between us braed hae roared
Sin' auld lang syne . . .

It lights up other things the partygoers may not have noticed: a young woman lying on the ground slashed to pieces by shrapnel, motionless except for her eyes rolling wildly until they come to rest upon her husband kneeling to comfort her; an old black Austin hit by a rocket and incinerated so quickly, the windshield has melted onto the driver's face; a baker's family huddled apparently asleep in the doorway of a bakery, except that the lower half of the baker's body has been blown away and his hands clutch the air with curled fingers like dead chicken's feet.

The score has changed, too, from McIntyre's skirling into the wail of sirens. This is New Year on the other side of Phnom Penh, in Pochentong Market. A man is running down the street; he is taking photographs. Normally, he would also be stopping to make notes in his neat, cautious hand, but a few minutes earlier he helped to extract a little girl from under a pile of bricks, and the pages of his notebook are too sticky with her blood to pry apart.

This is a matter of anxiety to Dith Pran. Tomorrow when he gets back from Bangkok, Sydney will ask him where is his firsthand report on the rocket attack on Pochentong Market. He does not want to let Sydney down. In the last two years, Sydney has introduced him to a world he hardly knew existed, a world of scoops and exclusives and deadlines, of clattering Telex machines and breakneck taxi rides. It is a litany of urgency that makes his heart pound and his blood race; it spins the earth faster under his feet, almost fast enough to leave his gods behind.

Get up and go! is the lesson Sydney Schanberg has taught him. Don't reflect, act! If you stop and look around, the world won't wait for you to catch up!

In the middle of this desolation, it is easier not to think. There is too much suffering. People are working hard not to think about it: the firemen by carrying hoses and finding a hydrant that can still provide water pressure; the ambulance men by giving first aid and running stretchers back; the victims who are busy dying or coping with shock. The only people who have time to reflect are the bereaved, the survivors. They are the ones who are weeping.

Pran asks himself what Sydney would be doing. Sydney would be calm, impassive, detached. He would not have tears in his eyes like Pran: it would prevent him getting a clear picture. Those shrieks he would identify correctly not as human shrieks but as the shriek of corrugated iron being dragged across metal. Sydney would not let a blood-sodden notebook stop him from getting out the facts.

Dith Pran stands in the carnage of Pochentong Market and wipes his eyes. He sees scores of cardboard boxes lying in the ruins of a shoe shop. He hurries over. He flings out shoes and tissue paper. On the inside of shoebox lids, he starts composing his story.

Sydney Schanberg's attention was first drawn to the New Year offensive when he saw the flight departures board at the Don Muang International Airport, Bangkok. The flight to Phnom Penh had been delayed by an hour, and the Air France plane that he'd booked on had been replaced by an Air Camboge Caravelle.

The Cambodian air hostesses claimed to know nothing, but they knew enough to take away everybody's glass and double-check the seat belts before the approach run. Out of the window Schanberg at first could see only the flat lime-green paddy fields he'd been looking at since they'd come away from the dark, forested hills and valleys of western Cambodia. Then he saw the city and the spirals of white smoke. And the plane put its nose down and dived with a terrible shudder of its engines at a forty-degree angle toward Pochentong Market.

At first Schanberg thought they'd been hit. *New York Times* Bureau Chief Killed in Plane Crash. In smaller print: Shares last two weeks of his life with wife and daughters. He closed his eyes tightly; when he opened them again, the Caravelle was down and jolting the length of a dirt-strewn runway toward the airport. Soldiers and airport workers were walling the terminal building with sandbags. The ground crew that came out to the plane had flak jackets on.

He had returned to a city under siege.

The immigration official's face was smooth and guileless. Like the faces of most educated Cambodians, including Pran, it gave away nothing with a smile.

"You have grown a beard, Mr. Schanberg," he said politely.

"It's an old photograph."

"You are a journalist? I hope you tell truth about us."

"I try to give the facts," Schanberg replied.

Outside, the heat was like a poultice. There was no sign of Pran, or of Sarun and the Mercedes: just taxis and cycles and barefooted boys under the wilting banana palms, and a plume of smoke going up into the hard blue sky. Schanberg looked at his watch impatiently. He could smell the burning; he wanted to get to work. A grinning urchin with a Martini parasol—an umbrella in the wet season, sunshade in the dry—tugged at the hem of his jacket. He nodded, scowling, and clambered into an ancient Peugeot taxi, handing the kid a few riels for his enterprise.

Traveling through the Pochentong Market, he saw the scale of the rocket attack; the smoldering houses, the shattered shop fronts. But life was already returning to normal with the speed that never failed to amaze him in the East, like skin healing instantly over a deep wound. Fruit and vegetable stalls were back in business selling bananas, melons, mangoes, sweet potatoes, Chinese cabbage, and sugar cane, laid out on trestles balanced on the rubble of arcades that yesterday had sheltered them. Pigs' heads and bundles of yellow tobacco lay side by side. An elderly Chinese woman was sitting on an up-turned Sanyo TV, stitching the hem of a girl's frock. The crowds pushed around her, bargaining for bomb-damaged goods.

Farther in, the long, brimming corridors of the shanty-towns stewed in the heat, hiding their poverty behind the rusty, sun-stained houses that fronted the highway. The first French villas appeared, discreet little yellow-ocher Toulouse bungalows once occupied by the French artisans who had laid out Phnom Penh's wide boulevards, its parks and gardens and squares, and transformed it into the pretti-est of Indochina's capital cities.

That had all gone now. Much of it was going by the time of Schanberg's first trip in 1972. The flame trees that lined the boulevards were being hacked down for firewood. The jacaranda trees in the parks, the jasmine, and the hibiscus were being cut back by soldiers in case they could harbor Communist snipers. Now, two years later, what trees were left were dying for a different reason. Their bark was being stripped by starving refugees to be boiled and eaten.

Phnom Penh was no longer beautiful. The main government buildings had sandbags and plank barricades up against their French neocolonial architecture. In the post office square, the café tables had been replaced by rolls of barbed wire. The scent of jasmine and bougainvillaea had been smothered in the exhaust of Army trucks grinding out toward the battlefields. But this was what Schanberg had come for. As someone whose closest brush with danger in the last two weeks had been a trip in a tourist sampan on the Chao Phraya River, he felt the adrenaline sparking in his veins. He paid off the cab at the Hotel Phnom, flipped a coin at a blind match-seller who deftly caught it and put it in his begging bowl, and went up to his room.

It was dark. He opened the shutters enough to let a wedge of sunlight in. A heap of bedclothes shuddered and spoke.

"Shut the fucking blinds, will ya?"

It was a voice Schanberg recognized. He threw the shutters wide. The bedclothes heaved in agony, and a face appeared, blinking, bleary-eyed, a mask of suffering trying to contain a hangover that clamored for head room. A single bloodshot eye opened and focused.

"Hey, Syd, sorry, I'm sorry, I thought you were the houseboy."

Schanberg didn't reply. He picked up his bag and strode into the bathroom. Al Rockoff made a bid to sit up and clamped a hand to his bandaged forehead. With the other, he fumbled blindly for a painkiller on the bedside table. Schanberg shouted from the bathroom.

"What's all this shit?"

"I was developing some film. Sorry, Syd. I'm sorry. But listen, Syd. I'm feeling abnormal. If you wanna shout, I'm gonna have to come back later—"

"I don't want to shout," Schanberg shouted. "I want to be in a good mood! But things aren't going according to plan." He came out of the bathroom and emptied the remains of his bag on the bed—a change of clothes, a Nikon camera, cartons of film, and an airmail copy of *The New York Times*. "My plane's delayed . . . I get a pilot who thinks the way to avoid rockets is to fly vertical . . . no fucking car at the airport . . . back here, all I want to do is work, I got you."

"Happy New Year," murmured Rockoff weakly.

Schanberg was dialing. He glanced at the photographer. "How'd you get in here, anyway?"

"Came over the balcony . . ."

"Hello? Is Pran there? Sydney Schanberg. No, I just came from the airport. Sure. I understand. Okay. Okay, I'll wait." His eyes strayed around the room. Everything looked pretty much as he'd left it—the battered portable Olivetti on the table, the sharpened pencils beside it, the typing paper and envelopes, the neat stacks of news clippings, a photograph.

Everything was in order, except for the wreck in the bed. Schanberg gestured at the white turban Rockoff was holding to his head. "What exactly is that?"

Rockoff grunted. "Sanitary napkin. I had it soaked in ice."

Schanberg had to smile. He shook his head. "I don't know how you breathe, Al."

"Mr. Sahnber?" Dith Pran's son was back on the

60

phone. "He coming. He say have story on Pochentong rocket attack. Many photographs."

"Okay. Fine. Listen. Tell him I'll be at the Café Central. Tell him I'll meet him in forty minutes at the Café Central. Thanks. Okay."

He put the phone down. Rockoff had managed to get the other eye open.

"Come on," said Schanberg. "I'll buy you breakfast."

At the café, Schanberg closed his eyes, put his nose down to the coffee, and was back in Paris in the late 1950s on a Harvard travel grant, gloating at Europe like a little boy in a candy store. If he opened his eyes slowly, it was still Paris: the chunky porcelain, the yellow, scalloped awning overhead, the bushes in the little tubs ranged along the terrace, the rustle of newspapers, the couple of Army officers playing chess at the next table.

Look over the bushes, though, and the vision was gone. Trishaws and Honda motorbikes vied for passage in the street below. A fish truck was unloading live oysters, crabs, and eels. Two young girls in straw hats and purple sarongs were selling bunches of jasmine at the café tables on the sidewalk. Opposite, a couple of Chinese sat under a yellow umbrella in a great array of U.S. Army surplus goods, including a row of enormous boots, made for American feet, that were curling in the sun. A Buddhist monk in barley-sugar robes critically examined an Army-issue can of mosquito repellent. A garish poster in the window of a closed-down *patisserie* proclaimed a special late-night showing of "Do You Believe In Swedish Sin?"

Rockoff was looking at Schanberg's holiday snaps. He had assembled himself into a white T-shirt and jeans;

with his trusty sunglasses and two Nikons slung around his neck, he was ready for the day. He held out a picture.

"Who's this?"

"That's my youngest daughter. That's in Chiang-Mai. She's buying me a yellow silk good-luck rose. I brought it back with me."

"Very nice. Nice trees. This looks like a very nice holiday. So how was Singapore?"

"Bangkok. Singapore's where I live."

"Yeah." Rockoff seemed more interested in the people. He was gazing at a snap of Schanberg's wife wrapped in a silk sarong. "You know, Syd," he said slowly, "I never think of you as a family man."

A waiter arrived. Schanberg interrupted. "You want something else? You want some eggs?"

"I can't eat eggs. You ever seen where they come from? I'll have another café complet. And some aspirin."

"Oeufs brouillés avec du jambon et encore un café complet, s'il vous plaît. Et est-ce que vous avez des aspirines?"

"Oui, monsieur." The waiter left to serve a cameraman sitting farther along the terrace. All the pros were trickling back into Phnom Penh; it meant they smelled a storm. At the next table, one of the Cambodian officers knocked over his White King and stood to leave. Schanberg yawned. Even through the awning, the heat was like a dose of Valium. Across the street a man in sandals and baggy trousers sat slumped under a tamarind tree, dazed with heat—or else just starving, like that little boy with gaunt features, maybe thirteen or fourteen, weakly holding onto his mother's hand like a child of four. Schanberg picked

up a local paper from the Army officer's chair. EX-CASINO CHIEF FOUND STABBED IN BROTHEL, ran the headline in French. You had to go to an inside page to find news of the war.

Rockoff was still on the subject of eggs. "Anything I eat's gotta be a hundred percent dead. That's why I could never eat an oyster. I read somewhere they squeeze the lemon juice on just to stun 'em. As far as I'm concerned, an unconscious oyster's just as horrible as the fucker wide-awake . . . Syd!" Rockoff hadn't raised his voice, but Schanberg's eyes flashed up. "Syd, there's a guy just thrown something off the back of a bike."

The grenade went off before they hit the floor. It was followed in quick succession by two more. There was a moment's dead silence, broken by the winding of the cameraman's Arriflex. The yellow awning above Schanberg's head slowly blotched with pink.

He followed Rockoff down the stairs, ran out into pandemonium. The Honda bike had disappeared. The two officers must have reached the fish truck about the same time as the grenades. They lay in crystals of bright red ice, in a red froth of flapping fish and chunks of eel, unrecognizable things. What was still was dead. What was moving was dying.

Rockoff darted in and out, snapping pictures. The cameraman was focused on one of the Army officers who had flapped with the fish for a minute then fallen still. Next door, a cycle repair shop had caught fire. Under the pall of thick, black smoke from the burning tires crouched the starving boy Schanberg had seen from the terrace. Blood covered his vest from a shrapnel wound, but he was trying to move his sticklike limbs toward his mother, who could no longer hold his hand. Shrapnel had opened her throat, and she lay staring sightlessly at his pleading face. Schanberg knelt and took a photograph as two medical orderlies came up to lift the child away.

The street had filled with a blare of people. Cameras were flashing; stretchers were being carried through. A tablecloth had blown off the café terrace; someone picked it up and laid it over the mother's face. It was Pran.

"You got here," said Schanberg.

"What happen?"

"KR. Three grenades off the back of a Honda. I need a reaction from a senior Cambodian minister . . . comment on the new campaign of terrorism, plus on the opening of the dry season offensive by the Khmer Rouge . . ."

Pran was scribbling in his notebook, lips pursed. He said, "Lon Nol is at medal ceremony—"

"Where?"

"Independence Place. It start at eleven thirty, very soon."

The little boy was screaming in the ambulance. Schanberg tried to remember what he was going to say. An old woman was carried past on a stretcher, her arm over her face so as not to have to look at what was left of her legs. Rockoff came up to them, out of breath.

"Syd, can I borrow some film?"

Schanberg tossed him a couple of rolls. His moment of forgetfulness was over. He'd learned to recognize it—a delayed reaction to shock. He'd got it down to a few seconds now; he hardly noticed it. Pran was waiting. He clapped him on the shoulder. "Let's go," he said.

Sarun was waiting with the car in a side street. Over the whir of the small battery fan strapped to the dashboard he was apologizing profusely for something. Pran explained.

"The blood on the seat. I'm sorry, Sydney. I took someone to hospital from Pochentong Market. Sarun have no time to clean the car." He stopped and a look of extreme concern came over his face. Crawling over into the backseat beside Schanberg, he took out a handkerchief, spat on it, and began scrubbing vigorously at a bloodstain on Schanberg's jacket. "Sydney, I'm sorry," he repeated. In front, Sarun let out a high-pitched groan.

News of the terrorist attack had reached Independence Square, and security was tight. The armored personnel carriers clanking slowly around the perimeter were ostensibly on parade. The soldiers in them, though, had their rifles at their shoulder and were scanning the windows in the buildings overlooking the place. The passes Schanberg and Pran showed were sufficient to take them through to a roped-off enclosure next to a dais, in front of which three lines of Cambodian soldiers, for once in uniforms that fitted, were standing at attention.

Marshal Lon Nol, Sihanouk's successor as ruler of Cambodia, was standing on the dais. His military khaki uniform was baggy around the hips; his plump cheeks had hollowed, giving a morose expression to his normally round, amiable face. Surrounded by his customary clique of henchmen, he was at that moment shaking the hand of a portly man whose uniform was heavily decorated.

Schanberg shook his head in disbelief. This portly man was considered the most corrupt of all Lon Nol's army commanders. He sold his soldiers' rice to the Thais, and thousands of rounds of ammunition each year to the Khmer Rouge. Lon Nol, who knew he had White House backing whatever he did, kept him in power. Schanberg noticed the tall, crew-cut figure of Lincoln, close enough in front to smell his hair cream. He edged toward him. Lon Nol had finally released his associate's hand; a trumpet blared uncertainly, and the army commander twitched a smile.

"He doesn't look too happy," said Schanberg.

Lincoln nodded. "Maybe he was hoping for an air ticket."

The marshal was being handed a sash to put around the neck of one of his cronies. "It's Lon Nol who needs the air ticket," murmured Schanberg.

"I agree."

"Is there any progress in that direction?"

"No."

"Off the record."

"Off the record, Sydney, still no. Lon Nol is the Nixon Doctrine incarnate, I need hardly tell you. He represents the determination of the White House to go on fighting Communism in Southeast Asia. Since Congress won't let the President fight it to the last American, he's fighting it to the last Cambodian instead. Lon Nol's incompetence is the White House's guarantee he can go on fighting the good fight and give Congress the finger at the same time."

"Which is why Kissinger's refused to talk to Khieu Samphan?"

Another trumpet blast, and the investiture was over. Lincoln took Schanberg's arm and walked him out of the enclosure. "Sydney, I wanted to talk with you about that—"

"It's a well-known fact!" Schanberg was indignant. "We all know the Ambassador sent cables to Kissinger saying that Khieu Samphan, leader of the Khmer Rouge, was on a foreign tour and would Kissinger please see him as a last hope for Cambodia, and Kissinger cabled back refusing—''

"I know. I know. I'm not denying it. But Kissinger got so angry when the story leaked out, we all thought we'd be getting our fourth head of mission in two years. So do me a big favor, Sydney. Keep off the subject of Kissinger for a while, okay? If you've got to stick your pen nib in somebody, try the Pentagon; it doesn't scream so loudly."

Lincoln never said anything without a reason. Schanberg glanced around swiftly at the disappearing soldiers and the APCs and artillery slowly trundling out of Independence Place. With a light laugh he said, "Someone put a rumor around that even if this lot goes up the spout, Congress won't raise any further military aid?"

Lincoln grinned, as if acknowledging a pro. "You know I wouldn't know anything about that, Sydney. But I guess you'll already be aware that the Pentagon just discovered an 'error' in their bookkeeping? They reckon they owe the Cambodian government something like twenty-one million dollars." He glanced around, letting that sink in. Nobody was in earshot. Schanberg's assistant was talking to a Cambodian aide. He went on casually, "Apparently our embassy screwed up in the military accounts department. So the Pentagon is going to pay Lon Nol's debts in military hardware. You should check it out. Especially since the United States embassy in Phnom Penh doesn't possess a department of military accounts. As ever, Sydney—''

"Hold it, James," said Schanberg, thinking fast.

But Lincoln had disappeared, like the proverbial Cheshire cat, leaving in the air a smile more cynical than anything Alice would have understood.

*   *   *

Through the weeks of the dry season, Phnom Penh grew weaker and more distended, like one of its starving children. Refugees from the Khmer Rouge terror swelled its empty belly and pressed toward the heart of the city, setting up their cardboard houses behind bushes in the parks or stretching polyethylene between tombstones in the cemeteries and sleeping restlessly over the dead.

The hotels were filled, too, with journalists, photographers, and TV crews and with the hyenas and vultures who feed off every society in a state of terminal decay: French and German speculators offering contemptible prices for the Khmer treasures of Cambodians panicked into exile; Filipinos hawking cut-rate drugs; Australian and Indonesian contractors charging exorbitant fees to freight out rich families to Thailand where they could get a plane to their relatives in the South of France. A former U.S. military officer reappeared in Phnom Penh as a Singapore-based arms dealer, offering to buy back from Cambodian officers weaponry they'd been given under the American aid program. There were many more like him, mass-market equivalents of the Chinese stall-keeper on the sidewalk of Monivong Boulevard handing over a brand-new M-16 in exchange for a ten dollar bill.

"Aid is opium," observed Schanberg. By the light of the ancient copper lamp he could see Barry Morgan sitting on the teak floor a few feet away. Opposite him on the rush matting were lying two other figures, less familiar. Their faces seemed to change each time the lamp threw shadows. "The more you have, the more you want," he went on, as if discovering a great truth. "The more you want, the more you need. We have given Cambodia too many pipes of opium. The withdrawal symptoms will be terminal.''

"You think it is the fault of the Americans? I disagree.'' It was an educated Cambodian voice that spoke out of the shadows. The bare-breasted girl had called him Excellency. Schanberg wished he could recognize the face. "I fought in the First Indochina war against the French. Now I am fighting the Chinese-backed Communists. Next time, it could be the Vietnamese. The fault is colonialism. The United States does not intend to rule the Khmer people. Its aim is to help us fight off colonizers and rule ourselves.''

He broke off as the girl came in from the corridor with a tray of fresh opium pipes. Schanberg felt a stab of uneasiness. All the Cambodian politicians he'd met shared this same serene detachment, this belief that American hearts ruled American heads. He watched as the girl knelt in the middle of the floor. She was naked except for a green silk sarong wrapped around her stomach and thighs. Her hair, black as liquid graphite, flowed down her back and around her small ears and delicate jaw.

She smoldered the opium over a flame and inserted it delicately into a platinum pipe. With a graceful movement she offered it to the Excellency, who shook his head, and then to the other figure propped against the cushions. An elderly man with a silver mustache; he thanked her in fluent Khmer and then ordered another whiskey in French.

Morgan, with uncharacteristic tact, had moved the conversation on. "There's an obelisk in London, in the

Mall, to the glory of the British Marines," he told them. "And there's a plaque depicting a Marine shoving his bayonet through a Chinaman's gut. He's so shocked, his pigtail's sticking up like an exclamation mark. Underneath, it says, 'Shanghai Campaign 1898.' "

He went on solemnly as the girl knelt very close to him, supporting the pipe for him to inhale through. "It's totally bloody insane, don't you think? Imagine seeing that in Peking. A plaque of a Chinaman sticking his bayonet through an Englishman halfway up Regent Street. A bowler hat levitating in shock. And underneath, 'The Central London Campaign 1898.' " He breathed deeply. "God knows what we were doing in China in the first place."

The French diplomat chuckled. "Protecting your opium trade, my friend."

"That was bayonets in hand-to-hand fighting," Schanberg said. "The Chinese forgave you. What about the Khmer Rouge? Five years of saturation bombing. Thousands of gallons of napalm. Tens of thousands of them blown up or incinerated. No means of retaliation; nothing to turn their fury on except their own people. Do you think they're going to forget and forgive?"

There was no reply. Morgan was gazing into the girl's eyes. In Khmer he whispered, "Thank you." She giggled and said something back and giggled again, flickering a pink tongue at him between betel-red lips.

"What are you laughing for?" asked Morgan, laughing, as she nuzzled him.

"You should learn Khmer, my friend," murmured the Excellency, a little sadly.

"Hatred," said the French delegate. He drained his whiskey glass and put it down with a sharp tap on the matting. "To answer your question about the Khmer Rouge. And when they win, as they assuredly will, it will be the victory of men in whom hate has driven out every other emotion."

The girl rose without a sound and picked up his glass. When she went out with the tray, Morgan got to his feet and followed her. There was silence in the room. The opium was spinning webs in Schanberg's brain. He felt drawn into the fatalism of this ancient country. Hatred would pass. Love was stronger than hatred. When the Excellency spoke, he listened to him with a new respect.

"We shall negotiate," said the cultured Cambodian voice. "At the end of the dry season, when the Khmer Rouge is tired. We shall invite them into the government, within the constitutional framework. There will be no retribution."

Tears came into Schanberg's eyes. The magnanimity of it. That was the way wars should be fought. Only the mandarin from the U.N. appeared unmoved. "I think it was Byron," he remarked, "was it not? Who said, 'Now hatred is by far the longest pleasure/Men Love in haste, but they detest at leisure'?" He sucked on the opium pipe and expelled a deep breath—almost a sigh.

It looked like the furnishings from all the villas in Phnom Penh were up for sale, and the street sellers were going crazy. Refrigerators, TV sets, air conditioners, record players, and U.S. Army surplus still in its Department of Defense wrappers spilled off the sidewalk. People milled around them, bidding silly money and screaming with laughter. Sarun, driving the Mercedes at a walking pace, his nylon shirt dripping with sweat, was telling a joke in

Khmer. Schanberg sat in the back beside Pran, a newspaper over his face.

"Ask him why he always tells jokes when we're in a hurry," he said.

Pran translated and elicited a high-pitched cackle from Sarun. "He say because laughter travel faster than sorrow."

Schanberg grunted. They pulled up at a red light, and he lifted off the newspaper. Small boys were gathering like flies at the windows with black-market gasoline in wine bottles. *Essence? Essence? Voulez-vous acheter d'essence?* In fact, they were nearer the U.S. Embassy than he'd thought. But now the chanting changed. It was louder and angrier. And in English.

"No more American aid! Peace in Cambodia!"

Schanberg tapped Sarun on the shoulder and jumped out of the car. Pran followed him. Between them and the embassy gates the street was filling with Cambodian students shouting protests and waving banners: Lon Nol Must Go! Peace With Honor! Americans, Go Home!

"Americans have stolen the middle way!" they shouted. "Why must we be for Lon Nol or the Khmer Rouge? Where is the middle way?"

Schanberg and Pran forced a path through them. The U.S. Marines behind the locked iron gates of the embassy stood at attention and stared ahead with an expression of indifference. This was nothing to do with them. Far be it from the United States to interfere in the internal problems of a foreign state. As Schanberg knew, so stretched now were Lon Nol's troops, the Joint Chiefs had tried to get the marshal to announce general mobilization. But that would have meant calling up middle-class students like these, which would have destroyed Lon Nol's political power base in an instant. So his army trucks continued to scour the poorer streets to press peasant youths into battle while the wealthy purchased "lop-lop" papers, declaring them insane and draft-exempt. And the students demonstrated.

Schanberg, his back to the embassy fence, didn't feel at liberty to raise this issue. Notebook in hand, he beckoned over a moon-faced student in sneakers and sports shirt, wearing tortoiseshell spectacles. The boy, knuckles white around his banner, answered Schanberg's questions with other questions.

"Why do you support this government? Why do you support Lon Nol? Why do you Americans keep this war going? We want to negotiate. Khmer Rouge is Cambodian—why can't Cambodians talk to Cambodians?"

If there were answers, Schanberg was saved from having to give them. Armored trucks had drawn up at either end of the street. Cambodian military police were advancing in a pincer movement, flailing out with riot sticks and knocking to the ground any students too slow to escape. Another line behind them hauled the demonstrators to their feet and bundled them into the trucks.

Pran scribbled nervously. The moon-faced student was suddenly felled from behind and carried away. As the embassy gate was opened and Schanberg was pulled inside, he saw the tortoiseshell spectacles lying on the sidewalk.

"Sydney!"

Pran had no embassy pass. He needed Sydney to get him in. The Marines were coming forward.

"Sydney!"

Schanberg didn't hear him. He was running up the steps and through the doors, already ten minutes late for the press conference.

The jeep careened down Highway 1, dodging the rocket holes. At the wheel was Joe Marocco, an American military adviser. Schanberg sat beside him. In the back, Rockoff and Swain hung on for dear life with Pran sandwiched uncomfortably between them.

Marocco was talking about the war. "Our information is the VC have stepped up weapon supplies," he shouted. "This time last year the KR were running out of fight!"

"What about Lon Nol's supplies?" shouted Schanberg.

"What's that?"

"I hear that the Pentagon will be supplying twenty-one million dollars worth of military equipment, despite the wishes of Congress."

Marocco lifted two fingers from the wheel. Schanberg smiled grimly. At the press conference the assembled journalists had been told what they had expected to hear: that there could be a bloodbath if the Khmer Rouge came to power; the the U.S. was trying by all possible means to find a controlled solution to the conflict; and that the airlift—flying in fuel and ammunition from Thailand and rice from Saigon—made up for the loss of the Mekong to the KR. Efforts to get the White House to sanction an attempt at negotiations between the Khmer Rouge and Lon Nol had evidently come to nothing. All the emphasis was on extracting enough extra American aid to see them through the dry-season offensive.

A dead bullock lay with its hindquarters across the raised dike road, and the jeep swerved to miss it, hitting a puddle instead and sending most of the rancid water into the backseat. "Hey! Take it easy, will ya," screeched Rockoff, shielding his precious cameras. "What's the fuckin' hurry, anyway?"

"Nobody's going to hit him with a speeding ticket," said Swain.

"I'm not worried about his ticket. I'm worried about mine. On a big toe. In a fridge . . ."

"Ah," said Pran.

They had crossed the United Nations bridge and driven through the Chbar Ampou Market a few minutes earlier. The front line was less than five minutes drive ahead of them, past a continuous straggle of refugees. "Before the push last week, this was all Khmer Rouge territory!" shouted Marocco, staring fixedly ahead. "Maybe tomorrow they'll cut the road again!"

There were no more complaints about the speed. They passed more dead animals and three bodies lying at the side of the road under a shroud of transparent plastic sheeting. A burned-out truck with its nose down in the rice paddy still had its consignment of shop dummies in the back, charred and twisted in an obscene parody of human corpses.

The road now passed through trees. Swain pointed out to Schanberg one or two of the stilt huts with thatched roofs. Not so long ago they had been bordellos, patronized by the French planters whose decaying colonial mansions could still be seen at the end of overgrown drives. Now nothing moved in the vivid green landscape that did not have a weapon in its hand.

From one of the sandbagged military posts at the side of the highway, a soldier flagged them down. Marocco took out his Smith & Wesson revolver and drove past before braking. The soldier ran up.

"Have you cigarettes?" he asked, flashing a row of blackened teeth.

Schanberg tossed him a packet of Bastos. Sitting on the sandbags were three giggling girl soldiers—fifteen years old at most—wearing oversize fatigues. They were awkwardly holding on to brand-new M-16s but were clearly more interested in the lipstick they'd been trying on and in the Paul McCartney track from the *Band on the Run* album blaring out of the small transistor radio. Rockoff took pictures of them with their lipsticked faces, and they shrieked with laughter as though death were far away. Schanberg was beginning to smile as well. Then he noticed Pran, sitting very still, with tears in his eyes. Swain had seen Pran, too, and appreciated the pitiful sadness of the scene.

"Here today, gone tomorrow," said Marocco somberly, and put the jeep into gear.

After about a mile, Swain broke the silence.

"Did you see those M-16s?" he said. "They still had their bloody dust caps on."

They could see the front now, defined by the ugly billows of black smoke gushing into the cloudless sky. They came from a burning factory at the edge of one of the last village enclaves outside Phnom Penh still defended by the armed forces of the Khmer Republic. A Coca-Cola factory, it had been rocketed since early that morning by the KR. Half its roof had come off. The rest was a litter of concrete rubble, smashed crates, exploding cans, and burning oil slicks around twisted machinery. A tall aluminum pole had been sliced in two and bent double like a broken twig. A neon sign on the end, almost touching the ground, was still flashing redly BUVEZ COKE.

Marocco stopped the jeep by an overturned truck near the gates. The scene that greeted them made Schanberg think of etchings he had seen at college out of Goya's *Disasters of War*. In the fitful shadows cast by the pall of smoke, two small boys carried a dead dog on a pole over toward a dismal fire, walking around the shell craters that pocked the rubble-strewn ground. Beside the blackened stump of a tree crouched the family of a young soldier at the front. The wife, hardly older than the girl soldiers they had passed, was suckling a baby under a rough plank structure she had erected to shield him from the midday sun. The mother was washing clothes in a plastic bowl. The only way Schanberg could tell them from refugees was that the shirt the mother was scrubbing was an old French military khaki.

In single file, Joe Marocco leading, they trailed past bullock carts and cooking fires and huddled, shapeless figures, toward the front line. "We should be up with them before they break for lunch," remarked Marocco.

"Before they break for lunch?" Swain sounded incredulous.

"That's right. Lon Nol's artillery officers work a strict daily schedule. 0630 hours to 1300 hours, except Saturday and Sunday, which are rest days. That means the army attacks KR positions in the late morning, then usually retreats with heavy losses in the late afternoon because of lack of artillery cover."

"And at night?"

"Only the Communists fight at night."

Schanberg had heard it all before. One reason the Cambodian army's kill ratio was as low as the worst troops in Vietnam was that it went to war as it might have sown rice or gone into the office. The Khmer Rouge could time their watches by its attacks; to ambush it was as easy as ambushing a postman on his morning rounds. Burdened by the incompetence of their officers and the corruption of their commanders, the troops fought mechanically; it was a wonder they fought at all. Before the early seventies, the only experience these gentle people had had of mechanized warfare was of serving as extras in Prince Sihanouk's patriotic home movies. As a result, they first went to battle against the Vietnamese with bugles and a standard bearer and were ambushed and massacred by the thousands.

"Over here!" yelled Marocco. Rockoff, who had stopped to photograph a little girl holding the reins of a bullock cart, her refugee parents loading bundles behind her, turned and trotted after him. The chatter of light machine-gun fire guided them to a low brick wall reinforced with sandbags. About thirty exhausted soldiers, none of them looking over eighteen, lay peering over. As the journalists arrived, four of them got up and ran crouching past a crippled antitank gun to a ruined house one hundred yards farther along. Ahead was open country, a couple of football fields long, and then a row of sugar palms seen dimly through the swirling smoke.

This was the front line.

A couple of officers squatted on the ground drinking Coca-Cola and listened to a field radio barking out commands in Khmer. They stared in disbelief as the journalists came up. One of them, a huge Buddhist monk wrapped in dirty yellow cotton, shook his head and muttered.

Pran translated for the military adviser. "He says he thought you went home."

"No, sir!" Marocco assayed a smile. He stepped forward and thrust out his hand. "Made in the U.S.A."

The monk's face contorted. He slapped at the proffered hand. Then, before Marocco could take offense, he smiled with tears in his eyes and clasped the military adviser in a warm embrace.

"He says you have come in time to help," Pran translated again.

Marocco disengaged himself. His sunglasses had come off, and Schanberg could read in his eyes a Judas-look of embarrassment, guilt, and sorrow. "I can't help," he said angrily. "I'm an adviser."

They went forward to a machine-gun nest, Schanberg in the lead. The sergeant in command was about twenty, barefooted like the others and carrying a green umbrella as a mark of authority. There was a bloody bandage around his head, and on his blue jeans a long stain of oil and blood. He bowed politely to the group and returned to an M-60 machine gun, which was chattering fruitlessly at the distant row of palms.

"This scene's crazy," grumbled Rockoff. He had moved aside to take a picture of a goat blown in half but still tethered to a flagpole. "Fucking lot of us gonna get boiled."

There was a sudden whistle of mortars. Schanberg and Pran dived to the ground. Machine guns opened up from the tree line, and their M-60 hacked in reply. On the ground beside them, the field radio was warbling furiously. Pran translated above the din, *"Why don't you go forward!"*

The bloodstained sergeant, clumsy with fatigue, grabbed

the phone and screamed at the invisible colonel hundreds of yards behind the line. *"Why don't you come down here yourself and find out!"*

Khmer Rouge mortar fire had increased. Shells were coming down behind and in front of them. The military adviser looked at his watch in puzzlement; this was not how it was supposed to be. The radio squawked, and gouts of earth and burning building rose in the air, coming down over them as a yellow rain of atomized brick.

Next to Schanberg a crate of Coke exploded in slivers of flying glass. *"Why don't you go forward!"* screamed the radio. Looking down, he saw a line of blood welling up and starting to advance across the palm of his hand. As the earth shuddered around them, Pran took Schanberg's hand and sucked away the blood.

"Danger of poison," he said, and took out his handkerchief to bind the wound.

Schanberg looked at his number two in astonishment. They were under shellfire, and here was Pran doctoring him like a hospital case. With the nicest smile he had, Schanberg very gently pulled his hand away. "That's okay for now," he said.

A mortar explosion fifteen yards down the line batted them to the ground. Red sandbags rose slowly in the air and opened, spilling out human guts. Two soldiers scrambled out of the rain of blasted dirt, soundlessly crying. They wore sweatbands; one of them had rubber shower clogs on his feet. With one accord they threw down their rifles and ran. The young sergeant screamed after them in a harsh, hopeless voice as they vanished in the haze.

The shelling rose to a crescendo, like New York subway trains crashing down a long track. The military adviser was a hundred yards back through the smoke, pointing at his watch and yelling. This was a major push by the Khmer Rouge. Schanberg grabbed at Pran and ran for his life.

Some of the shells had been targeted on the refugees. They ran through screaming children, swaying carts, panicking animals. Rockoff was way ahead, cameras flying. Swain was with him.

Schanberg looked over his shoulder and saw shapes moving near the deserted machine-gun post. He stopped and threw himself down in another gun emplacement between two walls of Coca-Cola crates. Pran shouted at him.

"Come on, Sydney!"

"Go on!" yelled Schanberg. He thrust his arm at the jeep. "Go ahead! I'll catch you!" He stared at the distant line of sugar palms. Black insects were scuttling out between them and across the green paddy. Now they were swarming in the ruined house beyond the sandbags, which five minutes ago had been part of the free world.

"Khmer Rouge!" whispered a voice beside him. Pran had come back.

Together they stared, fascinated and fearful. The figures had dark faces and long black hair. Perhaps they were women. A building burst into flames, and the smoke obscured them. When it lifted, the black figures were gone. A car horn sounded; it was time to make a run for it.

As they ran, crouching low, there was another explosion. The bullock cart Rockoff had photographed was covered in blood. The girl had let the reins slip from her hand. One of the beasts was dead. The other one, blood pouring from its neck, was struggling to stand. The little girl had not turned around to see what was left of her parents. Eyes screwed shut, fingers in both ears, she was screaming at the top of her voice.

Schanberg sat eating his shrimp cocktail by candlelight. With the electricity cut, as it was with increasing frequency this March, the dining room of the Hotel Phnom looked more than usual like a mausoleum to past glories. Above Schanberg's head, a baroque chandelier tinkled in the breeze from the louvered windows. On each damask tablecloth sat candles that threw shadows on the paneled walls. At this late hour, Schanberg was the only customer, and there was no sound except for the chandelier and the tap of his spoon on the cut-glass dish.

He was getting used to solitude. Apart from Pran, he now lived entirely with his work and his thoughts. Cambodia filled his thoughts—the people and the war. On his rare trips back to Singapore and his family, he woke up each morning thinking of circling helicopters. The cries of children playing in the schoolyard down the road would make him shut the windows and turn up the radio to drown out the memory of other, sharper cries of pain. The only thing that penetrated his remoteness was one of his daughters giving him her traditional good-bye present of a yellow silk rose and speaking with a trembling bottom lip: "Daddy, I love you. But I keep losing you. Just when I'm getting to know you again, I lose you."

Schanberg wiped the tiredness out of his eyes and pushed away the food. A waiter approached noiselessly with a cold chicken curry; he waved that away, too, and lit a cigarette. It was too hot to eat. Tobacco, alcohol, vitamin pills, it was all he seemed to live on just now. When he'd first come out to Cambodia, a novice war reporter, and latched on to some of the experienced correspondents who didn't mind his questions, their intake of stimulants had been the one trick he'd tried to avoid copying. Since then, he'd learned what the omnipresence of war did to the nervous system. It keyed you up, and it calloused you at the same time. A full stomach was the worst thing to take to some of the sights he'd had to cover.

It had been hard enough last Sunday in Pran's apartment, trying to swallow the food Ser Moeun put before him. It was only the second time he'd accepted having a meal in their home; Pran's wife had plainly gone to great trouble, buying delicacies in the market and setting them out in bowls around the curry—and halfway through he'd had to put his chopsticks down and ask if he could smoke. With his extravagant politeness, Pran had stopped eating and joined him. Ser Moeun picked up the dishes with a disappointed smile and took them into the kitchen.

"My father always smoke at table," said Pran with a giggle. "My mother, she make very hot curry and he always says, 'Smoke after fire'!"

"How are your people, Pran?"

His assistant lowered his eyes to the brightly polished table. It hadn't been a tactful question, Schanberg realized as soon as he'd asked it. Pran's parents lived in an outlying part of the township of Siem Reap, up north near the temples of Angkor Wat. His father was a senior public works official, responsible for supervising road building in the Siem Reap district. The whole area was currently under fierce assault by the Khmer Rouge.

"My father is very sad. His whole life has been with making roads. He built the modern road to Angkor Wat, when I worked in the hotel there in 1967 as tour guide. He used to say, 'My roads are bring Siem Reap into twentieth century.' Now he says, 'My roads are gone. American planes bombed them. Then the Vietnamese and the Khmer Rouge bomb them. Now they are fit only for bullock carts.' ''

Schanberg remembered the old man. They had gone up to Angkor Wat three years ago when you could still get there, and Pran had shown him the Auberge Royale des Temples where he used to work, and the pagoda into which he'd moved his family in 1970 when the fighting around his own house had got so intense that he'd feared for their lives. It was then that Pran had joined the local militia. He'd worn khaki and learned how to handle a Thompson submachine gun before deciding he stood a better chance of survival if he came down to Phnom Penh to look for work. With his grasp of French and English (self-taught) it wasn't long before every newsman in the capital wanted to hire him. Japanese reporters, television crews from the BBC and ORTF . . . it was luck, really, that the *Times* bureau chief in Saigon, Craig Whitney, had snapped him up on one of his early visits and recommended him to Schanberg.

Ser Moeun brought them tea. Schanberg felt her anxious gaze upon him; he suspected he'd been asked to dinner to discuss what plans he had if the U.S. pulled out. But Pran already knew his family would be looked after. There was nothing else to say, at least until he got word from the embassy. In the meantime, Schanberg wasn't about to behave like this was some kind of farewell dinner. His eye caught Pran's small molded-plastic souvenir of the Statue of Liberty on the windowsill. ''You still got that thing Craig gave you," he said, nodding at it. With a laugh, he raised his glass of tea. "Here's to life, liberty, and the pursuit of happiness!"

"To life and liberty and to happiness," said Pran with a solemn frown.

That was five days ago. Since then, there hadn't been much to toast, even with a glass of tea. The U.S. airlift wasn't compensating for the loss of the Mekong. The poor were starving. Inflation was running so high that teachers at the university were out on strike because their salaries weren't enough to pay their fare home. A rocket had landed outside the Hotel Monorom, hurling bits of the doorkeeper into the lap of an American TV reporter. Worse still, a school in the middle of Phnom Penh had received a direct hit, killing ten children outright and wounding many more. He had arrived with Pran shortly after the blast and watched the cameramen filming close-up as the small, mangled bodies were carried out into the street. The Khmer Rouge had issued repeated statements, via Sihanouk, warning all foreigners to quit the city immediately. Meanwhile, the best restaurants continued to serve Puligny Montrachet and escargots by candlelight, and Lon Nol was proceeding with his plans to construct a new parking lot-cum-zoo, perhaps to take care of the three sacred elephants Prince Sihanouk left in his care. . . .

Schanberg stubbed out his cigarette. The swinging doors opened behind him; he turned, expecting to see Pran. But it was Swain and the Red Cross doctor from Aberdeen, Gordon McIntyre, dressed in tennis whites and swinging rackets. McIntyre was red in the face.

"I lose the first set, and the bloody floodlights go out,"

grumbled Swain, pulling up a chair. "And the Cercle Sportif bar is crawling with rich French business types comparing notes on the souvenirs they're snatching up to take out of the country."

"They call it 'rescuing from the Khmer Rouge,' " added McIntyre dryly. "And it goes without saying, it's a better investment to rescue a seventeenth-century bronze meditating Buddha from the Khmer Rouge than it is to rescue your chauffeur."

Schanberg smiled and said nothing. The two Brits talked at him for a bit longer, then left him to his thoughts. Pran interrupted them, flourishing Telex messages.

"Sydney! I think Communists have capture Neak Luong."

"That's verified?"

"No. It's a rumor. On the street."

Schanberg ran his eye down the Telex sheet. It reported another attempt by Kissinger and President Ford to shift the blame to Congress, if Cambodia fell, for withdrawing aid at this "critical moment" in the struggle. "The President declared that they needed urgently to address the moral question of whether the United States would deliberately abandon a small country in the midst of its life-and-death struggle," he read out in a soft voice. "He said it had always been a cornerstone of American policy to aid its allies, so long as they were willing and able to carry the burden of their own self-defense. Cambodia, said the President, has been such an ally."

Schanberg laid the statement down on the white cloth. "We're running out of time," he murmured, half to himself. "If Neak Luong has fallen, it means thousands of KR, plus captured artillery, make straight for us here. There's nothing to stop them."

Pran said nothing. Schanberg looked up at him. Pran's face in the candlelight looked drawn and distant.

"What's the matter?" he asked.

"Something I hear tonight, Sydney. Khmer Rouge have attack Siem Reap. They have taken the village with my parents in."

A waiter was moving from table to table, blowing out the candles. Schanberg followed him with his eyes. "Let's go get a drink," he said.

"Bar's closed, Sydney."

"I don't give a shit if the bar's closed. We'll open it."

A machine gun chattered. One of the poolside journalists, Sy Jules, threw himself to the ground and rolled sideways into a bomb crater. Sarun, in the Mercedes, gave a squeak of fear, swerved, and braked to a halt. Jules climbed out of the crater and blew dust off the sleeve of his combat jacket.

"Okay. Let's take it from the top," he called.

His television crew, a director and two technicians, set up the shot with a view of the Mekong in the distance. Sy Jules spoke furtively into the microphone. "Behind me, some 600 yards away, the Communists have taken and hold the Mekong. From here, with captured 105-millimeter artillery, they rain death into the city at will. But the armed forces of the Khmer Republic, under the leadership of Marshal Lon Nol, are putting up a spirited fight. Informed sources are agreed that if this present offensive can be resisted until the monsoons arrive in four weeks' time, the Communists will never be able to mount a major assault again. But, as a senior U.S. official put it to me last night, 'We know very damned little about the Khmer Rouge.' "

On cue, the director pushed a button on a tape recorder, and a burst of machine-gun fire echoed down the street. Covered by the TV camera, Sy Jules replayed his dramatic bid for safety. Raising his head, he spoke hoarsely into the mike.

"This is Sy Jules. Pinned down in the fighting. Somewhere in a western suburb of the besieged city of Phnom Penh . . ."

Schanberg, grinning, wound down the Mercedes window and flicked out his cigarette. Sarun drove him the remaining few hundred yards to the United States Embassy. The mission was like Macy's at Christmas sale time. Frantically busy secretaries clacked down the corridors carrying folders by the armful. Orderlies manhandled desks and filing cabinets down the stairs. Slade went past Schanberg in the lobby, talking urgently to a workman.

He found James Lincoln in his office on the second floor. On the wall was a large map of Cambodia dotted with little black pins. Opposite, President Ford grinned out of his photograph between two rubber plants on a filing cabinet. It reminded Schanberg of the schoolroom in Neak Luong.

Lincoln was emptying his drawers. An enormous heap of newspaper cuttings and pictures on the floor was steadily getting higher. On his desk beside two plastic garbage bags was a much smaller pile. "How about a yard sale?" suggested the *New York Times* man.

"Who'd buy any of this? I'm half-inclined to leave it to Intelligence. They're setting up an operations center on this floor in the event of a rocket attack on the top story." Lincoln opened another file and groaned. "Christ, there's some shit been through here in the last few years. Mostly at the speed of dysentery. Look at this . . . 1972 . . . care for a snap of me and the doc?''

Schanberg grimaced, and Lincoln threw Kissinger's picture onto the pile of rubbish on the floor. ''He's not the best-loved man in this embassy right now,'' the diplomat said with bitterness.

''Why?''

''He won't allow us to evacuate from Pochentong. It was pointed out to him that at the rate the Communists were closing in from the north, it was our last chance to get out on fixed-wing aircraft. Kissinger wouldn't budge. That means the last of us will have to go out by choppers from the center of Phnom Penh. Not a morale-raising spectacle for the average Cambodian.''

''Maybe Kissinger still thinks there's a chance to negotiate?''

Lincoln emptied the rest of the folder on the floor with such a look of hopelessness that Schanberg felt a stab of sympathy for him. He knew what caused it. The final, last-minute plan, conceived by the French and backed both here and in Saigon, had been to bring back Sihanouk to form a coalition government in Phnom Penh. Sihanouk was willing. But the dead hand of the Nixon Doctrine could not drop Lon Nol now. The plan had fallen through, and with it, any real hope of a controlled solution in Cambodia.

Lincoln was holding a picture of Sihanouk that many wire services had carried. It showed him smiling broadly with his arms around the shoulders of two Khmer Rouge leaders, Ieng Sary and Khieu Samphan. ''You know he got in touch with us,'' he said abruptly.

''Sihanouk?''

"Yeah. Not to negotiate. He wants all his old home movies sent to him in Peking. He says they constitute a 'unique cultural record' of what life was like in old Cambodia!"

Schanberg laughed aloud.

"He also told our man in Peking that the KR wants to model the country on Stalinist Albania," added Lincoln somberly. "So he could just be right."

He went back to the filing cabinet. Schanberg moved over to the desk and glanced at the topmost paper on the pile. He looked up to find Lincoln watching him.

"Sorry, James. There's something inexplicable about the back of your neck that automatically turns my eyes upside down—"

"It's called force of habit. You can read it if you like."

"I already did."

Lincoln returned his grin. They were both old hands at this game. "I'm keeping that for historical reasons," he explained. "The first news report I ever saw mentioning the Khmer Rouge by name. What's the date? 1969? There were four thousand of them then. Six years and a war later and we've got seventy thousand of them baying at the gates. This country had a lot of faults and a lot of strengths, and the sad thing is, we've only played to the faults."

He emptied another folder on the floor without looking at its contents. Outside in the corridor, Schanberg heard a voice say, "It's documented, Will. The children were swung against trees. The women were nailed alive to the walls of their houses. The men were hung up and burned—"

Lincoln and Schanberg looked at each other in silence as the voices retreated down the neon-lit corridor. The diplomat unpacked the garbage bags and handed one to Schanberg. Together they shoveled in six years of commentary on a country that was ceasing to exist.

"I tell you, Sydney, I'll be damned glad to get out of here." Lincoln ran a cord around the neck of the garbage bag and pulled it tight. "I think it's getting to all of us. Someone upstairs in Intelligence had a heart attack last week, though he survived it. The Ambassador's got high blood pressure. Tom Bailey, his deputy, had emergency treatment for bleeding ulcers. Someone else down the corridor drinks himself into a coma every night. There's a lot of whiskey drowning a lot of sorrows around here."

"What about the airlift?" Schanberg knotted the neck of his bag.

"We're taking it with us. 'Drawdown' is the technical expression."

Schanberg thought for a moment. "That means two hundred thousand people starve to death. *Minimum*."

"I know that, Sydney. What else do we do? Just tell me, what else do we do? Forgive the pun, but we're either living or we're staying. . . ."

Schanberg hoisted his bag and followed Lincoln to the door. The diplomat stooped and picked up a letter that had escaped the holocaust. He grinned. " 'Dear Sir, My family and I'—and dig the date, this is a month ago—'My family and I are planning a touring vacation in Southeast Asia and anticipate about two weeks in Cambodia—' "

"Oh, Mr. Schanberg—"

They had reached the lobby. Schanberg was accosted by an assistant from Personnel wearing half-moon glasses and carrying a clipboard. The heading on it read "Operation Good Samaritan."

"Mr. Schanberg, I didn't receive a list of your dependents?"

"Sorry, I been busy. Here."

They went down another flight to the basement. Lincoln continued, " 'We would be grateful for any tour information or brochures. Thanking you in advance, Wendell Payne.' Wendell lives in Potlatch, South Carolina!"

Both men laughed, partly with relief, to know it was possible to share a joke, to recapture the feeling of being human. It didn't last long. Schanberg glanced at Lincoln and saw the worry lines settle back in place.

"In here," said Lincoln.

He opened a soundproof door, and they walked into a deafening low-pitched whine. Three big paper shredders were being fed by men in overalls. A couple of supermarket trolleys filled with plastic bags were waiting to be unloaded. A portly man in slacks and dark glasses was standing guard; Schanberg recognized him as one of the CIA contingent at the embassy who frequented the Cercle Sportif. So this was where the secrets went, minced in metal and spewed out the other end in fine white ribbons that even the Khmer Rouge wouldn't be able to stick together again.

The CIA man took their bags and flapped his hands at them to go away.

"What happens to the shredded paper?" asked Schanberg as they went back up the stairs.

"It gets incinerated," replied Lincoln. "But not yet. The official line is that the sight of white smoke pouring out of the embassy chimney might be interpreted by the city as a symbol of surrender.''

They threaded their way through the crates and packing cases that crowded the reception area. A large bronze eagle that had hung on the Ambassador's wall was being wrapped in several layers of tissue paper before being crated up. Lincoln handed Schanberg a booklet from a tall stack by the front desk. On the front in large letters were the words, ''Standard Instruction and Advice to Civilians in Emergency.''

Schanberg looked at him. Lincoln reddened. ''You know, Sydney,'' he said awkwardly, ''there could be a bloodbath. This thing's dragged on too long for it to be all sweetness and light. . . .''

Schanberg nodded. He thought of Pran. All of a sudden he wanted to be away from this building, away from these people, out in the open air.

''Thanks, James,'' he said.

Lincoln accompanied him to the main door. On his doleful face there was the suspicion of a grim smile. ''After what the KR has been through, I don't think they're going to be affectionate toward Westerners,'' he said. ''I guess you know that.''

''I guess I do,'' said Sydney Schanberg.

The Mercedes was waiting. Schanberg got in and opened the SAFE booklet. He did not want to look at Sarun. ''Hotel Phnom,'' he said.

The booklet was full of generalities. Schanberg flicked through exhortations to register for evacuation, to keep clear of crowds, to keep one's radio tuned to American Forces Radio. There was a special section on what to bring with you to your allocated helicopter on "departure": ". . . two changes of clothing, a raincoat, a sewing kit and an umbrella, a can opener, insect repellent, Band-Aids, your marriage certificate, a power of attorney, and your will. Unfortunately, you cannot take your automobile with you." Schanberg looked at the back of Sarun's neck, as plump as the bags of rubbish he'd knotted with cord in Lincoln's office. He threw the SAFE booklet out of the window, on top of a pile of U.S. Army surplus being sold on the sidewalk.

"Hotel!" cried Sarun, beaming. "Very quick!"

The hotel lobby was as full of packing cases as the embassy, except that each of them had a large red cross stamped on the side. Threading his way through was Sy Jules, carrying several bags and two cases trimmed with Florentine leather. His shell-crater report was plainly the last his audience could expect from their man in Phnom Penh. He would be on the next flight to Saigon. As he passed a group of grizzled French *colons* arguing in excited voices with the hotel manager, one of his bags split. Out fell an exquisite lacquer-and-gold tiger with ruby eyes.

"Damnation!" said Sy Jules.

Schanberg avoided him and headed for the stairs and went up to his room.

The bed was unmade. Stale cigarette smoke hung in the air. A drift of sound came from the swimming pool; Schanberg opened the peeling white shutters and went out on his balcony.

The chlorinator had gone wrong days ago, and nobody had turned up to mend it, but people still splashed around in the yellowing water. A girl in a red bikini was putting suntan lotion on her ankles, watched by a fat Cambodian colonel over his Pernod glass. The war groupies were out in force—lean, tanned girls who'd exchanged cable-knit sweaters for stained combat jackets and who got their kicks sporting mementoes of the dead heroes they'd fucked. Barry Morgan was in a small group of journalists surrounding one of these groupies at the poolside and trying to get her top off.

Schanberg placed a long-distance phone call and returned to the balcony. The scene fascinated and repelled him in equal measure. There was an atmosphere of feverish gaiety about: It reminded him of scenes in Stanley Kramer's film, *On the Beach*, or what it must have been like in Shanghai in 1947. Everybody had congregated for the final "bang bang," the last orgasm of a doomed country.

Out of sight of them, behind the frangipani trees, the Red Cross had already commandeered the private bungalows and were moving in surgical equipment. But that was for tomorrow. Today it was eat, drink, and be merry. Even old Desmond France was down there with his trousers rolled up, paddling his feet in the water and laughing hysterically with some diplomatic bag, her hair tinted mustard blond.

Only yesterday Schanberg had run into France at the General Post Office reading his copy over to some "informed source" who had Desmond on a short lead. His dispatch, for readers of the "London Daily Claptrap," had been one of "guarded optimism." Apparently there were "good grounds for hope" that political moves in Phnom Penh would "open the door to peace negotiations." Lon Nol's ousting two days before had "removed a critical stumbling block," and Prime Minister Long Boret's new cabinet included figures "who could, if necessary, enter into talks with the Khmer Rouge."

Schanberg had liked that "if necessary." It suggested a monocled Victorian industrialist deigning to talk to a delegation of uppity coal miners, first rolling up the hall carpet so they wouldn't spread coal dust over his thick-pile Wilton.

The phone rang. Schanberg rushed into the bedroom. His daughter's voice seemed to come at him from the other side of the world. "Hello, honey. It's Daddy. Yes. Yes, I'm fine. That's what I want to talk to Mummy about. All right, you go get her. That's right, honey. I'm waiting."

He shook out a cigarette and lit it with a hand that trembled slightly. He knew what his wife would say. He knew he would disagree. But he had to give her the chance to convince him. He owed her that.

"Hello? No, everything's fine. What? I can't hear you. What? That's what I want to talk to you about. I said, that's what I want to talk to you about. Hello? Hello?"

The line was a storm of static, gusting with voices. An operator came on; Schanberg shouted at her. "No! I haven't finished. Jesus, I'm trying to make a call to Singapore! Will you get off the line! Hello! Shit!"

Schanberg smashed the phone down in a fury. He picked it up again and morse-coded the button. "Hello! I was talking to Singapore. I was cut off. This call is vital. Would you please reconnect me. *Schanberg*. It took me twelve hours to get through. Yes. All right, I'll wait."

He dumped the receiver and went and lay on the bed. A couple of flies were buzzing around the yellow rose he'd put in a toothpaste mug on the table. After a minute, he got up and went out on the balcony again.

The girl in the red bikini had turned over and was

sunning her bronzed back. Some of the Cambodian army officers had left; their place had been taken by more Western newsmen and black marketeers, plus a few weirdos Schanberg couldn't place at all—probably the trawl from the posters embassy staff had pinned up in every brothel and seedy drug parlor in the city, offering expatriates a free ride home.

A small band of journalists, drinking whiskey in the shade of the sugar palms, were singing a song to the tune of "She Was Poor but She Was Honest":

> Oh, will there be a dreadful bloodbath
> When the Khmer Rouge comes to town?
> Yes, there'll be a dreadful bloodbath
> When the Khmer Rouge comes to town!

White-uniformed Cambodian waiters, holding trays, watched them with puzzled grins on their faces. Schanberg, looking over and beyond the palms, realized with an unpleasant shock that they had a wider audience. Hundreds of refugees had scaled the wall that stretched right around the Hotel Phnom's gardens. They sat quietly with their bundles on top of the wall or peered over it with dark faces, listening to the song, watching the swimmers through the trees. A little girl with a topknot had seen *The New York Times* man and was waving to him, the emperor on his balcony.

Schanberg raised his hand and dropped it. The emperor had no clothes. He went inside to run a bath, closing the shutters behind him.

The heat is stifling. The electric fan on the sideboard clatters but hardly seems to move the air. Muffled squeaks

97

come from the bedroom—Dith Pran has sent the four
children in there to watch a Tom and Jerry cartoon on the
TV. Now he sits at table with Ser Moeun, his wife, empty
bowls between them, listening to the fan and the ticking of
a Donald Duck alarm clock on the fridge next to the
sideboard. He has come to the end. He can't think of
anything more to say.

Ser Moeun has stopped crying. She wipes her eyes with
a corner of her sarong and gathers up the bowls as she
does every night. Tonight her limbs are weak; she cannot
get up. She puts the bowls down on the coarse-weaved cloth
and bows her head.

"It is up to Sydney," Dith Pran repeats in Khmer.

"Yes."

"If he needs me, I have to stay."

"Yes."

"I have a duty. It is . . ." Pran searches. There is a
word for *professional* in Khmer, but it does not have the
portentous associations it has in the West. "I am called to
be a journalist," he finishes simply.

"Yes. Why can you not be a journalist in America?"

Ser Moeun twists the rings on her fingers. Tears have
started to flow again down her round cheeks. Pran frowns.
How can he explain something to his wife that he can
barely explain to himself? Journalism is not a trade, like
teaching, or guiding tourists around the ruins of Angkor
Wat. It involves the spirit of a man. To reveal the truth in
a war, you have to be brave and quick-thinking, but you
also have to *understand*. And like any process of under-
standing—like becoming a priest of Buddha, for example—it
first demands a dedication of the spirit. To *belong* you

have first to *share*, to share whatever comes along, even fear, pain, grief.

"They will kill you!"

Ser Moeun is sobbing. Pran shakes his head. Like many women, she has a habit of letting her imagination carry her ahead of the facts. "I have done nothing to the Khmer Rouge," he tells her. "I have nothing to fear from them. They will need people like me, people who are educated. You heard what Khieu Samphan said on the radio. 'Every Cambodian has his role in national society regardless of the past.' "

Ser Moeun gazes across at the painted wooden Buddha squatting behind the fan. Eyes half-closed, head slightly averted, he is obviously doing his best to keep out of this conversation. But his non-committal expression may also be because he is reflecting on one of his Twelve Commandments, the one that forbids his disciples to use words that conceal the truth. For all his words of comfort to Ser Moeun, Pran is unhappily conscious of the fact that nobody has any idea what the Khmer Rouge will do when they take Phnom Penh.

There are some of his friends who choose to believe the reassuring speeches of Sihanouk and Samphan. Sarun is one of them. There are others, like Nhiek Sann who works as an interpreter in the Ministry of Industry, Mines, and Tourism, who believe that the victorious Khmer Rouge will be more brutal than their worst imaginings. One of his friends, an aide to Prime Minister Long Boret, had actually shared a Paris flat in the 1950s with Saloth Sar, who now calls himself Pol Pot. He claims to have known him well, but when people ask him about Pol Pot's revolutionary ideology he only shrugs his shoulders in confusion.

Next to the Buddha is a framed photograph of Pran and Sydney Schanberg at the seaside, down at Kompong Som on the Gulf of Siam, in early 1973. They are both wearing baggy shorts and have their arms around each other. Big smiles for the camera. Pran's own eyes fill with tears at the thought of what lies ahead. He blinks them back.

"I think Sydney will not want me to stay," he says.

Ser Moeun stands up without looking at him and takes the bowls and spoons into their tiny kitchen. She runs the tap full on so that Pran will not hear her tears. There are other pictures of Sydney in the room. One of them, propped up behind a Yogi Bear, is of Sydney crossing a river near Battambang. His notebook is under his arm; he is casually smoking a cigarette. He looks like the 1850s French explorer who rediscovered Angkor Wat and brought the French into Cambodia in place of the Vietnamese. Except that Sydney has no time for relics of the past. He is a man of today, a man of angry will that drives him on, which is why he is to be admired and respected.

Pran gets up wearily. In its place of honor on the windowsill is the Statue of Liberty souvenir that Sydney noticed. He picks it up and holds it carefully, as he might hold the wooden statue of Buddha. Always he has thought that the confident sweep of the arm that holds the torch is signaling mankind's future. Now he knows it. He knows, too, what it was he was trying to say to Ser Moeun. Liberty is the freedom to make choices. That is the freedom Sydney has. He wants it, he will have it, too—the freedom to choose.

Shrieks of laughter come from the bedroom. It's time the children were going to sleep. Pran goes in just as the cartoon is ending. Tom has chased Jerry all over the attic, the floor is shaking under his heavy tread. But the little mouse hasn't given in. He lures Tom into a corner, the floor gives way, and the big, powerful cat is pinned, crushed, flattened, under falling timber. Tom struggles up and hobbles away from the unequal contest, glaring over his shoulder. Jerry preens his black whiskers; the house is his.

His daughter is laughing so much, she is crying. Pran picks her up and motions the others to bed. He cuddles the little girl, who puts her arms around his neck.

"How would you like to go on a journey?" he whispers in her ear.

Dawn broke as sticky and airless as the night before. Schanberg had hardly slept. Whenever he closed his eyes, he was surrounded by dark faces circling him in the darkness, faces peering and squinting at him over the brick wall that went around and around like the wheel of a bullock cart.

He got up early and took out his frustration on the typewriter. The call to Singapore still hadn't got through. The lights had failed; he worked by the light of a battery-powered lamp, distracted by the fat moths dive-bombng around his head and falling into his littered ashtray. There was an angry buzz from the air conditioning—that would be the next to go.

He lit another cigarette and returned to the Olivetti. The words weren't coming right. AFN Saigon had come through an hour ago with news of more spectacular collapses in South Vietnam. Da Nang was in Communist hands; now Nha Trang had followed. Communist forces had broken through the new government defense line drawn east of Tay Ninh and were heading south toward Bien Hoa and the capital. Not a line, not a word on the war situation in Cambodia.

Schanberg knew from bitter experience that news out of Cambodia always coincided with some upheaval elsewhere. The 1973 bombings had been effaced by Watergate. Now, in the moment of its greatest agony, it was once again to be relegated to a sideshow by the disasters in Vietnam. Nothing he wrote at this table would do more than head a side column on the front page of *The New York Times*. More probably, it would be appended to a full-length story on Vietnam, and when syndication was sold across the country, Cambodia, as usual, would get the bum's rush. Wendell Payne of Potlatch, South Carolina, was no different from the great majority of honest, God-fearing American citizens. If you told them there was a war on in Cambodia and America had something to do with it, they would have dropped their jaws in amazement.

He pulled a page from the typewriter, crumpled it, and started again. Sweat dripped on the keys. If only the distant rumbling was thunder before rain, and not always the dry crump of guns. "Hanoi is aiding the Khmer Rouge with more arms and ammunition than ever before," he typed, "but not with their sophisticated weapons, such as SAM-7 antiaircraft missiles, which could close down Pochentong Airport in minutes and bring Phnom Penh to its knees. The belief here is that the Vietnamese, traditional enemies of the Khmers, want Saigon to fall first before the Khmer Rouge succeeds."

The telephone rang. It was not the call Schanberg had been waiting for. "All right. Send him up," he said shortly, and poured another Scotch. Once the morning's Telexing was done, Pran could make himself useful. He could find out from his Cambodian liaison in the French Embassy what the feeling was about Valéry Giscard d'Estaing deciding to recognize the legitimacy of the Khmer Rouge.

There was a tentative knock on the door, Pran walked in, his blue cotton trousers flapping. Schanberg didn't look at him; he scowled at his typewriter.

"Where have you been?" he demanded. "You're late."

"They stop me because of curfew. It's dusk to dawn, Sydney."

Schanberg checked what he'd written so far and shoved it across the desk to Pran. "Put a hold on the last two paragraphs. I'll be over to the Telex office with corrections in an hour."

He switched off the lamp and opened the shutters, screwing up his eyes at the bright morning light. When he returned to the table, Pran was staring at him blankly. Schanberg sighed. He pointed at what he had written. "It starts with 'The French have recognized the insurgent government in Cambodia,' It ends with 'Preparing for this worst-case scenario, the *USS Hancock* and the *USS Okinawa* are now standing by in the Gulf of Siam.' "

"Sydney—"

"Okay?"

"They don't transmit today, Sydney."

Schanberg stared at his assistant. Pran hurried on, speaking in clipped, nervous tones. "The transmitter at Kambol got hit. They bring in auxiliary equipment. But no telephone or Telex today."

Schanberg went on staring in furious disbelief. Pran sucked in his cheeks.

"There was nothing I could do. . . ."

"Then what in the fuck am I doing this for?" Frustration and failure and whiskey-charged self-pity exploded in a bellow of rage. "You think this is how I want to spend my life? Hanging around every stinking diplomat with a bromide? Every stinking corrupt little politician, bribing them and kicking them and kissing their asses?" He stood up with a jerk that sent his chair crashing back on the frayed carpet and sent the typed pages flying. "Just tell me, what the fuck am I doing it for?"

He tore the new page out of his typewriter, screwed it in a ball, and flung it in the general direction of the refugees. Nothing worked in this damn country. They couldn't even fight a war and win. And Pran was on his fucking knees picking up the pages.

"They say maybe six P.M. we can file . . ." Pran ventured.

"Six P.M.? What do you think the newspaper is? A monthly magazine? I thought this was meant to be a partnership!" Raging, Schanberg retrieved a couple of pages Pran would have had to crawl under the table for. He hurt. He wanted to hurt back.

"Couldn't we try to update tomorrow?" Pran, frightened, was blinking rapidly.

"Don't ask me. I told you before, *don't ask me.*" A guided missile with its wires cut, he plunged at the nearest target. "You want to know something, find out yourself. Here are the pages. Here's a dictionary. Anything you don't understand, look it up. You wanna be a newspaper man, wanna be the best? Then look it up. Write it down. Read it!"

Pran stood there, holding the typed pages. The silence was louder than the moths, louder than the air conditioner. Schanberg paced through it, not looking at the Cambodian.

He came to a stop by the balcony. Men on ladders were painting a thick red cross on the tin roof of one of the hotel bungalows. In a cold, even voice he said, "I was at the embassy yesterday. I was told that when this place goes up, there is going to be a bloodbath. No question."

"Ah."

Schanberg looked at him. Pran was frowning in embarrassment at the pages. This wasn't the way he'd intended it to happen. He went on, in the same formal tone of voice, as if this procedural matter had distanced their friendship and opened a gulf between them. "I've arranged evacuation for you and your family. It's entirely up to you. Do you want to stay or do you want to leave?"

Pran was frowning at the pages. With a great effort of will, he looked Schanberg in the eye. "You stay?"

"That's none of your business. Do you want to stay or do you want to leave?"

Nothing moved in the room. Dith Pran gripped the pages with the hands of a drowning man. His throat was working. He blinked away the sudden brightness in his eyes and said, "I am journalist, too, Sydney."

They looked at each other. From his side of the gulf, Schanberg couldn't read Pran's face. He shrugged awkwardly. "Okay, take it easy, we don't have to decide right now." He hesitated. "There's some background we need on this story of France recognizing the Khmer Rouge," he said.

The breakfast room of the Hotel Phnom gave out onto the swimming pool. The group of journalists sat in lacquered rattan chairs with their backs to the window. The early-morning sun threw their shadows over trays of coffee cups set out on the serving table, and silver-plated coffeepots and milk jugs standing on hot plates. Al Rockoff chewed a slice of buttered toast with jam.

"Show us how it works, Des," he demanded.

"It works like any other walkie-talkie." Desmond France scowled at the photographers. When Lincoln had forced the damn machine on him yesterday, France had worn it under his shirt. Then everyone had accused him of wearing a pistol at his hip, like a Marine, so he'd tucked his shirt in and let the walkie-talkie dangle there, waiting to issue the word of command from the embassy.

A young Cambodian waiter with a pleasant smile filled their coffee cups and glided away as if it were just another morning. Desmond France sipped and slammed his cup down. "It's cold," he said violently. "Jesus Christ, it's typical."

"Typical of what?" asked Barry Morgan.

They were all exhausted, on edge, snapping at each other. France took the bait. "Of this bloody country, that's what. You try to help them, you give them everything they need, and look at them. They screw it up."

"That's the classic get-out line," drawled Jon Swain. "I think we're going to hear that one a few times." He leaned forward. "Desmond, did you ever hear the one about the Good Samaritan?"

"Bugger off, Jon."

Schanberg smiled. These two mixing it was always worth the price of admission.

"This guy gets mugged by thieves who take his watch and his wallet. Most of the cowardly types like me have been passing by on the other side, but then this Good Samaritan who's out on a jog sees what's happening. He rushes up and swings wildly at the thieves with his big stick. The thieves see it coming and duck. But the poor guy who's had his wallet stolen accidentally gets cracked on the head—so hard that he falls down and dies. So what does the Good Samaritan do? He goes away and prays for his soul!''

Al Rockoff and Schanberg joined in the laughter. France allowed himself a small smile. '' 'Cowardly types' like you would have let the muggers get away with murder,'' he observed.

Swain's reply was lost in a thunderous roar as two American F-4 fighter-bombers flew low overhead, rattling the coffee cups. Immediately afterward, Desmond's pocket began to whine. He took out the walkie-talkie and propped it against the toast rack.

"Four Zero Alpha. Four Zero Alpha. This is Tango. Assemble your group at my location. Repeat. Assemble your group at my location.''

It clicked off. The silence was broken by a discreet cough at Schanberg's elbow.

"More coffee, Mr. Schanberg, sir?''

Schanberg looked up at the familiar brown face. "No,'' he said awkwardly. "I have to go.''

He went back to his room, like the others. This was it. *We're either living or we're staying.* His resolution of the last few days wavered. To be on the safe side, he stuffed a change of clothes and some personal papers in his shoulder bag. AFN Saigon was reporting a story that Kissinger was offering to fly Sihanouk back to Phnom Penh, no strings attached. Well, it was too late now. He phoned Pran to give him details of the evacuation and went downstairs, through the lobby and out of the main doors, feeling the gaze of the hotel porters on the back of his neck.

At the foot of the steps, a beggar, shrapnel-blinded, was playing "Greensleeves" on a wooden flute. A boy held out a bowl. Grateful for once that there was no sign of Sarun and the Mercedes, Schanberg tossed some riels in it and hailed a cyclo.

"The American Embassy," he said, for the last time. The streets were full of Cambodians and Chinese going about their normal business, placidly secure in the protection of their ally, Uncle Sam. He settled farther back in the cracked leather seat, like a man on the run.

Outside the embassy, a small crowd had gathered. Faces were turned up to the sky from which five years of files and cables were falling slowly in gray flakes of ash. A youngster stood on one leg and scratched the other with his foot. There were no banners, no shouted protests. People took photographs of each other posing by the chain link fence. An old man plucked his whiskers in the mirror of a brand-new motorbike. The mood was one of curiosity more than fear. The American planes must be bringing reinforcements; they clapped and cheered. Anxiously smiling, the people of Phnom Penh were being drawn here to witness something they did not yet understand. When it was over, they still would not believe it.

Operation Eagle Pull had been quietly in progress ever since the start of the dry-season offensive. Non-vital embassy staff had been tiptoeing out of the country on scheduled flights in twos and threes. Their absence was noticed only by a few keen-eyed people like Schanberg, who saw the names scrubbed from the tennis tournament lists at the Cercle Sportif and who missed the familiar faces at the bar. Meanwhile, American diplomats were driven at high speed around the streets of the capital, opening a new ammunitions factory here, a new clinic there, as though by their intensified activity they could disguise the long good-bye.

The embassy itself began sprouting creepers of chicken wire, barbed wire, and rocket wire, which clambered in menacing thickets along the top of the perimeter fence and vaulted across the compound to the embassy roof where they intertwined with aerials, dipoles, reflectors, and a telecommunications antenna array until it was hard to uncluster security from intelligence systems, defense from attack.

Now that drawdown had become pull-out, the time for subterfuge was over. The main gate of the embassy was locked and barred. Behind the fence strode Marines, M-16s at the ready. A couple of flatbed trucks were parked in the forecourt, loading up with people and luggage. As Schanberg looked at the milling crowd, there was a roaring in his ears, and five U.S. Marine Jolly Green Giant helicopters came mashing down out of the hot sky. They swooped low over the embassy and landed in a cloud of dust on a football field a quarter of a mile away. It was nine o'clock. The evacuation had begun.

A Sea Stallion appeared out of nowhere and hovered thunderously over the incinerator smoke before settling in the embassy grounds like a fat metal bird in a nest of barbed wire. Marines jumped off, heavy-footed with guns and ammunition to help defend the mission against its allies. Schanberg crossed the boulevard to the main gate. There was no sign of Pran. The atmosphere was getting edgy. Lincoln's number two was on the sidewalk talking to a diminutive Cambodian woman toting a large shopping bag.

"Major Slade isn't here. I don't know where he is, honey."

"Major Slade, he sent me for his steaks! I have his groceries!" She held up the bag to prove this was all some mistake.

"Do you have money? Do you have any money?"

"Yes, money. Money for the housekeepings."

"Not any longer, sweetheart. You better hang onto it. Major Slade has gone away. No come back."

Schanberg turned away, hearing the tears start behind him. Pran's ancient green Renault, he couldn't miss it. It had to be somewhere here. Urgently, he pushed his way around to the side gate. It was guarded by Marines, bulging out of their civilian suits. A Marine sergeant stood checking off each evacuee, who was then issued with a brown tag recording his name and evacuation priority and sent to join one of the lines for the flatbed trucks.

The crowd was pushed back to allow through police outriders escorting a black limousine. A door opened, a middle-aged Cambodian was hustled through with his family and issued with tags. Schanberg recognized Saukham Khoy, the acting President. In his wake, he pushed forward and shouted a question.

"Has Dith Pran been through? Wife and four kids?"

The sergeant consulted his list and shook his head. "Thirty-two through thirty-seven. No, sir." He stepped in Schanberg's path and added, "Once you go in, sir, you can't come out again." Schanberg looked at his watch. Slade's disembodied voice boomed through loudspeakers. "At zero nine hundred thirty hours, no more evacuees accepted!'' The announcement was greeted by a push toward the side gate. The Marines stood shoulder to shoulder, although there was still more puzzlement than anger on the faces around them. A rich Chinese merchant, his family behind him, pushed diamonds in a twist of paper into the sergeant's hand. Schanberg didn't wait to see what effect this bribe would have. Running now, he got back to the main gate. Al Rockoff was there, taking pictures of a tall black Marine surrounded by a gaggle of fascinated Cambodian children. He hadn't seen Pran, either.

Schanberg gazed wildly up and down the road and back at the embassy. Through a filigree of ash he saw small figures on the embassy roof. The Stars and Stripes was lowered from the high flagpole. A Marine on the roof raised his M-16 and fired three blanks in the air, as if over a freshly dug grave.

U.S. jets screamed overhead, escorting four more Sea Stallion helicopters to the football field. Lincoln shouted at Schanberg from the other side of the embassy fence. ''Hurry it, Sydney! You've got about five minutes!''

''I'm waiting for Dith Pran!''

Lincoln shrugged and was gone.

The trickle of evacuees was dying. Most of the trucks had left. Carrying his youngest child in his arms, Pran pushed his way to the side entrance. Ser Moeun followed with the other three children. They carried their lives in two plastic bags and a suitcase.

''Dith Pran and family.''

''Who?'' The Marine sergeant scowled. A Sea Stallion returning to the *USS Okinawa* had blown Pran's words away.

''Dith Pran and family!''

A whistle shrilled. The detachment of Marines contracted into the embassy forecourt. The sergeant canceled his list with a stroke of the pencil and waved Pran back into Cambodia. The side gate closed.

In the forecourt, Desmond France was clambering onto the last truck. Pran shouted his name through cupped hands. France did not hear. The crowd pressed around him. Ser Moeun was making sobbing noises in her throat. Pran cried at the sergeant, "*You know me!*" Above him, whirring rotors beat toward freedom. The Marines followed France onto the truck, and it disappeared around the back of the embassy.

The crowd melted away. The spectacle was over. Pran saw Rockoff loping down the street.

"Al! Al! Help us!"

Another Sea Stallion low overhead. But Rockoff heard him. And saw him. And recognized him. And ran back to help.

The field was a billowing blur of dust and rotor blades. The squat black shapes rose, one by one, in a tight spiral over the city before heading westward to the Gulf of Siam. Carrying Pran's youngest son, Schanberg sprinted toward the dust and noise. Pran was at his heels carrying another of his children. Ser Moeun followed, head down, a scarf across her nose. The two oldest boys trundled the bags and suitcase across the baked earth.

Pran was stopped in his tracks by a machine gun held by a towering Marine.

"These are evacuees!" yelled Schanberg. The gun was turned on him. Another Sea Stallion spiraled skyward, blotting out the sun. In its shadow a black Cadillac drew up, pennants flapping in the dust storm. The Marine kept his finger on the trigger. A chauffeur opened the car door, and out stepped the United States Ambassador, bending in the wind. In his arms, wrapped in a shroud of transparent plastic, was the Stars and Stripes.

Schanberg nodded. That was the right stuff: keeping up appearances even though there was no one to witness this proud exit, apart from himself and Pran and a few Marines, and a gaggle of small Cambodian children by the touchline who were jumping up and down with joy shouting, "U.S. Number One!" Then Schanberg noticed a film cameraman, who had got out the other side of the Cadillac and positioned himself to record these final seconds of the American presence in the land they came to save.

His face drawn but his head held high, the Ambassador strode past them, cradling the U.S. flag in its protective polyethylene wrapping. Lincoln offered to take it from him; the Ambassador refused, tight-lipped. Slade, the last of the group, noticed Schanberg and marched up to his old enemy. For a moment, Schanberg thought he was going to hit him. Slade took his pistol out of its holster.

"Are you staying behind?" he asked.

Schanberg nodded. Dust stung his cheeks as another Sea Stallion thrashed into the sky. Slade held out his gun, butt end to the journalist. It looked ridiculously small in his big fist. "You better take this for protection," he said. "This time there's no Formosa to retreat to."

Schanberg felt his defenses slipping. He managed a grin. "No, thanks, I'd end up shooting my foot," he replied.

The haze of dust suddenly lifted, just as the Khmer Rouge renewed their artillery attack from across the Mekong after holding fire to let the Americans get out. It was a moment Schanberg committed to memory. The Ambassador, bent low in the door of the helicopter, had turned and raised his hand in farewell. The film camera-man was sprawled on the ground, shooting up at him. At the far end of the pitch, a goalpost had been hit by a Communist shell and was blazing. And the little children, seeing the diplomat wave his hand, were waving back at him. Schanberg could hear their voices, laughing and mimicking, *"Okay, bye-bye. Okay, bye-bye . . ."*

The helicopter door slammed. The marine lowered his machine gun and raced away from them. There were only two Sea Stallions left on the field now. The Marines were converging on one, backing into it defensively, ready to repel a last-minute assault. Pran and his family ran full tilt for the other. Schanberg reached it first and bundled each of the children on board. Hands reached down for Ser Moeun; the rotors were thudding faster and faster; there was no time left. Pran helped her up; she reached down and clasped his arm and cried out to him.

Schanberg stood back. Pran looked at him, and Schanberg shook his head. He was staying. What Pran did now was up to him. There was no time to discuss it. Pran was a free agent; he had to make up his own mind.

Pran looked up at his wife. Ser Moeun was pulled back into the shadow; the door was shut in his face. With a scream of motors, the Sea Stallion wrenched into the air.

The two men were left alone in the middle of the football field, which was suddenly the emptiest place in the world.

A group of the children came up to Schanberg and danced around him in a ring, holding hands. "Bye-bye!"

they chanted at the American, "bye-bye!" Schanberg hitched his camera bag on his shoulder and stole a look at his assistant. Pran was standing a little way apart, his lips pressed tight, his arms stiff by his sides. Red dust had settled over his best black shoes. Together they watched the helicopter circling above until it was a speck in the unforgiving blue.

Pran looks intently through the Renault windshield at the face of Ser Moeun. The road back to the Hotel Phnom is snarled with cycles and dispersing sightseers—he hardly sees them. In Ser Moeun's face, as she reaches down from the helicopter, is a look of desolation. She is terribly alone and terribly afraid, but he can see in her eyes that her fear is not for herself—it is for him.

Taking one hand off the wheel, Pran clasps the little Buddha hanging around his neck and presses it to his lips. Immediately he is calmer. Ser Moeun and he cannot be separated in the spirit however many oceans and continents she is being carried apart from him. That is his consolation for abandoning his family to foreigners in a foreign land.

He looks at Sydney sitting beside him, then quickly looks away. He had looked at Sydney when Ser Moeun was in the helicopter. He had and met his eyes and seen him give that small shake of the head. It had told him what in his heart he already knew: that Sydney was staying, and that he would not leave Sydney to stay on alone. But Ser Moeun was looking at him, crying out to him soundlessly in the panic of the engines . . . and his heart was confused.

So when the door slammed and the helicopter took them away, what he felt was not grief but anger at himself for his weakness. Sydney had worked out what he was going to do. Sydney's decisions never took him by surprise later on; as a proper journalist, he was prepared in his heart for every situation as it arose. Why was he, Pran, so indecisive? All he had worried about was getting Ser Moeun and the children out of Phnom Penh. After that, faced with the biggest decision of his career, he had . . . *waffled*.

He swings the car sharply onto the boulevard. Schanberg looks at him as if waking from a trance. He stretches his arms behind his head.

"We're going to be busy, you and I," he says quietly.

Pran half-grins back with a feeling of pride, his anger forgotten. He has a sudden vision of Sydney and him, the last defenders of the besieged city, alone in the barricaded General Post Office sending out Telex messages to the world while the Khmer Rouge batters on the doors in frustration. Revving the engine slightly, he turns the little green car into the drive of the Hotel Phnom. Men in overalls are draping its front balconies with Red Cross flags and dragging sheaves of barbed wire across the forecourt.

Schanberg gets out, delving in his camera bag, and bangs cheerfully on the Renault's roof. Halfway up the steps, underneath a large banner that reads "This Building Has Been Designated an International Security Zone," he turns around holding his Nikon.

"Smile!" he calls to Pran, and takes his photograph.

We're on our own now. That's what Schanberg had felt like saying. For Pran's sake he had put on a brave face in the car, but there was an emptiness in the city, which two and a half million refugees couldn't fill. The American exodus had left a vacuum. He felt like a scuba diver whose oxygen had switched off.

"*Vous n'êtes pas parti!*" Schanberg gave a thumbs-up to the hotel clerk and porter who had grins all over their faces at this proof that America had not utterly abandoned them.

Oxygen was the first thing he saw inside the lobby—canisters of it stacked against the fleur-de-lis wallpaper. A couple of women in nurse's uniforms were attacking a large box marked "Red Cross." Several more boxes were piled up by the coatroom. A hospital smell of formaldehyde had replaced the familiar aroma of stale coffee. On the receptionist's transistor radio, the strains of the First World War French marching song, "*Sambre et Meuse,*" rounded off the siege atmosphere.

"*Apporte-moi des oeufs brouillés et du jambon auprès de la piscine,*" he ordered. He strolled through the breakfast room—where three hours ago Tango had told Four Zero Alpha they had lift-off—and out to the pool.

Even here, in this last redoubt of good living, the war was seeping in. Somewhere a mynah bird was chattering, and the jacaranda trees were heavy with bluish-purple blossoms, but the swimming pool had turned a vinaigrette color and had beer bottles and cigarette packets floating in it. The refugees had come nearer, too, since last night. They were down inside the garden now, in gypsy huddles all along the wall with their cooking pots and mattress bundles. The ashes of camp fires sent up a haze of gray smoke.

Oblivious to all this, two elderly French *colons* were sitting by the pool playing a game of chess. Farther along, a lanky figure lounged in a faded green deck chair, hidden behind an airmail copy of the London *Times*.

"Jon?" hazarded Schanberg.

"Princess Anne and Captain Mark Phillips must've had a tough weekend," said Jon Swain without lowering the paper. "The horse trials at Badminton had to be abandoned because of heavy rain."

"It's a lousy world," said Schanberg, sitting beside him and picking up a newspaper to shield his eyes from the sun. "What else is new?"

"Forty-two degrees and partly cloudy in London." He paused. "Scared bloody stiff, aren't you?"

"What else is new?" said Schanberg again with a smile. He took out a cigarette and lit it with a hand that was trembling slightly. A handful of French and Swedish journalists came out of the breakfast room and stood staring at the refugees. Behind them, the two Red Cross nurses wheeled a stainless-steel trolley laden with plastic-wrapped surgical instruments down the path of the requisitioned bungalow.

"If it gets to be a run-out," said Swain evenly, "I was told our best bet is the French Embassy."

"Who told you that?"

"The British Embassy."

"That makes sense." Schanberg yawned. His eyes were up close to a large cartoon on his newspaper hat. He brought it down to study. Drawn in bold strokes was a satanic, scowling figure wearing black pajamas and labeled "The Dangerous Khmer." He stood over a bath full of Cambodian children, lathering them with a bar of soap shaped like a mortar and marked "Made in the USA." Dozens of shell cases littered the bathroom floor. In the background a tophatted Uncle Sam squatted on a lavatory, shitting himself. A grotesque caricature of President Ford dressed as a weeping nursemaid was bringing in fresh bombs for the bloodbath. The caption, in French, read *"Savon pour le Bain."*

A soft tread approached along the paving. *"Sûr la table, s'il vous plaît,"* commanded Schanberg. But it was not the waiter.

"KR has taken Samrong Teav," announced Pran, squinting down at his notebook with its neat, cramped writing. "That is very close to Pochentong Airport. Two miles."

"Okay," said Schanberg.

"Good for you," said Swain, interrupting. He had put the *Times* down and was looking at Dith Pran with frank admiration. "Jesus, Pran, you could have been halfway to America by now."

"Okay, go on," repeated Schanberg, scowling.

"They have no radio contact with Arey Khsat. That is government stronghold on the Mekong, two miles from here. They think KR have overran Arey Khsat. And Communists have attacked along the Bassac River to within five miles of Phnom Penh."

"What's the word on AFN Saigon about the American evacuation?"

Pran shook his head. Swain butted in. "I listened at ten o'clock. The lead story is that Josephine Baker is dead. Born the daughter of a St. Louis washerwoman, she became a legend of the Paris music halls and the highest-paid entertainer in Europe. If the Americans have evacuated Phnom Penh, it hasn't made the news yet."

"Long Boret has gone on radio," offered Pran.

"What's he got to say?"

"The premier says that Saukham Khoy is a coward for going with the Americans. The leadership is now with a committee of ministers and generals that wants to talk to the Khmer Rouge."

Schanberg was scribbling busily in the margins of his newspaper hat. "Poor bastards," he said softly. "Not enough government left even to arrange a decent surrender. . . ."

As he spoke, there was a sudden shriek across the sky. Schanberg, Swain, and Pran dived to the ground, coffee cups and saucers shattering around them. Fast out of the north, with a noise like a tear in sheet metal, came a T-28 fighter bomber. It screamed over them so low, Schanberg could see the weapon pylons. A moment later they were rocked by two explosions just two hundred yards away. A column of brown smoke leisurely toppled upward.

The French and Swedish journalists ran for their cameras. As he and Pran followed them inside, Schanberg noticed the refugees sitting as impassively and unmoving as pawns on the Frenchmen's chessboard. They had been through all this. Now it was the city dwellers' turn.

PRO: NOR SQUARE: 05120: PARA: AYE FEW MINUTES AFTER TEN RPT TEN AYEM THERE IS LOUD EXPLOSION NOT NOT FAR AWAY: AYE DEFECTING GOVERNMENT PILOT HAS JUST BOMBED MILITARY COMMAND HEADQUARTERS BEFORE FLYING OFF INTO INSURGENT TERRITORY: THE TWO RPT TWO BOMBS FELL ON AYE MILITARY TRANSPORT OFFICE KILLING SEVEN PERSONS AND WOUNDING MANY OTHERS: PARA: MORE: SCHANBERG:

Red Cross workers carrying the body of a seven-year-old boy in a polyethylene sheet, his blood lapping at the edges as they take him to the Red Cross ambulance. A large white concrete building that has collapsed upon itself in layers that look soft as cake; flames lick up from in between each layer. An elderly official in a dark pinstripe suit, his trousers blown off by the explosion, wanders around in a daze, waving helpers away; threads of blood come from under his jacket and trickle down his bare legs. An American woman journalist interrogates a Red Cross worker at the other end of the stretcher she is helping carry to the ambulance. A German television crew moves in like hunters; their cameraman pushes forward to the ambulance a sun-gun briefly flares, illuminating a chamber of horrors. An army officer's cap lies in the middle of the street; cyclo drivers ring their bells and go around it; nobody picks it up for fear of what might be left inside. . . .

PRO: NOR SQUARE: 05136: PARA: THE INSURGENTS ATTACK TO-DAY SEEMS TO BE COMING MOSTLY FROM THE NORTH AND NORTHWEST: REPORTS THAT THE INSURGENTS HAVE SHOWN THEMSELVES IN AYE NEIGHBORHOOD KNOWN AS TUOL KORK RPT TUOL KORK: BUT DIFFICULT TO GET COHERENT PICTURE EVEN THOUGH INSURGENT RING AROUND P.P. IS AYE TIGHT ONE AND ALL FRONTS VERY CLOSE: PRAN AND EYE RACE FROM FRONT TO FRONT: TRY TO TALK TO REFUGEES: TRY TO VISIT HOSPITALS: BUT NEVER SEEM ABLE TO COVER EVERY-THING: PARA: MORE: SCHANBERG:

Swabs and a stench of antiseptic in the Red Cross bungalow. Seven men and one woman on chairs in line to a wooden table, the syringe going into the upper arm and drawing out a pint of dark blood. Nurses on urgent errands opening and closing the batik curtain that separates off the candlelit corridor. Pran, eyes wide with fright, clenching his fist as the rubber tourniquet goes on. Schanberg, a pint lighter, following an English nurse into a room full of children, some injured, some starving, almost all with dysentery. Huge eyes in narrow, pinched faces, some anxious and trusting, others remote and serious as if approaching a mystery, too far gone for trust or mistrust. A little girl with a topknot who smiles and chirps when she sees Schanberg—perhaps recognizing him. *"U.S. number one. Okay!"* A French Red Cross doctor bends over her and marks a cross on her forehead with a red felt-tip pen, as one of the probable survivors. Schanberg can see only one ridge under the blanket where her legs should be and moves on down the room. In the corner, a baby with its belly swollen by starvation, its skin covered in sores, rests in his grandmother's lap and sucks vainly at her wrinkled dug. She sits quite still with her eyes closed, unable to look down at him any longer. Schanberg turns away, his eyes smarting. He cannot write this. He should look at the children to see what number stand a chance of living, but the red cross is on their forehead and he might meet their eyes. Pran stands at the door, watching him. He has a trustful look, like some of the children. They all think there is something he can do.

PRO: NOR SQUARE: 05142: AYEM: PARA: AYE TELEGRAM COMES FOR CAMBODIAN MILITARY LEADERS: ITS FROM LIEUTENANT COLONEL JACK DERING: RPT JACK DERING AYE FORMER ASSISTANT AT AMERICAN EMBASSY: IT SAYS: QUOTE EYE APOLOGIZE FOR MY COUNTRY'S TOTAL LACK OF CONSIDERATION FOR THE KHMER PEOPLE WHO FIGHT SO COURAGEOUSLY FOR THEIR FREEDOM: MY SHAME IS DEEP: UNQUOTE: PARA: MORE: SCHANBERG:

Ultraviolet light and a wall of sound. A heisted U.S. army generator powers Pink Floyd's *Dark Side of the Moon* and a Golden Bonanza pinball machine, maybe the last one working. A seedy basement bar with peeling evacuation posters becomes suddenly fashionable since the shelling started. Gordon McIntyre is at the long, chrome-plated counter. The barman pushes a purplish-colored drink in a long glass to Schanberg, sitting beside him.

"What's this?"

"The barman's latest cocktail, my friend. He's christened it 'Good-bye Uncle Sam.' "

Through the cigarette smoke Schanberg can see the barman grinning at him with a mouthful of gold teeth. "What's in it?"

"Bitters, mostly. It goes without saying."

The Pink Floyd stops in mid-synthesizer. Somebody has turned on the radio—AFN Saigon.

". . . flawless operation. By eleven hundred hours 276 people, including 159 Cambodians and other foreign nationals, had been airlifted out to safety from the beleaguered city. Secretary of Defense James R. Schlesinger lost no time in sending a message of congratulations to Pacific Commander Noel Gaylor in Honolulu, commending his forces for a safe and smooth operation."

The Pink Floyd returns with a high, screeching wail that ends in a cackle of laughter. Baby-faced Cambodian teen-agers are clicking solenoids and lighting explosions on Golden Bonanza. McIntyre is breathing in his ear, telling him his troubles. The tiredness talking.

"No blood left. All eleven hospitals drained of blood. I go out and I bargain for it. That's right, up and down the street. Here's a bowl of rice and a bit of fish, and can I have a pint of your blood, please? And they smile. A smiling people. But when I get back to the wards, oh, God. I give them blood, and they look at me, and they hate me for keeping them alive. Or so I sometimes think. Is that not your experience as a journalist, Mr. Schanberg? You look at their faces and you don't precisely know what they're thinking always, but it might be hate?''

Schanberg is thinking of Pran. He knows him, he realizes. He *knows* Pran, and that is worth a hundred books about Cambodia, a thousand articles, a lifetime of speculation. ''Not hatred, no,'' he says. ''It is grief. Grief. It doesn't stay on their faces, but it goes inside, and it stays inside for a long time. . . .'' He stops. McIntyre's head is resting on his arms. After forty-eight hours of propping his eyes open, he has given up the struggle.

PRO: NOR SQUARE: 05150: PARA: AT SEVEN-TWENTY: RPT: SEVEN-TWENTY AYEM THE INSURGENT CLANDESTINE RADIO AN-NOUNCES QUOTE THE REGIME OF THE TRAITORS IS FALLING UNQUOTE: GOVERNMENT DEFENSE LINES CONTINUE TO CRUM-BLE AS THE INSURGENTS CLOSE ON CAPITAL: ROAD TO AIRPORT IS CUT AND UNDER CONSTANT ARTILLERY ATTACK: YESTER-DAY PUSH COMING FROM NORTHWEST: TODAY COMING FROM ALL DIRECTIONS: PARA: MORE: SCHANBERG:

Who are the refugees, who the city people—none of them can tell any longer. Phnom Penh is divided into those who are fighting and those who are sheltering from the fight. Without effective relief organizations now the Americans have gone, malnutrition is everywhere. The zoo animals on Phnom Hill have been eaten, except for the two venerated tigers, which have mysteriously vanished. A teenage boy outside the Post Office begs for riels while his mother searches through garbage for plastic bags to sell. On their way there, this morning, Schanberg and Pran pass a bizarre procession of Cambodian men, women, and children marching shoulder to shoulder and singing an American hymn, "Meet Me at the River." A Southern Baptist missionary is leading them. He is offering them food and shelter in exchange for eternal life; they can hardly lose.

Passport, money, camera, film, extra notebooks, change of shirt and underwear, soap, toothbrush. Schanberg carries his survival kit in a blue Pan Am bag, Pran, in a knapsack. *Sauve qui peut*. The university is being turned into a fortress, with troops and half-tracks preparing for a last-ditch defense. The students barricade the stairs to classrooms and laboratories or climb up on the roof to watch the fighting on all sides. On the front lawn, two first-year students caress each other, giggles and endearments in the lee of the guns. The boy asks Pran to take a snapshot of them holding hands. He writes down his name and address. Keep the picture for us until after the war is over, he says, laughing.

PRO: NOR SQUARE: 05154: PARA: AYE CABLEGRAM BROUGHT IN FOR TRANSMISSION U.S.A. FROM THE CAPS NATIONAL BANK OF CAMBODIA CAPS TO THE IRVING TRUST COMPANY IN NEW YORK ASKING THE AMERICAN BANK TO CONFIRM THAT IT WAS CARRYING OUT AN EARLIER ORDER TO PAY DOLLARS ONE MILLION RPT ONE MILLION TO MARSHAL LON NOL: THE EARLIER ORDER WAS SENT ON APRIL ONE THE DAY THE MARSHAL WENT INTO EXILE: PARA: MORE: SCHANBERG:

The wires still sprout, along with a few weeds. Schanberg pushes at the gate—it is open—turns the handle on a side door, and walks into the embassy the way the Ambassador walked out. Faces stare at him from behind packing cases. Doors open a crack and swiftly shut again. Refugees have got in here, too. They lie on the desks and sofas and squat on the floor under the big chandelier. In little puddles on the floor are the remains of fish-cake packets and broiler-house steaks taken from the kitchen and guarded until they unfroze. Schanberg goes up the stairs, walks down carpeted corridors, pushes at doors. All is quiet up here. The Ambassador's office is just as he must have left it, even to the smell of insect repellent his secretary had sprayed every morning to kill any foreign body that moved. On the wall, an outline of unfaded paint marks where the eagle once hung.

On the shiny leather of the desk is a photocopied note that must have arrived just as the Ambassador was leaving. Schanberg examines it. Addressed to President Ford, it is from Prince Sirik Matak, one of the original leaders of the coup that ousted Sihanouk, and prime minister for almost the whole of Lon Nol's presidency.

Dear Excellency and friend,

   I thank you very sincerely for your letter and for your offer to transport me toward freedom. I cannot, alas, leave in such a cowardly fashion. As for you, and in particular for your great country, I never believed for a moment that you would have this sentiment of abandoning a people that has chosen liberty. You have refused us your protection, and we can do nothing about it. You leave, and it is my wish that you and your country will find happiness under the sky. But mark it well that if I shall die here on the spot and in my country that I love, it is too bad, because we are all born and must die one day. I have only committed this mistake of believing in you, the Americans. Please accept, Excellency, my dear friend, my faithful and friendly sentiments.

Sirik Matak.

At the bottom the Prince has written in his own hand: "*This is an open letter to President Ford and the people of America.*"

Schanberg folds it carefully and puts it in his pocket. The Ambassador's windows are open; he closes the shutters to help deflect shrapnel fragments. Then he leaves the darkened room and goes back down the stairs, taking care not to tread upon any of the refugees.

PRO: NOR SQUARE: 05160: PARA: BY MIDNIGHT RPT MIDNIGHT THE INSURGENTS REACH THE SOUTHERN EDGE OF PHNOM PENH AND AYE FIERCE BATTLE ERUPTS AT THE APPROACHES TO THE UNITED NATIONS BRIDGE IN AYE NEIGHBORHOOD NAMED CHBAR AMOU RPT CHBAR AMOU: PEOPLE FLEEING THE SCENE SAY GOVERNMENT FORCES USING APCS EQUIPPED WITH MORTARS AND HEAVY MACHINE GUNS TO TRY AND BLOCK INSURGENTS FROM CROSSING THE BRIDGE: PARA: MORE: SCHANBERG:

Flames and smoke and falling masonry. Pran and Schanberg in the Mercedes battling across the city in a wail of sirens, shuddering over scattered debris, bumping over fire hoses, skidding in muddy washes of water. Sarun backs up a narrow street under a canopy of smoke. A fifty-foot arc from a burst water main crashes against the back window. Through drapes of reddish water they see silhouettes running for their lives. The hissing might be steam, or it might be a rocket. As they cower, with arms over their heads, a menswear shop in front of them kneels ponderously like an elephant and collapses in a storm of smoke and raining glass. A jacket flies through the air, flapping empty sleeves. Naked tailors' dummies lie in the smoking timbers; some of the injured are bleeding and try to rise. As Pran and Schanberg and Sarun shake themselves, two white oxen come stampeding through the noise and smoke. Staring eyes and saliva through the shivered windshield, and they plunge on. But it is the end for the Mercedes. Sarun cannot work miracles. The car can go no farther. Nor can they.

PRO: NOR SQUARE: 15161: PARA::::

The chatter of the teleprinter echoed in Schanberg's head as he lay fully dressed on his unmade bed, blowing cigarette smoke out through the mosquito net. A blood vessel was throbbing above his left eye. He was too tired to sleep. When he closed his eyes, images of the dying city revolved in their pain and hopelessness like the refugees on the garden wall circled in his nightmare. He gave up and went downstairs to try to eat something.

Now that the Hotel Phnom had officially been declared a neutral zone, and the Red Cross had taken over the restaurant as a casualty clearing center, the dining tables had been moved out of the breakfast room along the edge of the pool.

The refugees, meanwhile, had advanced across the grass. Now they were congregated in small groups just on the other side of the pool, some lying asleep on their rush mats, others sitting perfectly still with their cooking pots and bundles, gazing across the green plastic cord that separated them from the Westerners dining in style across the water. McIntyre was there, wolfing down a cold chicken curry. Schanberg joined him, and ordered a plate of spaghetti.

"A classic demonstration of apartheid, wouldn't you say?" McIntyre jabbed with his fork at the refugees. Schanberg nodded, too tired to answer. Barry Morgan was sauntering past, hands deep in his pockets, his face and safari suit begrimed with soot, obviously just back from one of his exclusive I-Saved-an-Orphan-from-the-Khmer-Rouge eyewitness reports for his rag. Schanberg felt a twinge of irritation. For all his unpleasantness, there was no denying that Morgan was a good reporter, one of the best. A pity he had to parade the fact.

Morgan stopped at their table. His expression was sober. "The Commies are making a big push for the Monivong Bridge," he told them. "They've fired most of the houses nearby. Go up on the roof, you'll see what I mean."

Schanberg waited till Morgan had gone, then excused himself. In the lobby, he met Pran bringing the latest photographs. Together they went up the stairs, past the deserted top floor to the narrow walkway on top of the mansard roof, so far undamaged by the shelling.

The spectacle that confronted them had a kind of terrible grandeur, like a Victorian mural painting of hell. They were standing in a circle of flame, which thickened around the very edge of Phnom Penh. Fires of battle hemmed them in, turning the night sky orange. To the north and west, whole neighborhoods were burning. They could smell the smoke and hear the relentless percussion of battle, the sounds of mortars and machine guns and rockets sending tracer streaks across the sky.

Down there in the darkness, Cambodian was fighting Cambodian in a desperate last-ditch frenzy. The Khmer Rouge were winning because their leaders knew what they were fighting for, and for all of them it was the same thing. The Army of the Republic, deserted by its top leader, deserted by some of its senior officers, even, went on fighting like a headless chicken, because it was all there was left. None that Schanberg had found fought out of love for the Republic or fervent hatred of the Communist threat. They fought for themselves and for what remained of their families, and because there was nowhere else to go. They fought out of fear and because they had been told to fight.

The two newsmen gazed south toward the Bassac River where the flames raged highest of all, and the tiny blinks of light on the river were the searchlights of Naval gunboats weaving among the humped bodies in the river looking for survivors. The guns flashed like Morse lamps signaling a message of disaster.

Pran gripped the railing with both arms.

"It is finished," he said in a quiet voice. "It is finished. The war is over."

"Yes." Schanberg folded his arms. "Now only the killing is left."

PRO: NOR SQUARE: 15162: PARA: FOR THIRD STRAIGHT DAY REFUGEES ARE SURGING TOWARD THE CITY CENTER: CASUALTIES ARE HORRENDOUS THE HIGHEST NUMBER OF DEAD AND WOUNDED OF ANY DAY IN THE FIVE YEARS OF THIS WAR: PARA: TONIGHT THE GOVERNMENT RADIO ANNOUNCED THE

APPOINTMENT OF AYE NEW MINISTER OF STATE FOR INDUS-
TRY MINES AND TOURISM: RPT: TOURISM: PARA: MORE: SCHAN-
BERG:

It was an hour, still, before dawn. The cable office was
rancid with sweat and tobacco smoke. A Telex operator,
patchy with fatigue, clattered at the keyboards of one of the
last two teleprinters in Phnom Penh, pushing copy out through
an ancient Chinese-made transmitter, now that the main
transmission tower in the suburb of Kambol has been over-
run by the Khmer Rouge. Jon Swain and Al Rockoff slept
through the din, curled up on straw mats on the dusty
floor.

Schanberg was at a nearby table, pounding away at a
typewriter he could hardly focus on for tiredness. A wet
towel was wrapped around his head. Sarun brought him a
fresh cup of weak tea. The chauffeur's face was as round
and cheerful as ever, although he now wore suspenders to
keep up his gray flannel trousers. As the American's head
began to droop, he put the tea down and vigorously rubbed
his shoulders and pulled at his ears, a Cambodian massage
Schanberg had become familiar with. Two French journalists sat writing farther up the table. Barry Morgan had
brought a long think-piece into the office shortly after
midnight.

The Telex operators were even more exhausted than
Schanberg. Two of them had given up and gone next door
to catch some rest. The third was kept going only by Pran,
indomitable Pran, who joked with him and urged him on
as he had been doing, almost ceaselessly as it seemed to
the rest of them, since the Americans had left. It was Pran
who kept them here, Pran who persuaded them to carry out

repairs when a line went dead, who beseeched them, when the transmitter overheated, not to go home.

Outside, through the shutters, Schanberg could hear the faint shriek of shells and the thud of heavy explosions. The headless chicken was on its knees. He wrote, "Daybreak, five-fifty A.M. Having rejected last minute negotiations, the Communists gather themselves for a final assault on Phnom Penh. It is now only a matter of whether the government forces surrender before or after this beautiful city has been reduced to rubble and thousands more men, women, and children have died in the hand-to-hand fighting. Prime Minister Long Boret, interviewed a few hours ago by this correspondent, declared, 'The military situation has become impossible. We have no more material means. We feel completely abandoned.' "

. Schanberg tore the page out of the typewriter and gave it to Sarun, who put it on the clip. Pran took it and marked it up for the Telex operator who was completing a transmission for the *Le Monde* correspondent. Schanberg got up and paced the floor, lighting another cigarette to calm his nerves.

The loud, mechanical chatter barely paused as the Cambodian operator took *The New York Times* copy and started transmission across half the world:

PRO: NOR SQUARE: 15164: PA . . .

The Telex went dead. It was all over. In the cable office, the echoing silence was so sudden that it woke Swain, who uncurled his legs and sat up against the wall, blinking sleepily. This time Schanberg did not shout at Pran and Pran did not renew his negotiations with the Telex operator.

Instead, the *Times* bureau chief sat down and looked at his watch before he typed a few final words on the Olivetti: At five fifty-seven A.M., the Telex ceases to operate. End copy. Schanberg, Phnom Penh, April 17, 1975.

Then he went to the shutters and opened them. The sounds of shelling and gunfire had quieted. The dawn was breaking peacefully in a speckle of gray and blue streaked with pink, like a rainbow trout on the St. Regis in the Adirondacks where he sometimes got to fish. White flowers bloomed on the lychee trees in the post office courtyard. He realized with a shock that he could hear birdsong.

Time had run out on them. The Telex had been their link with sanity; it had given them a purpose in life. Now that this purpose was ended, they had nothing to do but observe and survive. That might not be so easy. As Schanberg caught Pran's eye, he knew they were both thinking the same thing. Every day new stories had emerged about the barbarism and brutality of the Khmer Rouge. Now they were the conquerors, would things be any different?

"I'm going back to clean up," he said to Pran. "You coming?"

Schanberg stood under the shower for a long time. The water pounded on his shoulders, softening the angry knots of tension in them. It trickled through his beard and ran down his untanned torso, which had not seen the sun in days or weeks. He cleared a space on the mirror and scrutinized himself. His face winked back at him. That was better. He was coming down off the high that had kept him going so tirelessly. The water was washing away a weight of professional responsibility greater than any he had borne before. Now his responsibility was to himself. And to Pran, of course.

He was shaving when there was a knock at the door. Pran came in, wearing a clean white shirt.

"They're coming, Sydney."

"Okay." If Pran could remain calm, so could he. He finished shaving. "Which way?"

"Down Monivong. They take Chrouy Changvar bridge twenty minutes ago."

Pran had a shoulder bag. Schanberg took his, which had not been unpacked since the U.S. evacuation. Somewhere a radio was still blaring martial music. The lobby downstairs was a turmoil of refugees, many of them government soldiers. In a desperate attempt to sustain the hotel's status as a neutral zone, a line of Red Cross workers and hotel staff at the main entrance was searching everybody they allowed in, and confiscating weapons. A huge packing case by the door already overflowed with rifles, pistols, knives, and chains.

Shouldering out against the tide, Schanberg and Pran found a space on top of the hotel steps and looked down Monivong Boulevard. A snowfall of white dazzled in the sunlight. Hundreds of white flags made from shirts and bedsheets fluttered from rooftops, lampposts, and shop windows. Strips of white cloth hung from the hotel railings. Jeeps and APCs packed with government soldiers drove slowly up the boulevard, with scraps of white fabric flying from their radio aerials and bouquets of yellow allamanda flowers in front of their headlights. Hundreds more government troops milled in the roadway. In the hotel forecourt, a soldier was hastily stripping off his uniform. His wife hovered anxiously beside him with a bundle of freshly laundered civilian clothes.

Pran nudged Schanberg's arm and pointed. Walking down the middle of the broad street, still some hundred and fifty yards away, came six men wearing black pajamas and red-checkered scarves. Behind them rolled a single tank, its turret gun swinging slowly from side to side.

At the head of a procession of trucks, jeeps, and APCs, the men in Khmer Rouge costume came steadily on. The crowd in front of them swayed uncertainly, caught up in conflicting emotions of fear and curiosity. A few of the braver spirits ran forward. The Khmer Rouge men returned their embrace and started waving.

Everything was going to be all right.

The crowd erupted in a great shout of joy and relief. Cheers and cries of "Peace!" drowned the distant rattle of small-arms fire. People ran out of their houses carrying children on their shoulders, or leaned from their windows and balconies waving white streamers and crying *"Cheyo Yotheas! Cheyo Yotheas!"*—"Long Live the Troops of Liberation!" Schanberg grabbed for Pran's hand and squeezed it. There were tears in his eyes. Maybe all was for the best after all.

Beckoning Pran to follow, he went down into the crowd. He badly wanted to interview these insurgents. The KR hadn't been like the Vietcong, who courted Western publicity. Twenty international journalists had made that mistake and crossed into KR territory and never came back. Now this unknown army was here in front of him, smiling and waving, helping their foes up into the trucks and draping their red-checkered scarves around their necks. The crowds were all at once unafraid; the soldiers tore the clips out of their rifles and tossed them in the air.

"C'est la paix! C'est la paix!"

Tank treads crushed the temple flowers strewn along the boulevard. A Buddhist monk had a KR scarf knotted around his neck; weeping and laughing, he was dragged on board a truck full of soldiers. Jeeps went past, overloaded with students, tooting horns and trailing white streamers. A man wearing neatly pressed black pajamas and a general's cap clambered on top of an APC; the crowd hailed him as a leader, cheering and waving white handkerchiefs.

"La guerre est finie! Nous sommes frères, tout le monde!"

The people around Schanberg went wild with joy. Perhaps only he and Pran saw the brown arm that reached up from the hatch and pulled the "officer" from his perch. They shared a moment's unease. This was all too good to be true. Something was wrong here . . . these men in fluffy, red-checkered scarves and black pajamas that looked as if they had been kept folded in a clothes chest for just this occasion. Pran set off to run alongside one of the KR trucks to try to find out what was going on. Schanberg pushed into the middle of the road and waved and shouted. Al Rockoff, who had been taking pictures from on top of a jeep filled with Khmer Rouge soldiers, scrambled down and joined him. His clothes were filthy. He was sucking at a gash on his wrist.

"What's the problem, Al?"

"I don't know. I don't like the look of this."

"Listen to it."

"Yeah. I know. But some of these people aren't for real."

Pran came running back, out of breath, excited. "Sydney! They hold press conference at noon."

"Took a swing through Keng Kang early this morning," Rockoff continued. "Practically got my ass shot off."

Petals of a temple flower thrown from a balcony fell off Schanberg's shoulder like wedding confetti. Tiredness was slowing his mind. There had to be some way of telling. He looked around. A soldier was walking toward them, leaning on a bicycle, an AK-47 propped in the front basket. He was wearing green fatigues over black Khmer Rouge pajamas. Schanberg signaled to Pran, who bowed to the man in greeting. The soldier stopped, unsmiling. The Mao cap he was wearing had a scorch mark on it. Around his neck dangled a cheap pair of field glasses.

Pran translated his answers. He was twenty-five. He had had ten years of education. He had been in the "movement" for five years. He answered in monosyllables, expressionlessly, off the blackboard of his mind.

"Ask him what his name is and his rank in the movement," demanded Schanberg.

To both questions the Khmer Rouge shook his head.

"Ask him if the Khmer Rouge take revenge and kill a lot of people?"

The soldier's eyes, black holes of nothing, stared at Rockoff's expensive camera. "He says that all those who have done corrupt things will definitely be punished." Before Pran had finished translating his answer, he had gone on his way.

Jon Swain came up to them, out of breath and out of film. "Talk about Hail the Conquerors," he gasped. "This is incredible."

Rockoff shook his head. He took out a handkerchief and

wound it around the cut on his wrist. "Khmer Rouge had some poor old French bastard back in Keng Kang," he said. "Screaming at him, 'You American? You American?' This isn't how it is. What you've been seeing is a PR exercise."

"Let's get the car," Schanberg told Pran. "I'm going to the hospital. I want to check this out." With the others, he went back through the hotel and out to the side entrance, hearing the rattle of machine-gun fire a few blocks distant. Away from the Monivong Boulevard parade, the mood was edgy. A premonition of fear and dread hung over the streets and seemed to drain the oxygen out of the air. Schanberg found he was breathing faster.

Sarun had "borrowed" a Renault from a civil servant who had fled the city the week before. Silent for once, he switched on the radio. Something had happened to the sultry tones of the government announcers. A new voice over the air, harsh and shrill, read a recorded message.

"We are ready to welcome you," Pran translated. "We enter Phnom Penh as conquerors. We have not come here to speak about peace with traitors. Those political criminals who have not fled the country will be tried and hanged for their crimes. However, Angka needs administrators in this period of transition. High-ranking government officials, civil and military, are requested to report instantly to the Information Ministry, carrying a white flag. Victory to the Revolution!"

Sarun switched off the shrill voice the second time around. There was silence in the car. Pran was sucking his cheeks nervously.

"What is Angka?" asked Swain.

"Angka is the Organization," Pran replied. "Now Angka rules."

"I think Long Boret got away by helicopter from the stadium," said Swain after a pause. "But I saw Prince Sirik Matak in the hotel. He said he didn't know what would happen to him and his family, but it was his duty to stay with his people. He said he'd been invited to run away and he'd refused."

Schanberg thought about the letter on the Ambassador's desk and was silent.

The Preah Keth Mealea Hospital, the biggest and most up-to-date civilian hospital in Phnom Penh, was housed in a dismal, barracklike set of cream-painted buildings on the banks of the Mekong. The Khmer Rouge had not shelled it, although for the previous forty-eight hours it had been within the range of their guns. Schanberg's first thought, when they got inside, was that it might have been kinder if they had.

If all the sufferings of the five-year war could have been concentrated into one place, that place was here. The Preah Keth Mealea had beds for six hundred. By now, more than two thousand injured and dying people, Cambodians and Chinese, filled the hospital to overflowing. They lay in beds or stretchers, or on the floor on foul-smelling mats. They sat on the stairs. They lay in the corridors. Orderlies mopped up the puddles of blood and splashed disinfectant around the corpses.

The main reception area was lined with stretcher cases left inside the main door by the ambulance teams who were working around the clock. Rows of patients, many with fearful shrapnel and burn wounds, lay looking up patiently at the newsmen as they walked among them, their shoes sticky with blood. Some had their relatives squatting silently beside them, wiping their foreheads and swatting the flies off their open sores. A Chinese doctor, moving mechanically now after two days and nights on duty, made his way down the line, tagging the cases who had a chance—as Schanberg had seen the Red Cross doctor do in the hotel bungalow—and abandoning the rest to die. A Red Cross nurse followed him with a clipboard, ticking off the hopeful and putting a cross against the rest.

"Where are all the doctors?" Swain asked her.

"No doctors."

"What do you mean, no doctors?"

"We have telephone doctors. They say they will come. But they don't come. No doctors for two days. Only Red Cross."

"Is Dr. McIntyre here?" Schanberg asked.

Another ambulance load had driven up to the door. The nurse pointed upstairs with her pencil and hurried on with her grisly task, a Recording Angel of man's inhumanity to man.

"It's like the Crimea, the bloody Crimea," said Swain as Schanberg led the way up the stairs. A rich, pink fluid, a mixture of blood and disinfectant, flowed down the steps and dribbled over the stairwell. An old man sitting on the stairs gave them a toothless grin and waved his stump of an arm wrapped in bloody bandages. Schanberg avoided catching Pran's eye. These were his people *in extremis*. He had never seen such suffering, nor such patience. It was their patience that cut him to the heart. That was it: The grief went inside, leaving a patience of spirit.

On the first floor, the noise and the stench were almost

unbearable. They were not in the Red Cross ward at all but in the corridor that led to it, and still they had to pick their way among the bodies and past the amputees who hopped from one wall to the other on crutches, their bloodstained trouser legs pinned up to their thighs. In the ward itself, there rose above the private moans of the wounded a high, persistent chanting. A very old woman, shriveled with age and pain, lay on a bloody bed on wheels chanting in delirium. Her legs had been amputated. The covers of her bed were saturated in mucus. Her withered arms brushed away real and imaginary flies while she sang in her agony. Around her, the casualties of the Khmer Rouge's last push for victory lay measuring out their lives in splints and bandages. A nurse was giving plasma to a Khmer Rouge soldier whose body was caked with blood. Only his lips were moving, whispering, "Water. Water."

Schanberg felt a terrible helplessness. It didn't make it easier that the others would be feeling the same. He forced himself to look at Pran. Frowning, Pran had his notebook out and was feverishly scribbling in it, as though this were a normal morning and he and Schanberg would be making for the Telex office as soon as they got out of this place. Schanberg recognized the look on his face and understood it with a shock of sympathy. It was a look of embarrassment. Pran was deeply embarrassed that they should be here, these Westerners, to witness the intimate spectacle of his own people stripped of their dignity and self-respect.

Rockoff, on bended knee, was showing one of his cameras to a little boy with an amputated left arm whose father, with his own arm amputated and wire holding together a deep, stitched wound on his thigh, was sharing the same bed. The nurse who had been supplying the plasma went up to him.

"Vous êtes le TV suédois?"

Rockoff looked at Schanberg, who shook his head. *"Non. Nous voulons trouver le docteur McIntyre."*

"Mais oui. Par ici."

She led the way past a row of stretcher beds lined up like supermarket trolleys, into a large room faced with white tiles. The operating theater was furnished with the latest in surgical technology, but the Preah Keth Mealea was a field hospital now: There was no time for the luxury of electrocardiographs and respirators. At the operating table, Gordon McIntyre was dressed in shorts and a surgical mask. The nurses had not been able to find him a gown or gloves to wear. With his bare hands, he was suturing the muscles and skin flaps over a stump of bone, which yesterday had been a man's leg.

He finished. Two of the orderlies wheeled the man away. By the time McIntyre had doused his blood-soaked arms and his steel instruments in a bowl of alcohol, another crumpled body had been put on the operating table. A little girl of about six, in pale blue dress, was shrieking in agony. Rockoff put his hands over his ears, Pran did the same.

"Ketamine, fifty milligrams," barked McIntyre, putting out his hand for the syringe. It didn't come. The nurse muttered something. McIntyre scowled. "What am I supposed to do? Sing her a damn lullaby? Gimme a hundred fifty milligrams Pentothal. Quick!"

While the nurse injected the child, McIntyre ripped open her dress with a scalpel. His scowl deepened. "God in heaven, she's got a piece of shrapnel in the spine. Have

142

you finished, woman?'' Mercifully, as the injection hit home, the dreadful screaming stopped. Schanberg watched as an intravenous drip was put in the girl's arm. Just before the oxygen mask went over her face, she widened her eyes and cried out twice in Khmer. Schanberg glanced at Pran.

"She said, 'Don't shoot me. Please don't shoot me,' " said Pran in a hoarse voice.

McIntyre was reading a label on the girl's wrist. "Blood group A. I'll have some A blood if you please, nurse."

"Il n'y a plus."

"How come there isn't any? You," called McIntyre, pointing to the nurse who had escorted the newsmen in. "Find me some plasma substitute. *Et vite!*" He seemed now to notice Schanberg and the others for the first time and spoke with the self-mocking air of a classroom lecturer. "Here we are, gentlemen. Plenty of blood around as you will see! Problem is, it's in the wrong fucking place."

Schanberg felt his eyes stinging. It was unbearable; it hurt all one's senses. Dante had written about scenes like this, and even Dante had neglected to describe the sickly smell. Pran had gone, unable to take it any longer; so had Rockoff. Schanberg followed them out and down some stairs. They passed the nurse, hurrying back with cartons of the plasma that just might save the girl's life.

Outside, away from the noise and stench, the blood and excrement, they inhaled the stifling midday heat like spring breezes. It was tempting to think that the worst was over, but Schanberg could still hear the death rattle of small-arms fire not very far away. For a moment, he thought he heard it coming from the hospital they'd just left, and he looked across at Swain. But he appeared not to have heard it; nor, plainly, had the others. Sarun had the doors of the Renault open; with relief he settled inside.

"Did you see all that wire?" asked Swain. "I asked the nurse. She said the Cambodian doctors had been suturing up the wounds so fast that the stitches would burst, and they were having to hold them together with wire—"

"Give me a break," pleaded Rockoff. There was one exposure left on the roll he'd used in the Preah Keth Mealea. Out of the window he took a picture of a fish eagle against the blue sky. At the click just behind him, Pran jumped. They all grinned. Anything to relieve the oppression of what they'd just seen.

They had left the hospital forecourt and were crossing a narrow bridge over a river channel when the tank bore down on them. Sarun slammed on the brake and reversed the car. The tank chased them down the street. Out of the turret climbed a soldier in a red-checkered scarf, waving and shouting in Khmer. Sarun stopped, his hands shaking on the wheel.

Before they could get out, the Khmer Rouge had surrounded them. Schanberg saw the weapons first: grenades, rifles, pistols, dripping from the black pajamas like fruit from trees. Then the faces, country boys he guessed, not more than kids but twisted with fury. Screaming at them.

Doors were flung open. The newsmen were dragged out and slammed against the side of the car. A KR officer of about thirty was waving a slab-sided .38 auto and shouting high-pitched abuse. Swain and Rockoff had their hands in the air. Schanberg, too. But the screaming went on. A rifle was barreled into Swain's stomach; he grunted with pain. The officer walked up to Schanberg and rammed his .38 into Schanberg's temple, hard enough to break the skin.

The safety catch snapped back. Schanberg felt his legs go weak. But the bullet didn't come. Instead the officer, his eyes coals of hate, tore off his camera and threw it on the sidewalk. Rockoff's cameras, Swain's notebooks, and a typewriter in the car were likewise hurled down and kicked away.

It happened so fast, they couldn't think, only react. Schanberg had seen anger before, he had seen hatred, but the blind animal violence of these peasant boys was something new. It was brutality born of ignorance, and it terrified him. He turned his head to find Pran. Pran would know how to deal with this. But Pran had a look of naked fear on his face such as Schanberg had never seen before, in all the difficult times they'd had together. He was mouthing to Schanberg over the roof of the car.

"Do what they say, Sydney. Everything they say!"

The street was beginning to fill with people. They looked like refugees, but Schanberg had no time to ask himself who they were or what they were doing there. An AK-47 in his ribs, he was being herded toward a captured armored personnel carrier parked outside the hospital. Its back door gaped open; the dark tomb of its interior was empty. Confused thoughts flashed through his mind. The KR could gun them down with nobody seeing. They could shut the door and toss a grenade through the roof. *We are journalists* . . . no, it would mean nothing to these hate-filled kids. They were Westerners, that was enough for them.

The rifles prodded them into the APC; Sarun, too. Only Pran remained outside. He was pleading with the KR officer. Schanberg could hear the raw fear in his voice. The officer was bellowing at him; Pran went on retreating.

On the pavement they could see the shadow of Pran's raised hands, as if he were hanging from wire.

Inside the APC, they were sweating. Rockoff whispered through clenched teeth, "Why doesn't he get in, for chrissake?"

Schanberg shook his head in disbelief. Any moment now they'd shoot Pran down in the street. Then Sarun spoke in a low voice. "He's trying to come in. They tell him, go away. They only want big people. . . ."

His words stunned them all. Far from trying to escape, Pran was pleading not to be separated from them. In effect, he was risking his own life in order to try to save theirs. It brought home to Schanberg, probably to all of them, the extreme danger they were in. Pran would not risk his life for nothing. He must know that they stood no chance without him.

The argument ended abruptly. Trembling, Pran climbed into the APC. The rear door slammed, and the officer and two of his robot soldiers got in at the front. With a painful jolt, the vehicle engaged gears and started moving.

They were in darkness, except for a shaft of sunlight through the hatch where one of the teenage thugs sat with his gun trained down on them. The heat was stifling. They sat on empty ammunition cases, keeping their feet off the floor where a pool of oil and water slapped from side to side as the APC jerked on its way. Where it was taking them was impossible to say. From the heightened volume of cheering outside, Schanberg guessed that they had rejoined the Monivong Boulevard. Probably the Khmer Rouge on top of the APC were waving and smiling to the crowds as they passed the Hotel Phnom. Barry Morgan and the others would be waving back, little knowing. . . . Self-pity engulfed him, and he looked to Pran, seated opposite, for reassurance. Pran had no reassurance to offer. He gestured for a cigarette; Schanberg brought out a packet of Pall Mall. Quick as a flash, Pran grabbed them and drowned them in the sump of oily water.

"Français!" he hissed. *"J'ai dit que vous êtes français!"*

Swain produced a pack of local Bastos. Pran took one with a shaking hand. In a moment he would have to pluck up courage for another violent argument with the Khmer Rouge. As he lit up, a tide of oily liquid surged forward. The APC was shuddering to a halt.

Bolts snapped. The rear door clanged open, filling the armored vault with blinding sunlight. Before the newsmen could adjust to it, two figures had been pushed inside, the rear door slammed and bolted again. The APC jolted on, with two more victims in its belly.

As they rolled across the city, the temperature inside rose to oven heat. The sweat ran down Schanberg's face and gathered in droplets in his beard. The two middle-aged Cambodians who had joined them were praying in a monotone. Schanberg recognized a Buddhist ritual that was used in moments of peril. They sat with their eyes closed tightly, chanting a mantra; one had a tiny gold Buddha in his mouth. Pran muttered to Schanberg, *"Ils sont officiers."*

"What's he say?" demanded Rockoff. The others sat in silence. None of them dared looked at the Khmer Rouge. Schanberg ran his hand across his lips in a sealing motion. They must speak nothing but French. Their lives depended on it. The shadow of the soldier's rifle cut across the rectangle of light from the hatch above him. Self-pity brought a lump to his throat. What had he, Sydney

Schanberg, a foreigner, done to deserve this hatred? He had hurt nobody. He had killed nobody. He was harmless: a journalist.

The noise of praying was contagious. Schanberg searched in his pockets and came up with a little crumpled yellow ball, damp with sweat. It was all that remained of his good-luck amulet, the yellow silk rose that his daughter had given him. He closed his fist over it tightly; it was the nearest he could get to prayer. Raising his head, he met Jon Swain's eyes and read in them the same terrible certainty—they were going to be executed. He opened his hand with the rose in it.

"*Voici la bonne chance,*" he muttered. Swain forced a sick smile. The APC clattered like a tumbril over paving stones and lurched to a halt. The rear door opened; the screaming started, and the rifles stabbing them out into the sun. They had reached the end of the road.

Men possessed by devils. Men who are eaten out inside so that no emotion, no warmth, no human feeling remains. Robots, these Khmer Rouge soldiers. Men-machines. The walking dead.

But as the trapdoor goes down and he sees the sandy bank sloping down to the Tonle Sap River, Pran knows it is the Westerners who are the walking dead. This riverbank, these deserted warehouses—it is a place of execution. The Khmer Rouge is about to shoot Sydney and the others in the back of the neck and roll their bodies into the river to join the other corpses rolling slowly like logs downstream to the Mekong.

Sydney has been very brave. He has not wept or cried out in fear. He was able even to joke with Monsieur Swain about his good-luck rose. It is a mystery how Sydney can be so brave without a belief in Buddha to give him strength. It must be, as Pran has always suspected, because Sydney *understands*. His idea of himself is total. He doesn't need gods to help him see his place in the scheme of things. Death is like another assignment.

Pran's life is forfeit now, as well. But he must not panic. He must keep calm, detached, observant—as Sydney has always told him. On the patch of ground between the warehouses is a table and a sunshade. Nine or ten Khmer Rouge soldiers in scarves and grubby black pajamas are sitting talking in the shade or strolling between the table and six Cambodian prisoners squatting in a line against a low wooden jetty, hands tied behind their backs. He recognizes one of them—a brigadier from the Seventh Division who led the defense of Pochentong Airport. Like the others, he is absorbed in praying to Buddha. The three Westerners, hands on their heads, are waiting to be led down beside them. So are Sarun and the two officers from the APC.

Pran searches around with mounting desperation. There is a man sitting at the table under the sunshade, a small man with flabby lips and little pig eyes set under a bulging forehead. He has the same callused hands and scruffy clothes as the others, but he has been giving orders. As Pran prays to Buddha for strength and courage, Pig Eyes questions the driver of the APC.

"Who are they?"

"Spies. We caught them." The officer who arrested them points to the clutter of cameras, typewriter, and notebooks that have been brought in evidence.

"Then Angka will sentence them. Leave us—"

"Please!" Pran steps forward. His heart is pounding. "Will you please report to your top authority? I was told by your top authority that he agreed to let me go around. I met them. I will meet them again this afternoon. It is essential that you report to your top authority!"

Pig Eyes swivels pale brown eyes and studies the interloper. Pran trembles, waiting for the screams of rage to begin. But Pig Eyes, it would seem, is of a quieter disposition. He simply dismisses the APC officer with a wave of his hand and snaps an order to his men. Their guns prod the three Western newsmen down to the wooden jetty. Pig Eyes gets up and strolls after them, tapping his fingers on his pistol in its holster.

Pran is left alone. He can walk away from here and live. Or he can follow this officer and go on pleading. He knows how the Khmer Rouge treats anybody who stands in their way. They murder with indifference. Nhiek Sann, his friend in the Ministry, was right when he said that the rebels would turn out to be more brutal than anyone could believe. He has Ser Moeun and the children to think of. He cannot throw his life away.

With faltering steps, Dith Pran advances toward Pig Eyes. He addresses his plea to the back of the officer's neck. "These men are international journalists. They are all Frenchmen. They all have permission from the top authority. Please! Please report to your top authority!"

Pig Eyes draws out his pistol and turns. A trigger pull from death, Pran forces a smile.

"These men are not American. Everybody French. These men are journalists, not spies. They are here to tell the world about your victory. Everybody's very happy about your victory."

The AK rifle seems to come from nowhere. Its muzzle bruises his stomach and knocks the wind out of him. Pig Eyes watches as the soldiers he's summoned pushes Pran against the warehouse wall, then he strolls down to where the Western devils are standing in a cage of guns. He selects Rockoff for scrutiny and stares him hard in the face. Rockoff stares back, the sweat running down his face. Pran prays that he won't open his mouth and give them all away.

Pig Eyes strolls back. The pale eyes are hard-staring Pran now. His head wobbles slightly like the rubber ball Pran's youngest child plays with, as if there's no skull in there, no brain. . . .

Pig Eyes speaks. "You are telling me lies."

"Please. These men don't support Lon Nol. They support Angka. That's why they're here—to see the victory of Angka. They will tell the world!"

"They are spies. You are all spies. You will be executed." He turns and shouts an order. As Pran watches, horrified, two KR soldiers march up to the Cambodian brigadier from the Seventh. One grabs his hair and pulls his head down; the other shoots him in the back of the neck. They go down the line of Cambodian prisoners, shooting each in turn. The bodies topple over, blood spurting up over the wooden jetty. In the emptiness, a racket of jungle birds rises into the afternoon sky as if carrying the prayers of the dead. Schanberg, the next in line, buries his face in his knees.

A motorbike with sidecar comes bumping down the track. Pig Eyes goes to meet it; Pran follows him, with his arms above his head. This one looks like some sort of officer, too. Pig Eyes is explaining the holdup. Both men look at Pran with a mixture of suspicion and contempt.

"I know you hate imperialists," Pran explains, trying to keep his voice from shaking. "If we were imperialists, we would not be staying here in Phnom Penh. We are newspapermen. We are writers. We want to tell the world the truth about your victory."

They look past Pran. He follows their gaze. Schanberg, Rockoff, and Swain are squatting under the KR guns, staring in their direction. Even from here, Pran can read their desperate intentness. They need him; he is the only one who can save their lives. And he needs them. He has tied his fate to Sydney and the others. They represent the only values he can live for now. The Khmer Rouge has destroyed the rest.

He turns back. He must plead and go on pleading. "They are French journalists! The French support Angka now. These men will tell everybody else to support Angka. It will make a good impression to let them go." His hands lowered now, he uses them to emphasize his arguments. For twenty minutes, he argues. The officers are unconvinced. Then Pran strikes lucky. The man on the motorbike comes from the northwest; it shows in his accent. Pran tells them he comes from Siem Reap—it is the man's own birthplace. They have names in common, people they both knew in the sixties. If Pran is telling the truth about this, he may be telling the truth about the Western spies. The officer from Siem Reap revs his motorbike: he will ask higher authority. He takes off for the city center in a trail of dust.

Pig Eyes has been scowling. Memories from the past have no place in Angka. He sends Pran back under guard to the warehouse wall to wait for the other officer's return.

Another hour passes. The Khmer Rouge soldiers are smoking and chattering. They have ripped the watches and gold chains off the corpses and ground the little images of Buddha underfoot; then, finding little else to do with the bodies, have dragged them down to the Tonle Sap and thrown them in the water along with all the other garbage floating by. Pig Eyes, sitting under the sunshade, is drinking orangeade and playing with a looted transistor radio. He picks up a disc jockey on AFN Saigon, and a cunning grin spreads across his melon features.

"American!" he shouts to the newsmen, turning up the radio. "U.S.A., yes?"

Nobody looks at him. Schanberg shrugs his shoulders, Pran wonders what he is thinking. Perhaps about his wife and daughters, although he's never talked much about them. He's talked more to Pran about his father in New York and what a struggle he had to get his grocery business established. So maybe he is thinking what a terrible blow it would be to his father if something happened to him. . . . But no. Pran frowns. He should know Sydney better by now. Sydney never brooded over things that could not be helped. Much more likely he will be thinking angry thoughts about all the good stories he is missing about the Khmer Rouge's entry into Phnom Penh.

Sarun—that was easy. Sarun would be fretting about whether his wife is safe, and whether she has been able to get to the shops to buy enough food for their next meal. Sarun always thought about his stomach when he was upset. Danger gave him an appetite. The other two Pran knows less well. Monsieur Swain is a very nice man but disconcerting. His character is so different from Sydney's, like light opposed to dark. He seems to get good stories without appearing to try very hard. Where Sydney is fierce, Monsieur Swain is casual, relaxed. How to work for him? It must be very difficult. Even now he is sitting with his hands on his head and his long legs stretched out—like a man enjoying the sun.

Al Rockoff . . . But before Pran can compose a reflection upon the photographer, he is distracted by a cackle of laughter from the soldiers. Barges are drifting past on the river, turning slowly in the current. Pran feels the hair rise on his scalp. They are full of dead men, Cambodians and Chinese. Some of them have been propped stiffly upright around the sides, like people enjoying a houseboat party. One man is hanging over the side, his arm trailing in the water as if he is enjoying the coolness on his wrist. But only the birds, the scavengers, are having a party.

More shouting and the sound of a motorbike. The officer from Siem Reap is returning. With an icy sensation of fear, Pran leans his head back against the warehouse wall and prays. This is the moment of truth for all of them. Opening his eyes, he sees Sydney watching him. There is a look on his face Pran has never seen before—a look of naked terror. The newsmen, he realizes, don't even know what he said to the officers before the motorbike went into town.

"Bring him here!"

The order is in Khmer. Pran stumbles over to the officers, nudged by his guard's Russian-made rifle. The man from Siem Reap questions him in a harsh voice.

"You say these men are French journalists. What papers do they work for?"

"*Le Monde*. The tall one for *L'Humanité*. The photographer works for a news agency, *Agence France-Presse*."

"What are their assignments?"

"They are here to report the collapse of Lon Nol's capitalist, American-backed regime and the arrival of the victorious Khmer Rouge in Phnom Penh."

"What were they doing at the hospital?"

For another five or ten minutes the questions are drilled at him. Pran answers with growing confidence. If—how did Sydney say?—their cover had been *blown on*, there would be none of these questions; they would all be dead by now. And the atmosphere is changing. Pig Eyes is getting bored. The man on the motorbike has put his gloves back on.

Pran has done it. He has done it! The Westerners will be set free. He has helped save Sydney's life, and Sarun's, and the others. And his own. He thinks of something he said to Ser Moeun that night at the table, with the children watching TV in the next room . . . or perhaps left unsaid, in case she felt cruelly excluded. *To belong you have first to share, no matter what the fear, the pain, the grief.* As Pig Eyes says something to the motorbike officer, Pran discreetly finds a moment to turn around, smile, and bite his lip. Sydney's expression says it all.

He belongs.

The afternoon was dying; the Tonle Sap River was covering its secrets in gold. Sunrise had reminded Schanberg of a St. Regis trout; the sunset made him think of burning, perhaps because he could smell it on the air. After the terrible hours in the heat, they had been allowed to sit in the shade of the warehouses. The guard had been relaxed, and they had been given drinks of orangeade—although the teenage psychotic in charge of Schanberg had made an

155

ugly game even of that, offering the bottle to him and pulling it away as he reached out until he'd forced him to beg for it. In New York City, kids like this strung up cats and set fire to them with the same cruel delight on their vacuous faces.

More prisoners had arrived and taken the newsmen's places in front of the wooden jetty. At least they would die in the dark. They had been waiting so long. Sarun had been keening to himself; now he looked to be asleep, rocked forward on his fat haunches. As far as he could tell, Pran was negotiating for the return of their belongings, scattered where the APC driver had left them. He must be very tired. He had been pleading for their lives for hours, it seemed, with what must have been incredible eloquence and cunning, as well as enormous guts. Schanberg had watched this persuasiveness at work before, on everybody from Prime Minister Long Boret to the Telex operators in the cable office—an oblique, appeasing hesitancy until Pran had gained their tolerance, when there would be jokes and smiles to win their confidence. It had got them some first-rate exclusives in the past few years; this time it had had to save their lives. It must have taken nerves of steel.

One of the KR officers shouted an order. The teenage psychotic shouldered his rifle and gestured them up toward the motorbike. Pran was tight-faced with anxiety. They were free; they wanted to praise him and embrace him, but that might be fatal. Schanberg understood and scowled the warning at Rockoff, who was humming "Auld Lang Syne" under his breath.

"S'il vous plaît, enlevez vos bagages," said Pran.

The teenage psychotic waved them back and distributed their stuff himself, with sarcastic little bows. Rockoff got his cameras and clutched them speechlessly, like a child. Swain got his camera and shoulder bag. His precious notebooks were missing, but he wasn't about to complain. Schanberg's shoulder bag had opened, the contents spilled in the dust. A money belt stuffed with dollars was handed over without interest; so were his notebooks, which somehow had survived. A pair of undershorts took the guard's fancy. He stretched them across his middle, giggling, and stuffed them into his pocket. Schanberg's passport was next, his United States passport, lying on the ground like a murder weapon. The guard picked it up.

Schanberg stared, rooted to the spot. Nobody else moved or spoke. The guard flicked through it, not six feet away from the officers talking behind him. Too ignorant to read, he was vastly amused by Schanberg's photograph. He held the passport in the air, comparing it with the real thing. Finally he handed it over. Schanberg palmed it, just as one of the officers turned around. He spoke, in Khmer, a phrase Schanberg could recognize.

"Let them go."

Without the Renault, the walk back into the city center was a long one. They were traveling against a human tide, a mass exodus such as none of them had ever seen or imagined. The refugee slums were being evacuated—that was their first impression. Hundreds of Cambodians were walking along the highway, men and women in straw hats carrying bundles and suitcases or crying children in their arms. Some trudged along with nothing at all, often pausing and looking eagerly backward as though they had been dispatched without a chance to wait for their families, vainly searching until the ones behind pushed them on.

Surely, though, these weren't only refugees? There were

157

many prosperous people, city dwellers, among them. Pran recognized a neighbor. He shouted to him across the moving river. The man did not look around. He raised his left arm in a gesture of greeting, or farewell, and plodded on his way. Pran tugged Schanberg's sleeves.

"They are all leaving. Everyone is leaving."

"That's impossible."

But as more crowds turned out of the side streets into the highway, turning a river into a torrent and a torrent into a flood, the impossible was taking place under Schanberg's eyes. The citizens of Phnom Penh were being made to abandon their houses and apartments, their shops and office buildings, and taking to the road with nothing more than a sack of food over their shoulders. A few had loaded their cars with supplies and valuables and, forbidden to start the engines, were pushing them along the highway. Most carried what they could on their backs—in some cases aged or bedridden parents who would otherwise be left by the roadside to die.

Khmer Rouge soldiers stood at the edge of this grim parade. They urged it on with threats and rifle butts, occasionally shooting their guns in the air. Rockoff began to take pictures of one who had looted watches strapped the length of his arm, and quickly thought better of it. Several times they heard loudspeaker vans in the distance; once, down a side street, they saw one, escorted by black-pajamaed figures, shrilling its message. Schanberg had never considered how ugly a language could be made to sound.

Pran translated. "They say the Americans are coming to bomb Phnom Penh. Everybody must leave their homes quickly. Everybody must go now before the Americans attack. They can return in a few days when Angka has restored order. Don't wait for family, don't lock up your home, Angka will take care of everything. Go ten, twelve miles, and come back in a few days when the city is okay again. Must leave now.''

The flood tide poured out onto the main railway tracks going north and south. The newsmen, heading for the city center, could not get through, so suffocating was the crush. They made a detour and crossed by footbridge a few hundred yards farther up. The sight that stretched away as far as they could see was so heart-rending that they could scarcely record it. To Swain it was a vision of horror that nothing in Vietnam had prepared him for. To Schanberg it seemed that he was standing on the lip of hell and looking down at the damned on their way to punishment.

The Khmer Rouge had spared nobody. An entire population shuffled beneath them, packed so tight they could move forward only in fits and starts. Western suits trod beside robed Buddhist monks with their black umbrellas. Bullock carts creaked along beside bicycles, topheavy with brightly colored bundles. Motorbikes and rickshaws, vans and pedicabs added to the confusion. A blind man stumbled forward with his hands outstretched, fastening upon shoulder after shoulder and shaken off.

Worst of all, the Khmer Rouge had emptied the hospitals. Cripples who could walk were made to walk. The very sick and the dying were pushed along in their hospital beds. Bandages unraveled and were trampled in the dust. Schanberg, on the footbridge, saw a man with his foot hanging by a thread of skin hobble past on a stick, dragging his foot after him. A shrapnel casualty with no legs at all levered himself along with his hands like a worm, bumping his belly on the track. Hospital beds were being wheeled along with their serum drips and plasma bottles jolting loose from the wretched creature under the sheet. Amputees were riding in wheelbarrows. A father carried his wounded baby son over his shoulder in a blood-soaked plastic bag; another had wrapped his child in a sheet and tied it around his neck in a sling. Schanberg saw one weeping couple, probably Chinese, carrying both their children in a stretcherbed: one still alive, the other infant parceled in brown paper and stowed at the foot of the bed.

A few, not many, raised their eyes to the footbridge with a flicker of hope that quickly died. What came up mostly to the newsmen was the speechlessness of this vast caravan of misery and the persistent sound, like rain, of children crying.

"Those bastards stole my wide-angle," said Rockoff.

From below, a Khmer Rouge soldier shouted angrily. They were too visible: Pran beckoned them urgently off the footbridge. The streets were emptier now as they approached the business quarter, except for the victorious Khmer Rouge. Drunken and joyous, they careened past in stolen cars and jeeps they weren't able to drive, jerking and shrieking the gears with cries of glee. Trucks piled with looted merchandise, hard liquor, bales of cloth, screeched past the shattered windows and, lying on the sidewalk, the broken bodies who had never made it to the great procession.

A group of soldiers had clustered like black insects around a yellow Buick and were shooting it up because they couldn't start the ignition. To avoid them, Schanberg and the others made a detour past the Information Ministry. A group of about fifty prisoners outside the building were being harangued by a senior KR officer. Schanberg recognized some of them—they were "the high officials" summoned earlier by radio to report for duty. Their strained faces, the armed guards surrounding them, were evidence enough that their first duty to the new republic would be to die for it.

As they watched, another senior KR officer—like all of them, he wore no insignia to show his rank—strolled up to the newsmen. Politely he suggested in Khmer that they should stay at the Information Ministry to be registered as foreign journalists. As politely, Pran declined. "I think this is where we remember a previous engagement," announced Schanberg. Smiling hard, the four men slipped away.

The Hotel Phnom they had left in a ferment of refugees. Now it was ominously quiet. The sign declaring it an International Zone had been torn down. Outside the main gate, soldiers sat in an army truck, their rocket launchers trained on the hotel. A solitary figure stood calmly on the steps, his silver mustache trim, his bearing distinguished. Schanberg recognized him as the U.N. official Henri Savarin.

"What's happening?" asked Schanberg when he had gotten his breath back.

"They gave me half an hour to empty the hotel," replied Savarin, hands clasped behind his back.

"When was that?"

"Twenty-five minutes ago."

They took one look at the rocket launchers and ran into the lobby. It was empty. They sprinted up the stairs and along the corridors. They were empty. Swain had lost his hotel key as well as his notebooks; while he and Pran tried to kick in the door of his room, Schanberg barged into his suite, followed by Rockoff.

"I'll get clothes," shouted Schanberg. "You get the food! It's in the cupboard!" Hastily he shoveled whole drawers into plastic bags set aside for just such an emergency.

Meanwhile, Rockoff was surveying the survival rations with an air of distaste. Pushing a cake and some sardines aside, he picked a can of Dinty Moore beef stew, a jar of Lipton's powdered iced tea, some cans of orange juice and peach slices, and a tin of wafers. "Chunky peanut butter," he observed, holding up a jar of the stuff. "Syd, did you ever see that film where two men stray on a nuclear test site and get blown up, and the only thing that saves them from radiation sickness is they've been eating peanut butter?"

Pran burst in. "Sydney! We've got to go, Sydney. It's half-hour!"

With bags and suitcases, they ran downstairs. From behind the hotel newsstand, incongruously still stacked with copies of *Newsweek* and *L'Express*, rose a member of the hotel staff who had somehow escaped the roundup. A hotel waiter, they all recognized him, he cried, "*Aidez-moi! Aidez-moi!*" in pitiful tones and ran after them to try to take their bags. But there was nothing any of them could do. They let him tag on and hurried into the darkening hotel gardens, the last people out.

The Red Cross had abandoned some of its vehicles in the hotel yard, after removing the keys. The newsmen threw what they had gathered up into a Toyota van, put it neutral, and pushed it out into Monivong Boulevard.

The French Embassy was the only place left to go.

The boulevard was littered with shoes and sandals lost in the crush of refugees who must have passed this way about an hour before. A middle-aged woman in a print dress was sitting on the sidewalk under a tree in a ring of odd shoes, calmly trying them on one by one. There was still a straggle of bemused refugees coming their way, under the guns of the men in scarves and black pajamas. One man of about Pran's age, wearing thick glasses, looked vaguely familiar.

"*Où vas-tu?*" cried Pran with a catch in his throat.

"*A mourir!*" Nhiek Sann, Pran's friend from the Ministry, replied, smiling.

Perhaps because of the Red Cross van they were pushing, no one molested the newsmen. Darkness had fallen in the time it took them to walk the half-mile to the embassy. The gates had been locked and barred against the mob; outside was pandemonium. Cambodians and foreigners were besieging the high iron fence—first passing their children over, hurling their belongings after them, and then climbing up themselves. Nations united in an effort to save themselves. A West German stood on the shoulders of a Swede. A Japanese was helped over by an Indian, snagging his camera cord and nearly strangling himself on the way down. A purple sari, a pair of nylon stockings, and a single trouser leg hung impaled on the spikes. A plump Pakistani diplomat broke his leg in the descent and screamed in pain; he screamed again when Rockoff fell on top of him.

Schanberg was the last over the fence and back into civilization. As he picked himself up, he was confronted by gendarmes with German shepherds, shouting hoarsely.

"*Par ici! Par ici!*"

They were being segregated. Caucasians and Japanese were dispatched into the embassy building. Asians, including Pran, were being kept in the compound. Tired and at the end of his resources, Schanberg could not comprehend this. Pran was with his group. He was one of them. "He goes with me!" he yelled, waving at the gendarmes and pointing at Pran. "This man goes with me!"

Pran hesitated in obvious embarrassment. He had Sarun with him, and another of their drivers. Schanberg saw he wasn't making it any easier for him. Brusquely, the gendarme pushed the American back into the ranks of the privileged. Looking back, he saw Pran raise his arm in farewell and disappear in the throng.

There were bodies everywhere. They lay full-length on the beautiful nineteenth-century Yunnan carpets and sprawled in the reproduction Louis Seize sofas and chairs. Two United Nations staff members lay underneath the grand piano, a third on top of it in a sleeping bag. Altogether there were twenty-two people staking out a claim for living space in the French Ambassador's drawing room known as the Salle de Reception—Red Cross and U.N. staff, journalists, and French doctors from the neighboring Calmette Hospital. This was the International Group. The *colons* were billeted in the central wing; the embassy staff, those that were left, stayed in the consulate.

To Schanberg it was like the tropical island in *Lord of the Flies*. Pushing for food and cushions and sleeping privileges, with no rules and no one in charge, they seemed to him to be reverting to children again, squabbling, greedy, competitive. Soon they would start defacing the paintings and carving their initials in the antique furniture. Stepping over legs and beer bellies, Schanberg went to the French windows and gazed out at the enormous compound, dotted with palms and tamarind trees, in which the embassy buildings were set.

At once, he was back in his dream of standing on his balcony at the hotel and looking out on hundreds of refugee faces peering at him darkly from the garden wall. Hundreds of Cambodians plus a few Vietnamese and Chinese were camped like gypsies on the grass. Every square inch of lawn was black with hungry and frightened figures, their faces visible in the light of cooking fires. Makeshift tents were going up with the aid of cuttings from the clumps of bamboo. The luckier families were camped inside the fifty or sixty cars left in the compound by embassy staff. A woman had already started chopping down the milky branch of a flowering frangipani for firewood.

He must find Pran and talk to him. They had a lot to say: there had been no opportunity on the walk back from their execution site. He stepped out into the humid night and began searching for him.

Most of the Asians out here were from the wealthier ranks of the city. A gem merchant whom Schanberg had patronized before his last visit to Singapore sat in affluent misery, surrounded by four pieces of Gucci luggage. A rich Vietnamese woman with lacquered hair had brought her poodle in and was trying to make it eat pieces of dried fish that she had cut up with a knife and fork. Some of the girls from Madame Butterfly's brothel were here, too, almost unrecognizable without their makeup.

He found Pran at last, sleeping on a rush mat under a tamarind. Sarun was beside him, perched in the fork of the tree, his face a mask of dejection. Schanberg squatted on the grass and looked at his assistant. Sleep had taken the worry lines away—Pran's features had softened to the dark, youthful smoothness that characterized most Cambodian faces, at least to a Western eye. Only a restless twitch of his elbow gave any indication of what he had been through or what he feared for the future. As Schanberg looked at him, he thought of what Pran had said on the way back, in his quiet voice: "You don't speak Khmer, and I cannot let you go off and get killed without someone talking to them and trying to get them to understand. Even if I get killed, I have to first try to say something to them. Because you and I are together. I was very scared, yes, because in the beginning I thought they were going to kill us, but my heart said I had to try this. I understand you and know your heart well. You would do the same thing for me."

Sarun slowly raised his head. Schanberg tried to smile at him, but there was too much anxiety. He whispered, "Everything okay?"

Sarun's round cheeks looked hollowed and shrunken in the semi-darkness. He gazed at Schanberg and shook his head. "Pran see *chauve-souris*," he said in a low voice.

"Bats?"

"Very bad." He shook his head again. "Sleep now, Sydney."

His shirt rolled up as a pillow, Sarun rested his head against the tree and closed his eyes. Pran stirred, but did not wake. Schanberg took off his own shirt and laid it across him; it could get cold before dawn at this time of year. Bare-chested, he walked back to the Salle de Reception and tried to sleep.

*　　*　　*

How long the night was, he had no idea. There was a time in it when his father's grocery shop was being robbed and he was powerless to help; he woke up with a start to hear the distant peal of burglar alarms as the insurgents ransacked the city. Then in the early hours, a great ginger bear of a man strode noisily into the drawing room. For a minute Schanberg listened to the moans of protest from the floor, then a booming Australian voice rang out.

"All right, you dozy bleeders! Where'm I supposed to sleep?"

A flashlight beamed up at the intruder. Schanberg grinned. It was Oscar, the freighter captain who had taken him and Pran to Neak Luong; he was swinging an enormous ruck-sack off his back and getting ready to drop it on whichever poor sod was under his feet. More growls of protest, the flashlight was switched off, and Oscar settled down for the night on the Ambassador's Chinese rug.

Schanberg was up at dawn. A French official had un-locked the double doors to the Ambassador's dining room; he helped Oscar collect up chairs for breakfast. Al Rockoff and Gordon McIntyre were sitting at the burnished mahog-any dinner table trying to tune a small transistor radio on to the BBC World Service. Jon Swain appeared from the kitchen with a huge pile of magnificent porcelain dinner plates, closely followed by a French journalist Schanberg vaguely recognized carrying a tray of knives and forks. As they set the table, a thin prattle came from the radio. McIntyre signaled for quiet.

". . . and that resistance continues in the northwestern province of Battambang. Reliable sources have been quoted as saying that the former premier, Prince Sirik Matak, one of the so-called Seven Traitors on the Khmer Rouge death list, fled to Thailand in one of the last helicopters to leave Phnom Penh—''

"That should please him," drawled Rockoff. "Think I'll stroll over and tell him; he's right next door."

McIntyre hissed for quiet. The English voice faded under a swelling of martial music; he twiddled the dial. A steaming cauldron appeared in the kitchen doorway, held in a beefy pair of arms.

"Right!" announced Oscar. "This'll put hairs on your chest." He banged the hot cauldron down on the rosewood table. "Jon, start dishing it out, willya? I'm going to wake those buggers up."

Swain took off the cauldron lid. A limp mess of rice and water steamed unpleasantly. "What is it?" he asked.

"Risotto." Oscar disappeared. A moment later Schanberg heard a bellow loud enough to span the Nullarbor desert— "Breakfast!!" He exchanged an amused look with Swain and went into the compound to collect Pran.

By the time he got back, the table was nearly full. Henri Savarin was at the head. Next to him sat the English nurse Schanberg had last seen tending wounded children in the Red Cross bungalow. Pran was hesitating on the periphery in an agony of embarrassment. Schanberg pulled a chair out and ladled rice gruel on a plate for him. Barry Morgan, sitting opposite, flushed a bright red.

"This is a journalist's table," he said, addressing Schanberg but staring at Pran.

"He is a journalist," said Schanberg, cold with anger. "And he sits here. And he eats at this table."

Pran kept his head down.

"If you want to start a soup kitchen, first buy the soup," muttered the Fleet Street man.

"Pardon me?"

Morgan's reply was drowned out by Oscar's voice at the other end of the table. "No arguments, gentlemen!" He waved the soup ladle like a policeman's nightstick. "Anyone who starts an argument around here is automatically arguing with me. Is that clear?"

Morgan stared at him. "You've got a lot to say for yourself—"

"That's because he's been democratically elected group leader," interjected Jon Swain. He winked at Schanberg.

"Since when?"

"We took a vote," said Schanberg, sitting down next to Pran. "Last night. When you were asleep, Barry. Sorry about that."

There was an edgy silence. Al Rockoff looked lazily down the table. "Who's got my croissant?" he demanded.

"You must have left her in bed, Al," said Swain without a moment's hesitation.

Even Pran grinned at that.

Breakfast was over, and Oscar had already organized a dishwashing detail, a bedding detail, and a sanitation detail when the Khmer Rouge arrived. The first the journalists knew of it was when the murmur of voices and the clatter of cooking pots in the compound suddenly ceased and a deathly hush descended. As Schanberg and Pran ran out of the Ambassador's lodge, the main gates were unbarred, and an insurgent officer and six of his men were allowed through. Pran stopped dead.

"They have come for us," he said in a hoarse voice.

Schanberg shook his head. "That's impossible. We're on French territory in here, that's an international convention. So long as you stay inside, you're safe."

He spoke with more conviction than he felt. Pran sensed it and turned back. Schanberg went on to the consulate where the vice-consul, Thibaut, was waiting for the Khmer Rouge officer at the top of the steps.

"This one's a general," said Henri Savarin, who had come up behind him.

"How do you know?" asked Schanberg.

"Four pens in his breast pocket. The more ball-point pens they have, the higher their rank. Or at least, the greater their authority inside Angka."

They were close enough to hear the exchange, in French, between Thibaut and the general—the first diplomatic contact yet made by the Khmer Rouge. Monsieur Thibaut had evidently claimed his right to offer political asylum because the KR general had raised his voice. "In a revolutionary war there are no such privileges! We are the masters now; this land belongs to us! If you expel the traitors, we will discuss the matter of the foreigners. If you do not, we shall come in after them, and we shall not answer for the consequences!"

Monsieur Thibaut raised his hands in evident distress. He seemed to be about to argue further. Schanberg felt Savarin go tense beside him. Then a man in a simple white shirt and cotton trousers came out of the consulate and spoke in a low voice in Thibaut's ear. Schanberg could catch only a phrase of what Prince Sirik Matak said: "I have been expecting this."

In a few minutes it was all over. Gendarmes escorted out of the consulate the three senior men left from the old regime whom the Khmer Rouge most wanted—Luong Nal, Minister of Health, Hong Buon Hor, President of the National Assembly, and Sirik Matak himself, together with their wives and children. As he watched the old Prince walk with ramrod back toward his certain execution, Schanberg remembered the letter he had found on the Ambassador's desk—*I have only committed this mistake of believing in you, the Americans. . . .* He had made another now, in turning to the French for sanctuary.

At the gate, Sirik Matak turned and shook hands with Thibaut. To a gendarme who wished him good luck he replied, "I am not afraid. I am ready to account for my actions." The Khmer Rouge had brought up a garbage truck; he was led around the back of it; followed by Luong Nal. It was the last anybody saw of them.

Hong Buon Hor, a much younger man, found it harder to control himself. His eyes staring wildly, he kept mumbling to himself while he patted his young daughter's hand as she clung to him. A Vietnamese woman with an Instamatic stepped in front of him and caught him full in the face with a flash. For a moment, Hong Buon Hor stood paralyzed. Then he cracked. Scuttling aimlessly, like a decapitated chicken, he ran into the crowd and out again. One of the Khmer Rouge escort snapped back his AK-47. There was a swirl of panic.

"Non!" shouted Thibaut.

The KR guns all around him wavered. Seizing his chance, the vice-consul dispatched three gendarmes with dogs to round up the President of the National Assembly. The Khmer Rouge soldiers hesitated. Thibaut had seconds to get this under control.

Hong Buon Hor had locked himself inside a Citroën Dyane and crawled under the seat. Rifle butts smashed the windows. Pleading for his life, his hands clutching at the seat covers, the broken windows, the door handles, the wretched figure was dragged out of the car and half-carried by the gendarmes to the gate.

Schanberg had no desire to see more. Nor had Savarin. They walked back across the compound. Schanberg told Savarin about Sirik Matak's letter. The U.N. official listened in silence.

"Don't give the Prince too much credit," he said when Schanberg had finished. "*Enfin,* he was the man who toppled Sihanouk. From that moment, Cambodia's fate was sealed. Don't forget, it was Lon Nol and Sirik Matak who at once declared war on the Vietcong."

"They had little choice by then," replied Schanberg.

"Because of your B-52 raids? Lon Nol and Sirik Matak could have started talks; they could have played for time. Sihanouk would have. He was always—how do you say *voltigeur?*—the man on the tightrope, yes. Instead they gave the Vietnamese Communists seventy-two hours to get their troops out of Cambodia, an impossible demand. Then they asked the Americans for arms. So you see why I have no tears for Sirik Matak. He has reaped his reward."

They were back in the drawing room. At the piano Barry Morgan was playing Beethoven's "Für Elise," his stubby fingers nicotine-yellow on the keys. Pran was sitting in the farthest corner of the room from him, his back to the window. Schanberg took a chair up to him. He lit a couple of cigarettes and passed one to Pran, who drew on it with a shaking hand.

"Where's Sarun?" asked Schanberg.

"He won't come, Sydney. He's afraid to be seen with Americans. And I think, maybe, it is better for both of us if I go outside, too."

"Why? Because of what Morgan said? You shouldn't

let a jerk like that get under your skin. You know what? He's just pissed off because you're working for me!"

Pran frowned and shook his head. "No, Sydney. It's not him."

"Sarun told me you were frightened by some bats. Is that what it is? C'mon, I'm right, I'm always right about you!"

Pran sighed. "They fly east in daylight. Very bad omen. And everybody say they will throw all Cambodians out."

"All right, I heard that too. And I heard a lot of other rumors as well. But they're all just rumors, Pran. Superstitions. Same as the bats."

Pran looked at him and looked away. "Same as a yellow rose, Sydney?"

"Okay." Schanberg nodded hard. He couldn't think of an answer to that. He gazed around. Rockoff had been put on hygiene detail by Oscar. He aimed the insecticide at the window behind Pran and pressed the button. A fly collapsed and died.

"Another U.S. Atrocity in Cambodia," Rockoff announced, "*New York Times* Indicts Nixon Doctrine." He shrugged and wandered off. Schanberg turned back to Pran.

"Stay around," he said gently. "You'll be okay. As much as any of us will be."

Pran sits in a wicker chair in the Ambassador's garden, apart from the others, and looks at the clouds. It is not only the bats that spell calamity. Pran is far too sophisticated not to believe in portents, even though he can't expect Sydney to understand them. He knows that the Buddhist law of karma applies to nations as much as to individuals—that the misdeeds of one epoch can be punished in another, in the same way that snowflakes, generations ago fallen on a mountainside, can issue as the avalanche that buries a village.

Not only the bats. For instance, the sacred sword. After Lon Nol's coup against Sihanouk five years ago, the Queen Mother had been required to draw the sacred sword from its scabbard to determine whether or not her son would return. It had come out not gleaming and lustrous but a filthy black. The Queen Mother had fainted. Not long afterward, while Pran was still working as a receptionist at the Auberge Royale de Temples opposite Angkor Wat, one of the most noble and ancient stone Khmer heads of the Buddha-in-repose had been stolen and sold in the West. All these things Sarun knows also. Which is why he grieves.

Pran lowers his gaze from the heavens and looks at Schanberg and Monsieur Savarin walking toward him across the grass. Wood smoke from the compound makes his eyes prickle. Sydney is always so optimistic, so positive. He has great respect for the Frenchman, perhaps because he has a silver mustache. But they talk together about history as if it conformed to a process of logic, as if one action done differently could have changed its course. If Prince Sihanouk had come back before Lon Nol, and Sirik Matak had closed the airports in 1970 . . . If the Americans had not given Lon Nol such generous support . . . If the Great Doctor (as Sydney always calls Mr. Kissinger) had got rid of Lon Nol and brought Sihanouk back one year, two years ago. Who is to blame? they ask. They will not understand that we are all to blame.

His boss leaves Monsieur Savarin and comes across the lawn toward him with a springy step. Pran begins to rise from his chair; Sydney waves him back and sits down beside him. There is a grave expression on his face.

"It's not looking so bad," he began. "Thibaut has had two meetings with the Khmer Rouge authorities—apparently they call themselves the Comité De La Ville—and he claims he's made pretty significant progress. No, there's no need to take notes. Thibaut says the Khmer Rouge he's met with are very intelligent, dedicated, and serious people, and it's encouraging they've taken time out to come and talk to him."

"That's good."

Pran tries to look enthusiastic, to please the American. But Sydney knows him better than that. "You're not convinced by any of this, are you?" he says.

There is much tenderness in his voice. Pran has a lump in his throat. He shakes his head without speaking. He feels embarrassed and almost humble that he should be the subject of such a great effort of sympathy from the man he admires above all others. They sit in silence for two or three minutes, apart from the rest of the world.

Sydney clears his throat. "I'm not bullshitting you, Pran, I honestly don't think they're interested in us. We're an inconvenience, that's all. There's people coming over that wall twenty-four hours a day. Why don't they shoot them? They don't want them. They're after the big guys. If there's anyone they hate, anyone they're after, it's the Americans. And I'm not worried. Except slightly!"

At the humor of his understatement, Sydney gives a bark of laughter. Pran follows suit, although as usual it comes out sounding more like a giggle. "Is that how I will find America?" he asks.

"I should hope not. We're gonna get you settled in with

Ser Moeun first. Find a good school for the kids, teach them history and English. Then it's a question of getting the *Times* to give you work. Don't worry, it'll sort itself out, you'll see.''

There is a loud explosion from the commercial quarter, which rattles the French windows and sets the glass spires tinkling on the Ambassador's chandelier. The Khmer Rouge soldiers outside the compound are tooting car horns. All day they have been trying to start abandoned cars and shooting them up when the attempt fails. Pran raises his head and sniffs the air. The monsoon is coming; he can smell it on the breeze. He asks, ''What was Monsieur Savarin saying to you about genocide?''

Sydney hesitates. ''That was his opinion about what the Khmer Rouge are doing.''

''Yes?''

''Sending everybody into the countryside. He thinks it will kill more people than if the fighting had gone on to the bitter end, because there's no food out there. It's April; the next rice crop isn't until December. Besides, he thinks that without outside help, the KR can only grow enough to feed thirty percent of the population. . . .''

''Khmer Rouge say the people will come back when all the problems are solved.''

Sydney is silent. Pran knows he doesn't believe it. Khieu Samphan had said on the radio, ''Every Cambodian has his role in national society.'' But Nhiek Sann had not believed him. And Nhiek Sann, under guard on Monivong Boulevard yesterday, seemed to know that he was going away to his death. Again, as Pran looks into the future, the clouds come over his mind. Sydney stands up and pats him on the shoulder.

"C'mon, my friend," he says. "Best thing for us is to do our jobs and to hope."

Another day went by, the second full day in the French Embassy. At the grand piano, Barry Morgan with a cigarette on his lip played "Für Elise" again and again until an international delegation persuaded him to vary it with "Limelight" and "Summertime." Squatting on the Chinese rug, the Red Cross nurses played bridge, disregarding all Rockoff's efforts to teach them strip poker. Oscar organized work details and ladled rice—almost the only food available now that the emergency supplies, like Schanberg's, had been consumed. Champagne there was in plenty, liberated from the Ambassador's cellar along with a good supply of Scotch whiskey, French wines, and Cuban cigars.

"If the fucking B-52s had dropped this stuff on the enemy instead of napalm, we could all have gone home," Rockoff muttered, squinting out through his dark glasses over the compound. The journalists in the International Group had commandeered an upstairs room with a balcony where most of them were sitting. McIntyre was fiddling with the radio, tuning and listening as intently as to a patient's heartbeat. Swain, long legs propped up on a tapestried stool, was reading *The Quiet American*. Schanberg, stretched out in the sun with a cigar, turned his head and scowled at Rockoff, who was sipping champagne.

"It's all right for you," Shanberg said. "What about my fucking Dundee cake? You come out of the hotel like some asshole spastic with a coupla tins of peach slices, leaving behind a whole brand-new Dundee cake! Here I sit ekeing out a miserable existence on a few grains of rice a day, thinking about my Dundee cake, not to mention my peanut butter, and what do you care?''

Rockoff sounded offended. ''They were top-quality peach slices,'' he argued. ''And what size pockets do I have to—''

''Hold it!'' McIntyre signaled for quiet. The BBC was coming through on a fading signal, with bad news from Vietnam. The Communists had advanced and were shelling Bien Hoa airfield. Secretary of State Kissinger had attacked the Soviet Union in a speech to newspaper editors. There were unconfirmed reports that Hanoi intended to push on for a total military victory . . . The signal faded. McIntyre urgently manipulated the dial. The reedy voice returned.

''. . . and that the situation in the French Embassy is increasingly precarious. Unconfirmed reports have said that the United Nations representatives confined in the embassy are entering into negotiations with the insurgent government. The UNICEF representative in Bangkok is quoted as saying that something must be done within a matter of hours if tragedy is to be averted. . . .''

The station faded out in a cackle of Burmese. Swain raised his head. ''Where are they getting all this crap?''

Rockoff lowered his dark glasses and assumed a conspiratorial air. ''See the little guy at the gate?''

The journalists all looked out over the balcony. A diminutive Khmer Rouge soldier stood guard at the main gate. Rockoff hissed, ''Don't all look at once! I have it from highly reliable bodies that this is none other than *Sy Jules*.''

Schanberg smiled. Swain played along. ''You're kidding me?''

"I'm deadly serious. He's disguised, of course, because the high-heeled boots looked a tad suspicious."

Schanberg's turn. "But how does he get copy out?"

"A type of specially trained hen," answered Rockoff, keeping a straight face, although Swain was already chuckling. "His TV network has commissioned these fowl to walk past the Khmer Rouge like they're regular chickens. They're crossing into Thailand day and night. . . ."

They all laughed aloud. Half a dozen Westerners on a balcony in the middle of an abandoned city, unwinding some of the tension that had screwed them up so tight these last few days. It was Barry Morgan, coming up to share whatever pittance of humor they'd discovered, who first saw the Russian truck draw up on the street outside.

By the time the newsmen got to the main gate, the dispute had become heated. The Soviet and East German diplomats, three men and three women, wanted to stay in their embassies—after all, had they not put a large poster up for the Khmer Rouge, "We are Communists, we are your Brothers, come forward with a French-speaking interpreter"? They had lost that argument. The Khmer Rouge had come forward but only to send them packing. What was worse, they had broken eggs from the Russians' fridge in front of their faces, thereby accusing them of backsliding since a true Khmer Communist does not commit the individualist act of eating an egg, he lets it hatch into a chicken he can eat communally with his fellows.

Now the argument was with the French officials who were prepared to let the Communists in but not with all the revisionist baggage stacked on their truck: two washing machines, a TV, and an American-made refrigerator. The Soviet chargé d'affaires, a band of white on his arm where

179

a Khmer soldier had liberated his wristwatch, was as angry as a radish, brandishing his fist. *"Nous demandons les avantages diplomatiques!"* Behind him the Khmer soldiers around the truck had already smashed the TV screen and a framed photograph of Brezhnev and were busy pulling the fridge onto the ground.

That argument was lost, too. The Russians and East Germans came in with only the cases they could carry. One flew open, spilling on the grass hundreds of smoked sausages. A cheer went up from the compound as a blond Russian of similar build to the sausages scrabbled to gather them back in.

"They are peasants, of course," the Soviet chargé d'affaires said to Thibaut once he had calmed down. As if in mocking reply, there was an enormous explosion a few streets away. In the sudden quiet that followed, pieces of paper began floating down out of the air. Schanberg picked one up: it was a ten-thousand-riel note. The insurgents must have blown up the Banque Khmer de Commerce. The idea bewildered him. What kind of regime was the Khmer Rouge proposing, that had no place for money in it?

Pran materialized at his side as unobtrusively as ever. To Schanberg's relief he was smiling and excited; all the old energy was back. In delight, he put an arm around Pran's shoulder. "What's new?"

"I manage to speak with KR officer. He was okay. He say the city is empty, everybody out. They search every building, burn down ones they cannot search. They fire grenades and B-40 rockets wherever they think snipers are there."

"Yes."

"Officer told me that Khmer Rouge are not Communists. They are"—he consulted his notebook—" 'Liberation Troops—Nationalists.' But everybody is brother-comrade now. No more towns and cities, exploiting rice farmers. Everybody must be farmer. That's all I got."

"That's good. That's very good. Well, I got news for you. Thibaut is opening discussions about an airlift. I'm serious. Keep your fingers crossed, we could all be in Thailand in a couple of days. What do you think of that?"

They grinned at each other like schoolboys. Pran said shyly, "I think—champagne?"

The clammy heat grew more and more stifling. In these last hours before the waters of the monsoon broke, everything sweated in the heat: the walls, the floors, the trees, the furniture . . . human skin most of all. Once they had emptied Phnom Penh, the insurgents had no further use for the city. They cut the electricity and turned off the water mains. The embassy compound, housing five hundred people without sanitation, began to look like a sewage farm. Any infection would have spread like the plague.

Driven indoors by the smell and the heat, the International Group sweltered in rooms no longer air-conditioned, fanning stubbled cheeks with bits of torn cardboard, thinking about their wives, about sex, about the airlift, most of all about food. . . .

"The cat was good," said Schanberg reflectively. With the help of a couple of French mercenary soldiers the previous night, they had strangled and skinned the embassy cat. "Curried is always best with cat. Makes it tender, like chicken." Louder, for Rockoff's benefit, "What I could really eat now is a peanut butter sandwich. Peanut

181

butter on rye, the slices forced apart by the intensity of filling . . .''

"I'm not listening," said the photographer. Lying on his tablecloth in the drawing room, he was reading an old copy of *Playboy*, very slowly, from the front.

"Or a fillet steak with fries and a crisp green salad . . ."

"Are you kidding?" Rockoff groaned. "When I get out of here, I'm gonna get a chair and spend a fortnight in front of a fridge. And I'm gonna employ a uniformed doorman to open it for me.''

A French official from the consulate, pink-cheeked and heavy-jowled, appeared in the doorway.

"Il y a quelqu'un qui parle français?"

Several of them did, but nobody wanted to say so. Schanberg shook his head at Pran. Eventually, Jon Swain stood up. *"Si vous voulez, monsieur."*

They went outside. Oscar returned to whittling a fork out of bamboo. Rockoff whistled, and the Australian growled at him. "Hurry it up. You read it daft.''

"I intend to undress this magazine slowly," said Rockoff. The Red Cross nurses in the corner bent deeper over their whist.

Swain returned alone. There was a tense expression on his face. He crossed to where Schanberg was sitting. "They've got some Red Cross instruction sheets they wanted translated. I said you'd give me a hand."

"Pran reads better than I do."

Pran stood up, ready to offer his services.

Swain pushed his hair back. He said awkwardly, "I think actually it would be simpler if I did it with you."

Pran sat down. Schanberg, scowling, followed Swain out into the entrance hall.

"What did you do that for?" he demanded as Swain closed the door behind them. "Poor guy, he's insecure enough as it is."

Swain glanced around. The opulent hall, like most other rooms in the ambassador's lodge, had by now been occupied by squatters from the compound, Asians and Europeans alike. He took Schanberg aside. "The Cambodians have got to leave, Sydney."

Schanberg stared at him.

"The KR have said no to the airlift. They've told Thibaut they no longer consider this as an embassy. They say it's an international regroupment center for all foreigners. The Cambodians have to go right now. The French are asking for everybody's passport in, to check. And everybody upstairs has to come down."

"Oh, God. No." Schanberg closed his eyes, his mind reeling. There had to be a way. Please, God, there had to be a way. Already the news was spreading. A Belgian woman, near to hysterics, ran through the hall crying out her husband's name. A Cambodian officer came down the stairs; she buried her face in his chest, hugging him and weeping.

"Ce n'est pas vrai! Ce n'est pas vrai!"

Schanberg went back into the drawing room, trying to think of what to say. Pran was missing. He hurried out to the compound. It was in pandemonium. Gendarmes were moving from encampment to encampment, giving out the news. Despair and fear were on every face. Cars were being loaded with possessions and pushed toward the main gate. A van had been pushed over a cooking fire: it lay on its side, its tires blazing. A Vietnamese woman, the one he had seen feeding her poodle on raw fish, ran up to Schanberg and tried to press gold earrings and an emerald necklace into his hands, begging him to give her shelter. Behind her as she spoke, the poodle was seized and loaded into a car as food for someone's journey.

Schanberg sent her away and walked on through the stink and misery, calling Pran's name. A Cambodian woman sat very still on an old steamer trunk, clasping two children in hooded raincoats who gazed up at Schanberg like two sad pixies. A Montagnard officer, one of the doomed, courageous mountain tribe who had fought both Vietnamese and the Khmer Rouge to preserve their identity, stood in his path. With his one good hand he tore open his shirt to reveal a grill of terrible scars across his chest and stomach.

"Five years I fought," he said with dignity. "I fought with the Americans. I lost my hand. I have these wounds. You are American. Please help us. Make them see—"

"Nothing. *Rien*. Nothing I can do," said Schanberg, spreading his hands. He hurried past the Montagnard, refusing to meet the censure in his eyes. When would these people learn that America was no more reliable than their native gods? Schanberg had no miracles to offer. He was as powerless as any of them.

He found Pran with Sarun, helping to load their few possessions onto the back of a Toyota truck. When they saw Schanberg, they stopped for a moment, almost expectantly. For the first time in their relationship, the man who gave the orders had no instructions to give. Whatever Schanberg had planned to say on the way over, he couldn't deliver it now. All he could think of was that a look had come back into Pran's eyes he dreaded to see again—a look of fatalism, which to Schanberg was the same as hopelessness. Perversely it seemed to give Pran an inner strength. He was quite calm. He took Schanberg's hand, smiling.

"I try to get to Thailand, Sydney. Maybe two, three weeks, maybe a bit more. If you get there first, leave message for me at Reuters."

Schanberg was breathing hard. "Give me an hour. Just give me an hour, will you? I need some time to think."

Pran looked around. Sarun had finished loading his stuff on the Toyota. In a moment it would be going, so they could leave before the line. The driver came up behind Pran and made Schanberg a traditional salute. "Good-bye Mr. Sahnba, sir," he said, tears rolling down his cheeks.

"Sarun . . ." Schanberg delved in his pockets and came up with a wad of twenty-dollar bills. "Take them. They might be worth a can of beans somewhere. Pran, wait a minute, there must be . . ." His voice tailed off; he didn't know what he was saying. The Toyota had started to move off. He looked at Pran with tear-filled eyes.

"No time, Sydney," said Pran. "Sydney, I got to go."

"Syd!" Rockoff was running toward them. Out of breath, he could hardly blurt the words out. "Syd. Swain's got an idea."

Pran hesitated. Schanberg looked at him, unable to speak. Sarun and the van were almost at the gate. If Pran stayed now, he was on his own. He gazed around, and back at Schanberg, his eyes full of fear and a desperate need for the American's advice. The glimmer of hope had sapped his defenses.

"Let's go for it," said Schanberg.

In the Ambassador's quarters, Vice-Consul Thibaut was standing on a table spelling out the Khmer Rouge leadership's instructions to a clamoring throng of Cambodians, Chinese, Vietnamese, and Westerners. He raised his arms for quiet. "*Je vous en prie*. There is one exception. The Cambodian wives and children of foreign male nationals are exempt. *C'est à dire*, a Frenchman may rest here, and so may his Cambodian wife and children, so long as they have French passports. A French woman may rest here, but her Cambodian husband and children will have to depart. They have permitted this latter group twenty-four hours for departure."

This was what the Belgian woman had known when she came screaming for her husband. Schanberg wondered how many would refuse evacuation and go out with their husbands into the countryside. But Thibaut hadn't finished. His voice breaking with emotion, he finished his address.

"I must tell you, the Khmer Rouge has demanded to search the embassy. I am not in a situation to 'negotiate from strength.' After very delicate bargaining, I have gained two days. They insist on knowing the identity and nationality of all foreigners. Therefore, I request of you to cede your passport or papers to your group leader. Your presence must be enregistered with my consular personnel by midday tomorrow. I am sorry. My assistants will respond to your questions."

Thibaut got down and hurried away, his face haggard. Swain beckoned Schanberg and the other two into the entrance hall. Here, as everywhere, families about to be separated were weeping and holding each other tightly as if they wanted to carry away an impression on their bodies of the ones they loved. Those who weren't crying were evolving desperate schemes, clutching at straws, building straw houses of hope to carry into the Khmer Rouge tempest that blew outside. Oblivious of the horror around them, the Soviet delegation, cushioned under the sweeping stairs, lunched off boiled eggs and vodka.

Swain's was one such scheme. He held two British passports in his hand, tied together with blue consular ribbon. "We think we can put a passport together for you," he said, looking intently at Pran.

"How?" asked Schanberg.

"Look." Swain untied the ribbon. "This first one's out of date but with a current visa. We knock out the Jon, knock out the Swain, and we get the two in the middle, Ancketill Brewer."

Pran was shaking. Schanberg knew how it must feel: like the man hanging on the side of the last helicopter out, after it leaves the ground. He could drop, now, and take his chances of surviving. He could hang on and maybe lose his grip. The name clearly worried him for a start; he tried pronouncing it.

"Hanketill Blewer?"

Swain nodded. "It's a bit of a mouthful. You'll have to practice. . . ."

Pran hesitated. The three newsmen stared at the Cambodian who had saved their lives, willing him to comply. For once, Pran was forced reluctantly to shake his head.

"I haven't got a picture," he told them, almost weeping. "I never got my identity papers back."

Rockoff made for the consulate. Schanberg headed into the compound, clutching dollars in his fist. As urgently as he had been pleaded to, he now pleaded back—for a Polaroid camera. There was a crush of Cambodians at the main gate. He pushed his way through, holding dollars in his upstretched hand, shouting for a camera. Outside the gate, a Khmer Rouge soldier was yelling through a bullhorn. Blank faces were turned on Schanberg. Nobody needed dollars anymore.

He ran back and saw Oscar by a half-dug sanitation trench, leaning on a spade. The huge Australian was holding a bundle in the crook of his arm; as Schanberg approached, he saw tears on the bearded face. The bundle was a baby.

"She said I would like him because he was very beautiful," Oscar explained. "She said he was her only child and he would die. . . . Shit!" With his right hand he thrust the spade a foot into the dry earth in a spasm of fury and frustration. "You know me, I've been a sailing man all my life, I'm not built for this kind of stuff. I haven't cried since I was a kid."

Two round brown eyes peered at Schanberg out of the white shawl. With an effort he said, "Oscar, I need your help. I got to get a Polaroid camera, fast."

Oscar raised his eyes from the bundle in his arm. "Try McIntyre," he said.

Back through the Salle de Reception. Up the stairs, two at a time. Down one corridor, then another, looking in offices converted into makeshift dormitories. He should have sent Pran out with his family in the helicopter. This would be the second time he'd encouraged him to gamble his life.

He found what he was looking for on the second floor. The absent Ambassador's bedroom had been converted into a clinic. A linen tablecloth on top of a Louis Philippe chest of drawers functioned as an operating table; a gilded lamp stand did service as a drip support. A badly wounded soldier had just been lifted off the table by two Red Cross nurses; another one was swabbing down the parquet floor with a strong solution of disinfectant. McIntyre, in a gauze mask, was bending over a feverish child.

"Gordon. Sorry. I need a Polaroid camera, you got one?"

"Yes. Don't come any closer. I have no film." McIntyre removed his stethoscope. "Also I have no emetine. And this child has amoebic dysentery."

He looked up. Schanberg had already disappeared.

"My name is Hank-at-ill Blewer." Pran sat in the kitchen, his head in his hands. His evident despair was beginning to infect all of them: Oscar, who sat at the table making glue out of cooked rice; Swain, beside him, using a razor blade with infinite care to ease his photograph off the old passport; Schanberg, boiling a kettle to help steam off the rest. Only the abandoned baby was unaffected. It lay in a cot Oscar had salvaged from the compound, fast asleep.

"Thought I'd see if it needed something," Oscar was telling them. "McIntyre was busy, so I took it to those frog doctors from the Calmette Hospital. Found three of the bleeders having lunch in the dining room. I couldn't believe my bleeding eyes. Cold chicken breasts, asparagus from the freezer, chilled white vino—Christ, imagine the Ritz on an emergency generator and you get the picture. I asked if there was a pediatrician in the house—offered to bring the world's press around to film their banquet—you should have seen 'em jump!" He peered into the cot. "I got it the best medical checkup this side of Bangkok."

The kettle was boiling. Schanberg held the carefully wrapped passport while the Englishman, with tweezers, carefully peeled out its written section. Both men knew

189

that without a photograph, what they were doing was hardly more than a masquerade. But there would be a photograph. *There would be a photograph*.

Pran looked up—not at the newsmen. The vice-consul, Thibaut, was in the kitchen doorway. He was pale, and there were dark rings under his eyes, but he carried himself with dignity. The others waited for him to speak.

"Messieurs, you will be pleased to hear that the Khmer Rouge Comité De La Ville has acceded to my urgent requests for food supplies. They will arrive in the morning. Also, I have a limited number of French passports. If you know a Frenchman who wishes someone to marry, I am prepared to backdate the passport to provide them with French nationality."

"Sir, what about these mixed families being separated?" asked Swain. "It's against every principle of justice and fair play."

Thibaut nodded. As Schanberg watched him, this veteran of the French Resistance, prisoner-of-war, and officer in the Indochina expeditionary force seemed to crumple a little inside his suit. "I try to save these people today," he replied. "I can do nothing. I am not a policeman. I had to turn them out. They could have been shot *sûr le coup*, and those believed responsible would be compromised." Thibaut's eyes welled with tears, his words coming out so softly that the newsmen had to strain to hear him. "It is a very sad thing to say. When we do such things, we are no longer men."

Unable to carry on, he turned away and walked off. He left behind a silence in the kitchen, which was not broken until Rockoff came in. His face was gloomy. He began to speak, then stopped. The faces turned to him, above all by

Pran, were so imploring that he seemed to change, mid-sentence, what he had been going to say.

"Well. There you go." He shrugged. "We're in luck."

"Oh, Al!" Pran's eyes lit up like a child's. "Thank you, Al!"

The photographer gave a thin smile. His eyes were anxious. "Syd, can we talk a moment?"

Rockoff led Schanberg out into the corridor that ran from the kitchen to the bathroom and lavatory cubicles. There was the sound of someone being sick. With a polite apology, a Frenchwoman with red-rimmed eyes led out past them her twelve-year-old Cambodian son. He was clasping her tightly; he had less than twenty-four hours to hold her hand.

"All I need's a developer," said Rockoff in a low voice. He was pacing up and down in agitation. "Some kind of powerful sulphide. I get that, I can improvise the rest."

"What about the fix?" asked Schanberg.

"Fuck the fix. Vinegar. Lemon juice. You could piss on it. What I need's a developer. Something to break down the emulsion. . . ." He punched his palm with frustration. "Where's McIntyre?"

"He hasn't got a thing. What about ammonia? You can get ammonia out of a fridge, can't you? What about car batteries?"

Rockoff kept shaking his head. "You're confusing me, Syd. I gotta think. There's a lot of stuff we can get first. That Swedish guy—Sundsvall—he's got a flashlight. We'll get a tray for the development tank . . . find a dark-room . . ."

The darkroom was the nastiest part. In the heat and

stench of one of the staff lavatories, the *New York Times* bureau chief was on his knees next to a water bucket, wrapping a sheet of colored cellophane around the flashlight Sundsvall had lent them. Rockoff returned empty-handed from his search for a sulphide.

"What are you going to use?" asked Schanberg.

"Fucked if I know." Rockoff inspected the lavatory cubicles for a possible darkroom. He recoiled from the smell, fanning the air. "Jesus Christ!"

"Need a bucket of disinfectant," remarked Schanberg. The next moment he was staggering under Rockoff's impetuous embrace.

"Syd! You bastard!"

"What?"

"Antiseptic! It's full of phenol! If we can get holda some caustic soda, we got to get an image!"

The antiseptic took hardly any time. The caustic soda took longer. By the time Rockoff got back to the kitchen and began stirring the mix together in a wide saucepan, the dusk was crowding them. Pran had gone outside. Schanberg, who had been on his feet all day, sat at the table watching the photographer. Swain, who had been out hunting for film, burst into the kitchen. "Two rolls, black and white," he announced in triumph, handing them to Rockoff.

The photographer took one look at them and shook his head. "Ilford. Sorry Jon, no good. It's got to be Kodak."

"Why?"

"Because the Kodak emulsion contains something called hydroquinone. It's a developer and antioxidant. It's the only film that has it, and it's what I need."

Suddenly it was very dark in there. Rockoff picked up the saucepan and stowed it in a high cupboard. "It's too late tonight," he said, seeing Schanberg's expression. "We'll take his picture in the morning; we'll have a few hours left. All I need now is the right film."

Schanberg walked out into the humid dusk. The Ambassador's flowering trees shriveled around him, stripped of their bark and branches by the refugees. Pran was standing in the lee of a burned-out van, staring across the fence. Paper money from the dynamited central bank lay in the ash of a cooking fire. The Khmer Rouge had stopped playing Keystone Kops on the road outside; beyond the gates, the city was dark and quiet except for the occasional rattle of small-arms fire.

"It's on for tomorrow morning," Schanberg told him. "First light. We'll have Al take your picture and stick it in the passport in time for the collection."

"Al has developer?"

"Yes. And the film. But he wants to get a better one."

"Thank you. Thank you, Sydney."

Schanberg couldn't read his eyes in the dark. "Don't thank me. I got you into this louse-up, remember?"

Pran knelt. He scrabbled up a mixture of earth and ash and began kneading it, like somebody washing their hands. "I could have go, Sydney," he said with firmness. "I could have go on the helicopter, I could have go with Sarun. I stay because I want to stay. Because I want to stay with you. I make the choice."

He let the earth slip between his fingers. Schanberg watched him. He asked, "Are the rains coming?"

"It's not for that. I talk yesterday to a man from the country. He say the Khmer Rouge in his village made everybody turn up the palm of their hand. Like so. People with rough skin are okay. People with smooth hands are *sambor bep*, the good-livers. They get executed."

"You believed him?"

"Yes. Dr. Macketire, did he tell you what happen in the Preah Keth Mealea? After we go, Dr. Macketire is operating on the little girl. Khmer Rouge break in, they smash all the plasma bottles, they cut the mask of oxygen on her face. Then they go through all the hospital to shoot the people who are dying. They tell the others, you have ten minutes before we blow up the hospital. So, yes, I believe him."

There was a crash of thunder. At the gate, the Khmer Rouge guard, startled, loosed off his rifle at the sky. Out of the blackness, the first few heavy drops fell, spattering their clothing and kicking up little puffs of dust. Pran grinned and threw back his head. Schanberg followed him, letting the warm rain drive through his beard. For a moment they all were at one: he and Pran; the Khmer Rouge guard; the dying trees; the soiled lawn. The monsoon had broken.

They ate by candlelight, the rain thudding at the high windows. Since fresh supplies were said to be arriving in the morning, Oscar had emptied the last two cans of stewed beef over the soggy mess of rice in the cauldron. Some of the tension seemed to have eased, allowing those present to dine more or less normally. They talked generally of all that was happening to the world around them, avoiding the specifics of their own survival.

After dinner the journalists and U.N. staff began to drift away. Oscar was deep in conversation with a Red Cross nurse who was looking after his baby. One of her colleagues,

194

tipsy on the last of the Ambassador's champagne, had carried a candle across to Barry Morgan at the piano and was shrieking with laughter at his improvised version of "Colonel Bogey." Pran had disappeared. Schanberg moved to sit beside Henri Savarin.

"You look wise, Henri, in this dim light," he said.

"I was thinking about Madame Chantal's," said the administrator. "There we could generalize about the world; it rarely touched us. Now we are in the middle of a human catastrophe, and it still seems unreal. Two and a half million people made homeless in twenty-four hours. As an evacuation, it ranks with the Jews from Babylon or the Ukrainians after the Second World War; there is nothing else to match it. We don't know why it has happened. We sit here in the middle of a holocaust, drinking champagne out of crystal goblets. It is like an opium dream. And tomorrow I marry a Cambodian woman, with two children, to whom I have spoken only once in my life."

Schanberg gazed at him in astonishment. Savarin stubbed out his cigar and stood up. "Will you do me the honor, tomorrow, to witness it? I hope so. For now, I shall go and try to sleep without dreaming."

He left the dining room before Schanberg had recovered. There would be time, surely, to ask him about camera film in the morning.

It has rained most of the night. By morning, a sky of galvanized iron has closed over the city. Water drips from the bare trees and abandoned cars and fills the sanitation trenches; it gathers up the yellow paper money and leaves it in million-riel deposits by the embassy fence. On the roof of the Ambassador's quarters, it lies in iron-gray sheets of water, reflecting nothing, not even Pran as he stands in one of them having his picture taken.

For the twentieth time he forces a smile. Al Rockoff, steadying the Nikon on a chair, clicks the shutter over the Rolleiflex lens. "That's great!" shouts Al. "Just keep smiling, Pran, boy! I'm gonna immortalize you in black and white!" All the time his hands keep moving, constantly adjusting the speed and exposure. Trying to get it right.

Pran doesn't want to be immortalized. All he wants is a bit longer to live. He knows there is something about the way he stands facing the camera and flinches when the shutter clicks that makes him look as if he is facing a firing squad. That thought must be in their minds, too. Sydney is pacing between the chair and the balustrade, looking up at the sky. Monsieur Swain is leaning against the fire exit door making faces at him to get him to relax. For Al it is the worst. Pran is a photographer, too; he knows what Al must be going through. Of all the combat photographs he has taken, mostly of death and suffering, this is one that may actually save a life—and for once he is without the proper facilities, at the mercy of whatever chemical solution he has had to settle for.

If it doesn't work . . . Pran looks down at his hands. Two days of rubbing in dirt has made them raw and painful; the calluses will soon appear. But what if the Khmer Rouge doesn't stop at the palms of your hands? What if they pull your lip up and examine your teeth, to see if they are the teeth of a peasant?

"Look up!" shouts Rockoff.

Pran looks up. He can't raise a smile. Like a rabbit caught in headlights, he stares at the camera. The shutter axes across. Without warning, the rain falls in a heavy drape, beating on his face and hands. He hears Al Rockoff say to Sydney, ''I had to use the Ilford.'' It must mean something, because Sydney has turned away and Pran cannot see his face.

Her name was Ang Van. Her two small daughters were still in their pixie hoods; Schanberg recognized them from the day before when he had gone out to see Pran for what he'd thought was the last time. Exhaustion and fear had made their mother almost beautiful; her black hair glistening from the rain, she stared at the Westerners in the Salle de Reception through enormous dark eyes, one arm around her children, the other clutching Savarin's jacket.

Barry Morgan, who had been dozing over the piano, woke up and began playing a two-finger melody.

> Yesterday, all my troubles
> Seemed so far away . . .

The inappropriateness of the song went unnoticed, although this was no time for sentimentality. There was nothing romantic about this wedding. If it saved three lives for one French passport, it had served its purpose; they would celebrate with an annulment when they reached Bangkok.

> Now it looks as though
> They're here to stay . . .

''The Consul needs two witnesses,'' said Savarin with an effort. ''Would you ask your friend for me?''

Schanberg was grateful. As Savarin had realized, it would take Pran's mind off the waiting. The four of them, followed by the two children, walked through the rain to the consulate.

"Her husband was one of Long Boret's chief aides," explained the U.N. official. "He tried to surrender directly to the Khmer Rouge and was shot."

Schanberg hesitated. "I didn't know you were single."

"Helene, my second wife, died three years ago of cancer. I lost my first wife in 1947, in Shanghai, when it surrendered to the Communists. It was what I saw then that made me join the United Nations."

Nothing more was said. Thibaut met them in the lobby of the consulate and took them up to the first floor to officiate at the brief ceremony. Pran guided Ang Van through the formalities, then stood back while Thibaut filled in the precious passport, carefully backdating it to April 12. Schanberg saw the expression on his assistant's face.

"It'll be your turn next," he said half-seriously.

"Yes, Sydney."

The two newsmen ran back through the deserted compound. Swain met them at the French doors. "Just trying to intensify the image," he said. "Theoretically, it should work."

Schanberg looked at his watch. "They'll be coming for the passports in thirty minutes."

"I know."

Swain raced back to the washrooms, Schanberg on his heels. One of the lavatory cubicles was cordoned off with a black curtain to keep out the daylight. As Swain went in, Schanberg caught a brief glimpse of Rockoff bending over

198

a large mixing bowl on the toilet. He handed Swain a flashlight wrapped in green cellophane. The curtain hid what followed.

"Go!" Schanberg heard the photographer shout. Two seconds of green light would be on the negative floating in the bowl.

"Go again!" Silence. "No good. Get rid of it. Have to try something else."

Rockoff came out of the cubicle wiping the perspiration off his face. Schanberg remembered something he'd just seen. "That generator in the consulate," he said. "Some of the electric lights are on."

They rushed back across the compound, Rockoff with the mixing bowl, Schanberg with the blackout curtain. The main gate was open. Gendarmes under black umbrellas were standing beside it, supervising the arrival of large Chinese-made trucks that rumbled through and parked on the muddy lawn. Inside the consulate, no questions were asked. A lavatory with electric light was found. Schanberg draped the black curtain. Rockoff snapped two thermometers over a saucer, pouring out the mercury. Swain unraveled a tampon and pulled out the cotton wool.

"Kill the light," said Rockoff. He took a negative out of the bowl and rubbed it with mercury. Laying it on a square of newspaper, he nodded at Swain. The Englishman flashed the green light.

"Again." Silence. Schanberg listened. Rockoff swore with a furious energy. The electric light went on, and he came out of the cubicle, shaking his head. "It *should* work, Syd. But it doesn't fucking work. I don't know what else is in the antiseptic—maybe something cutting something else out . . ."

The two men stared at each other. Both knew what this meant. They didn't want to put it into words. Rockoff ran his fingers through his hair. "I've tried everything," he said, more to himself than to Schanberg. "Everything I could think of, I've tried. The only other way's a dry process. But that means he's gotta sit absolutely still, in brilliant sunlight, for half an hour. Even if we got the sunlight, I don't think he's up to that right now. Plus I don't think I'd get any better than I got. . . ."

Schanberg looked at him. There was nothing to say.

"I'll try one more time, Syd. You go keep Oscar happy, pat his baby on the head. Just give me a couple minutes longer."

Schanberg walked back, very slowly, to the Salle de Reception. He waited to hear a yell of joy from Rockoff, running feet . . . but nothing pattered on the gravel except the rain. His watch said eleven fifty-five. In the Salle de Reception, the pink-cheeked French consular official had already arrived. Most of the others were clustered at the window, watching the last of the Chinese trucks turn into the compound with a grinding of gears. Pran was standing apart from them, his back to the wall, fingering a small object about the size of a roll of camera film. Schanberg thought it was the Buddha he prayed to for luck; as he came closer, he recognized the Statue of Liberty, the little plastic model Craig Whitney had given Pran as a joke souvenir. He hesitated.

Oscar's voice boomed out behind them.

"Okay, you lot, let's have your ears, as they say. It's been confirmed that people with families have been given another twenty-four hours. As you guessed, the trucks outside are for our evacuation—sorry about that—it'll be

to Thailand, and the date will be given us shortly.
Meanwhile, if you've all got your passports ready, I'll
collect them and hand them to this kind frog gentleman
here—''

''Syd!''

Rockoff was standing in the doorway. There was a
broad grin on his face. Schanberg bounded across the
room. ''Give us a hand with the car,'' said the photographer mysteriously. He raised two fingers in what might
have been a victory sign. ''Two minutes, Oscar!'' he
shouted.

The car, an abandoned Volkswagen, they pushed into
the Ambassador's garage. Swain sat in the driver's seat.
Rockoff crouched in front of it, holding a shoebox up to
one of the headlights. Schanberg, beside him, held a black
umbrella to cut out more of the light. ''Again!'' shouted
Rockoff. ''When I say go, give me ten seconds. Go!''

The headlights dazzled and cut. Rockoff made an inspec-
tion in the darkness. Pran stared up from the shoebox. The
three newsmen whooped with joy, and a large rat fled into
the darkness.

Oscar was still collecting up the passports when Schanberg
handed Ancketill Brewer his. ''Welcome to New York!''
he said. There was no reponse. The ordeal had been so
great that Pran was unable to show his gratitude. Together
with the other three, he handed his passport with its Ilford
photograph to Oscar, then went and sat on the floor, his
shoulders shaking. Schanberg went and sat beside him,
drained of emotion.

Now all they had to do was wait.

*   *   *

It seemed like long afterward, but was probably only a few minutes, that the pigs arrived. A Citroën sedan drove into the compound with two young Khmer Rouge soldiers on the luggage rack grinning through missing teeth. An officer put his head out of the window and barked an order; they jumped down, their looted ladies' overcoats trailing in the mud, and opened the Citroën's rear doors. The two huge pigs in the passenger seats didn't like the rain any more than the KR officer. The soldiers borrowed umbrellas from the two gendarmes standing by and prodded and poked them out of the car.

"They're laughing," said Schanberg at the window, in astonishment, witnessing the first human emotion he'd encountered from the Khmer Rouge since they marched past the Hotel Phnom. As he spoke, the officer in the front seat turned around and issued what was obviously a reprimand. Abashed, the two young soldiers tucked up their overcoats and climbed into the passenger seats. The Citroën drove away, leaving Oscar and Sundsvall, under black tarpaulins, to shepherd the pigs into a toolshed where they had left an unappetizing mixture of dog food and grain.

The rain stopped in the early afternoon. The International Group ventured out in twos and threes, like the animals on Ararat, to take stock of the situation. Oscar and McIntyre emerged from the toolshed and called for volunteers. When nobody responded, Oscar picked out a couple of reluctant assistants to help kill a pig.

Schanberg and Swain strolled across to lend a hand. As they'd expected, they found McIntyre doing most of the work. Noelle, the Red Cross nurse who assisted him in the operating theater, sheltered the doctor from the sun with an umbrella while he cut away the pig's face with a scalpel, slicing the cheek from the gums and tearing back the lips.

"Monsieur Swain? *S'il vous plaît, monsieur.*" It was the French consular official. Swain gladly surrendered the pig's hindquarter he had been grasping and went with the Frenchman a short way across the grass.

Schanberg watched them. He saw Swain wipe bloodied gloves on his white coat and take the official's umbrella. With a sinking heart, he saw the official search an inside pocket and bring out a passport. He saw Swain put out a hand and take it. He saw the Frenchman shrug and raise his arms in a gesture of apology. . . .

He went over. Swain handed him the passport without a word. At first glance, it was perfect. The blue ribbon. The name on the cover, Ancketill Brewer. He opened it, and that was that. It was all over. Pran's picture had oxidized. As Schanberg looked at it, in the sunlight, the faint image became fainter, more ghostlike, until only the shadow of eyes and hair could be seen; then they, too, disappeared, and Pran was no more.

The consular official was talking to him. "*J'en suis désolé . . .*" Schanberg paid no attention. Holding the passport, he sprinted across the compound and up the consulate steps. He found Thibaut in the Visa office, gazing out of the window at the dead city, a paper cup of coffee in his hand. On the desk was a heap of passports and visa documents, each one representing a life surrendered to the Khmer Rouge.

"I need your help," said Schanberg.

Thibaut turned and gave him a weary smile, perhaps of recognition, perhaps because he had heard that line so many times before in the last three days. Schanberg showed him the passport and made his pitch. "Ninety-five percent of them have never seen a passport before," he argued. "I had a Khmer Rouge soldier waving my passport in my face, he didn't know what it was. They're peasants. Hill people—"

Thibaut put up his hand to interrupt him. "The officer I am talking with was educated at the Sorbonne. He is facile in French, English, and Russian. If I give him this passport, Ancketill Brewer would be shot dead immediately. It could imperil everybody. I cannot permit that to arrive. I am sorry, Mr. Schanberg. Your friend must go."

Schanberg shook his head. There had to be a way. "What about the French passports?"

"I have finished them all. *Voilà tout!*" With a despairing sweep of his arm, Thibaut propelled the heap of passports to the floor. Schanberg took one last look at Ancketill Brewer, as if the face of Dith Pran might have reappeared out of the blankness, and threw the passport down with the others. *Voilà tout.* All their efforts, all their hopes—just so much wastepaper. *I am sorry, Mr. Schanberg, your friend must go.* A ghost to join the other ghosts beyond the perimeter fence.

Out in the compound, the sky had metaled over again. The pig, dismembered, had been carried inside, leaving bloodstains on the grass. Schanberg had no desire to go indoors. He wanted the rain to come down and wash him away, clean him of guilt, clean him of memory. But the rain was treacherous. It would wash away the blood and leave him unscathed—a witness, a survivor, a rememberer. He went inside to deliver the bad tidings and suffer the terrible disappointment on Pran's face.

The Salle de Reception was full of people he seemed to

see from a great distance. McIntyre had taken over from Barry Morgan at the piano and was playing a Bach fugue, slowly. Sundsvall was hunched over Rockoff's tattered *Playboy*. The Red Cross nurses were playing bridge. What right had any of them to make it to the border when Pran, this brave and modest man, was going to be surrendered to the Khmer Rouge? Especially what right did he, Schanberg, have to flee to safety and leave behind the man who had been his invaluable assistant, his companion and friend, the man who had saved his life?

He saw Swain but didn't speak to him. He went into the hall. Pran was standing at the top of the stairs, a string of water bottles around his neck. There was an intense, concentrated expression on his face. He ran down the stairs. It had to be that he knew already, that Swain had told him. At the bottom of the stairs, one hand on the banister, he spoke to Schanberg.

"My name is Ancketill *Brewer*!"

Schanberg dropped his eyes from the look of triumph on Pran's face. It took him a great effort to look up again. He laid his hand on top of Pran's. Still the words wouldn't come, only the tears. Through them, he shook his head.

They are alone. The room is dark. A solitary light at the embassy gate where a gendarme stands with a black umbrella. Schanberg leans forward in his chair, his head bowed between his shoulders. Pran watches him, a silhouette in the window.

"It's not your fault, Sydney."

"I made you stay."

"I stay because I want to. I am journalist, too, Sydney.

205

They won't treat me bad. I am educated man. They need educated people.''

"You think so?''

"You said it before. They're after the big guys.''

"I don't know. I don't know. We hate the Communists. Why should they like us back?''

"I don't hate Communists. I afraid of them, afraid of the Khmer Rouge. I don't hate.''

"I hate myself. I risked your life—for what? For a hundred hours of Telex messages before the fucking line went dead. That's it, a hundred hours. Christ Almighty, what a sacrifice!''

"It's all right, Sydney. I'll be okay. You get some sleep now. Okay?''

Silence. Rain. The night dissolves in rain. It hurts Pran to see the pain he's causing.

"Pran?''

"Yes.''

"You remember that rocket on the school . . . the Catholic Church we went in where the bodies were?''

"Yes.''

"You looked at the pictures in the nave. You asked me about the Catholic saints. You said, 'Is it true that the people who suffer will be saved?' And all those little children dead or wounded in the aisle. And I said, 'I don't know, but the bastards who make them suffer will sure as hell pay for it.' Well. I think we all pay for it. All of us.''

"Okay, Sydney. You sleep.''

Dawn. A hand was shaking his shoulder. Schanberg sat up automatically; there was a story to be done. He took the glass of tea Pran had brought him, as he'd taken it a thousand times before in Phnom Penh, Battambang, Kompong Chang, and drank it gratefully. Then he remembered. And he wept.

Pran said, "You have done everything you can for me. You have teach me. You have help me. You are my friend."

"We've tried everything. . . ." Schanberg could not go on. He put his arms around the Cambodian and embraced him. Pran's cheeks were wet.

"You tell my wife I love her, Syd. And look after her for me. She does not speak no English. I don't want any people to be bad to her."

Schanberg nodded. He held Pran tight and nodded.

They went downstairs. A few of the other Cambodians were packing. A rumor had gone around that the Khmer Rouge was coming into the embassy to search. In the dingy, early-morning light, the Salle de Reception had a barrack-room air. Gordon McIntyre's radio had picked up a stray BBC signal and was broadcasting grim news from South Vietnam. Xuan Loc had been abandoned. Bien Hoa, just north of Saigon itself, was falling. President Thieu had resigned. There was no news about Cambodia. Cambodia was yesterday.

Schanberg helped Pran pack a few essential belongings, including a blanket, into a small bag. Pran said something about journalists having to be good at packing; Schanberg nodded. He found some cigarettes and gave them to Pran, also 2,600 dollars from his money belt for bribe money. Swain arrived with some roast pork wrapped in one of the embassy's monogrammed napkins, plus a can of peaches and an old opener.

"Thank you, Monsieur Swain." Pran rummaged in his

bag and dug out a half bottle of Scotch. Swain refused with a smile. Schanberg could see what this was doing to him too. Rockoff had slipped away. Lying under the piano, all that could be seen of him was a pair of tennis shoes. Barry Morgan, lounging against the fireplace, looked on with a condescending air.

A French consular official with a clipboard arrived to check out the Cambodians who were being expelled. He asked Pran his name and crossed him off the list, as Schanberg had watched the Red Cross nurse at the Preah Keth Mealea cross off her list those who were beyond saving. Pran looked down at his hands. From across the compound came the harsh, metallic crackle of voices on loudspeakers, cutting through the rain.

They went to the windows. Several gendarmes and consular officials under umbrellas were in discussion around a Toyota truck. One of the officials broke away and walked with purposeful strides toward the Ambassador's lodge. Schanberg turned. Pran was already on his feet. He shouldered his bag with a brave carelessness, but there were tears running down his cheeks.

Nobody could look, except Barry Morgan. The Fleet Street man stubbed out his cigarette and remarked in a loud voice, "Beats me what he expected. Shouldn't have been kept on, of course. Sent my chap out with the Americans."

Shaking with fear and anger, Pran turned on him. "You make racist statement against *me*," he said, his voice fracturing with emotion. "As though *I* cannot choose. I stay because"—he looked around at Schanberg, his mouth working—"I stay because I know his heart. I love him like a brother. And I would do *anything* for him."

He waited for a reply. None came. "I am going now," he muttered, abashed at himself, and walked quickly to the door. Those who had to, followed him out into the rain.

It was a small group of outcasts, perhaps fifteen in all, who loaded their possessions into the gasless Toyota truck and began pushing it to the main gate. One of the women had left her baby with Noelle, the Red Cross nurse; it could be heard wailing in the drawing room. Pran would not look back; it was too dangerous. Everything on him that might link him to the foreign devils he had already destroyed. As he helped push the truck down the drive, it seemed that his steps were becoming heavier, his shoulders more rounded like a peasant's, as though he were auditioning for the part of a survivor. The loudspeakers bellowed out Angka's monotonous message.

Schanberg watched from the bottom of the steps, his hands plunged in his pockets. He had blown it. He had tried everything and had failed. He had been sent out by his paper to this country in Asia to report a war. Somehow the war had inflicted on him a personal defeat bigger than anything the United States was likely to suffer, here or in Saigon. He didn't understand it at all. He had to try to understand.

The Toyota truck freewheeled out into the vacant boulevard, taking with it the man who knew his heart. The loudspeakers fell silent. The gates clanged shut. Walking back, Schanberg felt something in his pocket. He took it out. Pran had returned to him the Statue of Liberty souvenir.

PART THREE

Cambodia and
the United States,
Winter 1975—Autumn 1979

Black. Yellow.

Black on yellow. Hard black shadows under the ferocious afternoon sun. Black clothes, yellow earth-stained hands: a crawling black multitude, crawling like dung beetles on upheaved clay.

The place is Dam Dek, east of Siem Reap, in what is now and forever known as Democratic Kampuchea. The time is the beginning of time. Year Zero of the Khmer revolution.

The Dam Dek work site gouges a deep white scar into the green jungle. It is like an open-cast mine without tractors, bulldozers, or machinery. Men and women, bent under conical straw hats, break the earth with hoes and pitchforks. They spade it into latticed baskets, one on each side of a wooden yoke, and stagger with the yoke to the top of a fifteen-foot-high earthen embankment where the

213

baskets are emptied. Angka overseers with bamboo staves patrol the endless lines of laborers. When one of them collapses under his burden and cannot rise, he is dragged away and not seen again. In a slave society, sickness is inefficiency, and inefficiency is punished by death.

In this wilderness of sky and earth and jungle, the only man-made color is blood-red. On top of the earthen dike, the blood-red flag of Democratic Kampuchea hangs motionless in the windless heat. Below, in an angle of shadow, a cauldron simmers over a wood fire. A Khmer Rouge guard, distinguished from the slaves by his red-checkered scarf, ladles a spoonful of rice gruel into the tin cans of a work detail. The fourth man in line bows meekly and carries his little can farther into the shade.

He has changed less than many. His face is thin, he has lost fifty pounds in weight, his legs are covered in purplish sores, his hair is matted with grit—but since by now most of the people he knows are dead, Dith Pran has reason to count himself lucky.

As every day, he tries to sip the gruel slowly. As every day, hunger and thirst overcome him, and he gulps it down. Pran has been transporting earth on this work site since long before dawn and will have to toil on until nine at night with only one more ninety-minute break in the evening. This gruel represents one-third of his day's allowance of one hundred fifty grams of rice. His sores, like his thinness, are the consequence of malnutrition. He has no energy left, not even enough to brush the buzzing flies off his legs.

But he is alive. He has fooled them. Those last days in the French Embassy, nine months ago, he clung to the hope that he need not live a lie. The journey north had showed him otherwise. It had taken him through a sacked and looted city. The university was in flames. Books from the Cathedral Library were burning on the precinct lawn. About four miles out, he saw five corpses lying by the roadside, their hands tied behind their backs. The Khmer guards said they were officers, army traitors—the one he recognized was a civilian. Farther on his group came across several more bodies in military uniform on the road; the Khmer Rouge had driven trucks over them and squashed them flat as pancakes. He knew he was walking into a trap.

On the fourth day, he decided on his plan. He threw away his Western-style clothes and the dollars Sydney had given him. He put on shorts and sandals, and a dirty shirt, and had his hair cut short. He was no longer a journalist and interpreter: He was an uneducated taxi driver from a working-class district of Phnom Penh, a poor family man who had become separated from his family in the mass exodus; a man of the people who spoke little and then in language obsequious or crude, who smiled often and in a bewildered way, particularly when the talk turned to politics—a man who was delighted to be called a fool.

Twenty miles farther on was the first big Khmer Rouge checkpoint. "Tell us the truth about who you are," said men with gentle faces, smiling. "No one will be punished." They believed his halting story and gave him an identity card. Thousands of others—civil servants, teachers, lawyers, military men—did tell the truth and were never to be seen again. The taxi driver, smiling, nodding, speaking only when spoken to, traveled on for another month and arrived in Dam Dek. He stayed there because it was worse farther on. Or so he'd been told. Now he was beginning to wonder.

An order is shouted in Khmer. Pran gets to his feet. Along the top of the earthwork come two senior cadres on squeaking, Chinese-made bicycles. They stop underneath the flagpole and inspect the work detail. The woman, stocky and square-shouldered in her black uniform, takes out an orange and begins peeling it. The man, a bloated figure with a face like a curry puff and two pens in his breast pocket to advertise his rank, summons up mechanical enthusiasm to make a speech he has made several times elsewhere.

"Angka is proud of you," he tells them. "The imperialist warmongers tried to destroy us by destroying our crops, but you have spat in their faces. Nothing defeats the Revolution. Now the harvest is almost upon us, and the assault season must begin. New work schedules will be issued by Angka. Today we make sacrifices so that tomorrow there will be plenty to eat. Angka has spoken!"

His speech is punctuated by clapping. Anybody who does not clap is an enemy of the Revolution. The stocky woman leads the applause, the orange in her mouth. Pran notices a small lizard by his right foot. Surreptitiously, he drops his hat over it. The speech over, the stocky woman spits orange peel down the embankment and cycles away. Pran crushes hat and lizard under his foot. His fellow slaves make surreptitious grabs for the orange peel.

All day and late into the evening, Pran carries earth and mud to the embankment. Its purpose is not clear to him, since the Khmer Rouge, having dispensed with engineers, have no idea how to build proper dams or irrigation canals. But the thought is dangerous—to ask questions, even silently, is the mark of an educated man. In any case, he is too exhausted to care.

Under the watchful eye of Khmer Rouge guards, his work detail shuffles back to Dam Dek village, hardly more than a settlement of thatched huts in a jungle clearing. They are pushed on past the cooking fires of the old villagers to the covered market in the middle of Dam Dek, which the Khmer Rouge have taken over as a meeting place. There Pran leaves his yoke and stumbles on alone to his hut on stilts at the far end of the village.

He is too tired to eat. But he must eat. He inspects his pride and joy: his few square feet of garden in which he grows tomatoes and tobacco and a row of squash plants. The tomato he has had his eye on for three days is now ready to eat. He kneels and picks it, and drags his feet up the four slatted steps.

The rush matting on the floor is flaked with white mud. Grasping one of the hut's supporting bamboo poles, Pran lowers himself to the floor. He has no furniture; just two tin plates, a cooking pot, and drying tobacco leaves hanging from the thatched roof. He places the tomato on the floor and looks at it for a minute. Then he removes the hessian bag he carries at his waist and empties its contents into the cooking pot: four live snails and the lizard, already dry and shrunken.

Exhaustion is unwinding him like a broken spring. With the edge of a tin plate, he cuts the tomato in half. One half he leaves on the plate, the other he puts in his mouth. He masticates slowly. Then he curls up on the matting and covers his eyes with his hands. The last tomato seed is scarcely swallowed before he is fast asleep.

Immediately, as it seems, he is forced out of sleep by

the screeching clamor of voices on the public address system. For a moment, he lies there, listening to the shrill commands. Get up! Attend the meeting in the village hall! It is time to participate in the work of the Revolution! Sleep claims him; he wants to close his eyes. But this would be suicidal. The Revolution never sleeps. Groggy with tiredness, not knowing if it is night or morning, Pran pulls himself up and gropes in the darkness for his rubber Ho Chi Minh sandals.

Three times a week the indoctrination meetings take place in the roofed village market. The men of Dam Dek sit on one side, the women on the other. The children sit cross-legged at the front. Beyond the children, under electric light from a specially rigged generator, sit twelve sleek cadres of the Khmer Rouge. Pran recognizes two of them from today . . . or yesterday: the stocky, masculine-looking woman and the big-head with the curry-puff features. The loudspeaker directly above his head, haranguing him, keeps him just this side of consciousness. The woman is at the microphone.

"Look forward! Always look forward! Never look back! The new Kampuchea demands your loyalty! You must set yourselves higher goals, higher production targets! Our imperialist enemies destroyed the land. You must make it good again. Help Angka, and Angka will feed you. . . ."

Where does all the rice go? Pran can only guess. Even with last month's bad harvest and probably a block on all rice imports, one hundred fifty grams a day is not enough to live on. In the eight months he has been in Dam Dek, forty villagers have died of starvation, mostly old people and children. That is ten percent of the village. If this figure is repeated across Cambodia, 700,000 people must have died of starvation since the Khmer Rouge victory—many more of his countrymen than were killed in the whole course of the war . . . and yet there are surpluses! He has seen them. He has been on a transport to one of the communal storage depots and seen enough rice there to feed the whole province of Siem Reap for a month. So where does the extra rice go? It is a mystery . . . his eyes begin to close. A mystery . . .

And again the loudspeaker jars him awake before the cadre on the platform has witnessed his disgrace. ". . . that only Angka will feed you. Buddha will not feed you. Your sacrifices must be to Angka. You must work hard to become a good revolutionary. If you stay in the middle of the path, if you look over your shoulder, the wheel of Revolution will crush you. To build our new society, one million people will be enough. One million people who are pure and hard. . . . So Angka says to you—harden yourselves! If you fall, pick yourselves up and start working again!"

It is pitch-black outside. There is no hint of the dawn. The woman cadre leaves the microphone and is replaced by a teenage boy, two pens in his pocket to denote his high rank, who exhorts them in the same high monotone. The children gaze up at him from the floor, unblinking. Pran feels a shudder run through him. Could they be the "pure and hard" to whom the cadre are referring?

These five- to nine-years-olds are the blank sheets of paper on which the Khmer Rouge write their terrible instructions: to regard Angka as their mother and father; to rid themselves of all human emotions not directed toward Angka; to learn to spy upon all enemies of Angka, even if they be their parents, with the promised reward of being allowed to take part in their execution.

Pran stares at the babes sitting cross-legged in front of him. How lucky he is to have none of his own with him. He has witnessed the indoctrination they receive every day from the Khmer Rouge cadre—the hour-long "education class" from eleven to twelve in which they learn to hate their enemies and to sing revolutionary songs while a cadre moves softly among them asking questions about their parents. *Do they give you anything extra to eat? What do they say about the Revolution?* And the children are happy. They would volunteer for the class if they could. It gives them an hour of rest from what they do the rest of the day, which is to collect twenty to thirty kilograms of oxen and buffalo manure to be mixed with human shit to make fertilizer.

Everybody is clapping. Pran claps, too, fearful that he has joined in too late and his inattention has been noticed. He turns his head and grins foolishly at the row behind him. There are spies everywhere making their rounds—not only children. Angka warns that even under the huts at night there are spies, and for once Angka can be believed. Grinning, he applauds the Khmer Rouge cadre for their wise and benevolent remarks. Across the paddy fields, above the banana palms, there is the faint glimmer of a red dawn, crushed into the horizon.

The dry season. Food is almost nonexistent. In Dam Dek, they are down to one spoonful of rice per day. To survive, Pran grubs for lizards, scorpions, snails; he tears off and chews the bark of young trees. A good meal is fish gruel and a mush of banana leaves. News has reached him that his father and his brothers in Siem Reap have died, two of his brothers executed for having fought in Lon Nol's army. A quick death might be preferable to what he sees around him. People are collapsing and dying as they work, harnessed to plows in the paddy fields or knee-deep in the mud of an irrigation trench. Above them, on high bamboo poles, stream the blood-red flags of Democratic Kampuchea. Their sacrifice will not be in vain, the flags remind them. If five million Cambodians die for the Revolution, there will still be one million left, pure and hard, to inaugurate the new Khmer nation in which all enemies of democracy are dead and all internal contradictions have been eliminated.

The elite survivors will be the young army of the Khmer Rouge, the children who have no memory of the past, who have been disciplined to have no conscience and no compassion, nor any love or loyalty or faith except toward Angka. To Pran the very words they use have an unfamiliar ring. People are *opakar* or "instruments," carrying out Angka's bidding. The Khmer nation is *machine*, in the French or English sense of a man-made engine organized down to its smallest cog. But the great machine has run out of oil to nourish it. The instruments are being ground down. . . .

The taxi driver is in the jungle, cutting branches with an ax. The wood is dry; when the ax strikes it, it snaps with the sound of bones. It costs Pran a great effort to lift the ax above his head. He cannot control its downswing and several times misses the wood completely, burying the blade in the soil. A child of nine or ten watches him without expression. Pran grins at him in a foolish way and works on, not daring to speak. His own younger children might have become like this.

221

Gathering up a bundle of small logs, he carries them to the ox cart waiting on the track at the edge of the clearing. The child watches him. He tries to imagine them in America, Ser Moeun and the children. He imagines tall buildings of glass and metal soaring up toward the sky, and fast cars with chrome bumpers and tires that squeal like pigs. Food everywhere, even in the shop windows; food being thrown away. New York as Sydney has described it to him: mountains of glass, valleys of concrete, a great rushing wind of many thousands of people hurrying from place to place—deep-voiced Americans six foot high with long noses, who dine on slabs of meat. Everything bright, metallic, hard-edged . . . and somewhere in this bright hardness, his family, praying to Buddha for his survival, finding it as impossible to comprehend what was happening to him as he did them.

He swings the ax. Bones splinter. He must calm himself. Sydney has promised they'll be all right: Ser Moeun will be looked after, the children will go to a good school and be taught English and history—so be it. What is meant to happen will happen, as surely as this ax will strike. It is why he has never changed his name along with his identity, despite the risk that someone will recognize him and betray him to the cadre. If Buddha has chosen to protect Dith Pran, Buddha will protect him.

A gong sounds in the distance. Bending with aching back, Pran gathers up a final bundle of logs. To his surprise the cart is still stationary on the track, the oxen shaking their heads and pricking their ears restlessly. The driver is asleep. Watched by the small boy, Pran unloads his logs and slaps the driver on the leg. The man wakes with a start. Old enough to be Pran's father, he sends him a look of pathetic gratitude and wields his stick. The cart moves off, Pran following. The boy has disappeared.

The track leads out of the trees along the verge of waterless paddy fields. Four figures in black are yoked to a plow, and pulling it across the heavy earth under the bullying supervision of a guard. One of the women is a schoolteacher—Pran knows this because she bravely offered to give the village children lessons in arithmetic. For some reason the cadre did not shoot her out of hand; instead, they are working her to death in the fields, while in the meetinghouse the children sing revolutionary songs and learn that two plus two equals six if Angka so wishes it.

The track has become a road. Pran and the ox-cart driver pass a burned-out convoy of military vehicles. Ahead of them Pran sees the nine-year-old. His steps falter. Two guards are on the road. The child points. A guard steps forward with a curt order for Pran and takes the old man by the arm. Obediently, Pran takes the reins and leads the oxen on. The driver is dragged behind a blackened APC. Pran sees nothing and hears nothing, but the young boy runs back smiling.

At length he reaches the construction site on the hill where a new and grander meetinghouse is being built; he unloads the wood. By the time he gets back to Dam Dek, it is late in the evening. Men are washing their clothes in what water remains in the riverbed and staining them black again with the makhoeur fruit. Somewhere an owl hoots. For a moment, this is Cambodia as it has always been, a land of tranquillity and green calm, revolving around Buddha and the seasons and the villagers' plot of cultivable earth.

Wearily Pran shuffles toward what he calls his home. The sight that greets him is enough to make him howl with rage. The Khmer Rouge is laying waste the vegetable plots. As he gets there, a boy kicks up his squash plants and, before his eyes, uproots his precious tomato plant and throws it into a wheelbarrow.

"Why . . ." Pran begins, and is immediately silenced by the look on the boy's face. *Never argue; never tell the truth.* In his anger he has almost forgotten the two vital rules that have so far protected him. He changes his expression to one of polite bemusement.

"It will no longer be necessary for the individual to supplement his diet!" declares the boy, shrilly parroting his instructions from the cadre. "Angka will supply everything!"

Angka will supply . . . It might be possible to go on enduring, if Angka would just supply the time to sleep. But the voices come at him again, dragging him from broken dreams. Meetings . . . more meetings . . . the harsh electric light, the children rubbing their eyes, the cadre intently watching every face for marks of weakness, marks of guilt. They are held in a hallucinatory no-time between one day and the next, like the continuation of a terrible dream that began when you reached your hut at night and lay down on the rush matting. They sapped your resistance. They made it harder to lie.

Tonight in the meeting place there are more empty chairs: the ox-cart driver's is one of them. Pran moves up a row. It is wise to sit neither at the back where you are under suspicion, nor at the front where every trembling of the eyelids is visible to the cadre. He is late, but his excuse is accepted. The most senior and most hated cadre in

Dam Dek, a dwarf of a man with a bulbous head set deep between up-sloping shoulders, had sent him on an urgent mission to get penicillin tablets, the only small bottle of them in the village. When Pran returned with them, the cadre fed them to his Siamese cat, which had an infected leg. Then Pran had to hold the animal while the dwarf bandaged it.

Such examples as this of selfless sacrifice are the theme of tonight's lesson in political education. Curry Puff is at the microphone. "We must exercise greater revolutionary vigilance and severity! Angka has identified a sickness that must be exterminated. It is a memory sickness. Let us examine ourselves! Do we reflect upon life in prerevolutionary Kampuchea? It is a sign of individualist tendencies. Root them out! Be like the ox, strong and obedient. The ox eats and pulls the plow. It does not waste its time in futile thought! Enemies surround us—the enemy is also inside us! No one can be trusted. Be vigilant, or others will be vigilant for you!"

Pran lowers his head and raises it again. The platform is a blur of black and white. Curry Puff is giving examples of individualist tendencies; he shouts out a name. In the row opposite Pran, a girl stands up. It is the schoolteacher.

"See, comrades. This woman wanted to keep her child when Angka came for him. She thought she could look after him better than Angka! She put herself above Angka! That is an example of where individualist tendencies can lead!"

Pran steals a look at her. Despite a scab on her lip and the dust of the plow graying her hair, she is unmistakably beautiful. Perhaps because she is still young, she has managed through all her griefs and humiliations to retain her supple femininity; she carries herself with a dignity that must be an affront to the Khmer Rouge for whom beauty is a danger sign of individualism. Pran glances fearfully at the cadre on the platform and back to the woman. He has seen her somewhere before. She reminds him of someone: She reminds him of the girl riding on the motorcycle who came up to them in the ruins of Neak Luong, her hair tied back in a scarf—Rosa. But . . . he has surely seen her somewhere since then.

Curry Puff has finished without calling Rosa up for punishment or execution. She sits down, one thin hand clasping the chair in front for support. Pran is too tired to work out where he has seen her. The only thought his mind can form is that beauty survives, and he is still capable of recognizing it. As his eyelids flutter, the boom of a gong brings the meeting to an end. The people of Dam Dek struggle to their feet for the National Anthem of their new homeland.

> Bright red blood which covers towns and plains
> Of Kampuchea, the motherland,
> Sublime blood of workers and peasants,
> Sublime blood of revolutionary men and women fighters!
>
> The blood changing into unrelenting hatred
> And resolute struggle
> On April 17th, under the Flag of the Revolution,
> Free from slavery!

Another harvest passes, and another dry season. It is early in Year Two of the Revolution, and the nightmare has closed in. Pran has cut wood, fished and plowed, and carried earth to build up paddy embankments in time for

226

the monsoon rains. Land crabs in the paddy he eats alive. Rats he traps in a hessian bag and takes home to skin and cook on a bamboo spit over a fire. His face is puffy with malnutrition; his teeth are rattling in his skull. To walk any distance he needs the support of a stick.

The mass executions have started. Every day Pran sees men and women, their hands tied behind their backs, led off by armed Khmer Rouge guards. Trucks take them out of the village and beyond the hill where the new meeting-house is almost completed, into the western jungle. According to the tales that filter back, the victims are beaten to death with axes and pitchforks, hammers and iron bars, in order to save valuable ammunition. There were huge craters in the western forest, made by American bombs. Now these have been completely filled with bodies, and instead the Khmer Rouge stand on either side of freshly dug trenches and bludgeon the line of men, women, and children into the trench, one by one—sometimes hardly bothering to shovel the earth over them, so that after they have gone, arms and legs still stick out of the ground. . . .

Today, in the pelting rain, he has been sent out with the bullock cart to collect firewood for the cadre. As he leads the animals along the banked track, beside the bent, black figures with rolled-up trousers planting rice in the paddy, he stoops with painful slowness to wrench sticks and branches from the mud and throw them on the back of the cart. Every thirty yards he passes a young Khmer Rouge soldier with a AK-47, standing guard. It is the young ones he fears most, the guards aged between twelve and fifteen. They seem to have no emotions except loyalty to Angka. They are as disciplined as machines, killing machines. Only in killing are they allowed to find pleasure. As Pran shuffles past them, he lowers his head and bows his shoulders submissively.

He is thinking about Rosa. The mystery of Rosa has found an explanation, and the thought of it fills him with anxiety. She is the wife of his friend Nhiek Sann, whom he last saw in Phnom Penh on the day of the Khmer Rouge victory, being led away to his death. But Nhiek Sann did not die. He threw away his glasses and his Western clothes and disguised himself, as Pran did. It took him almost two years to obtain the news that his wife was alive in a nearby village. At the end of the last dry season, Pran met Nhiek Sann dredging a canal to the paddy—he had somehow received his cadre's permission to transfer.

The meeting gave them no pleasure: it filled them both with dread. But Nhiek Sann remains in the greater danger. It is, in any case, Khmer Rouge policy to separate husbands and wives, but for Nhiek Sann to tell the Dam Dek cadre he is married to the schoolteacher would risk both their lives for nothing. Pran thinks of them both with pity as well as apprehension. Twice he has seen them working in the same paddy. Each time they have exchanged glances—he can guess the intensity of feeling that passes between them. But no speech. To speak, in full view of the guards, would be a fatal mistake.

Pran himself has spoken only once to Nhiek Sann's wife. By chance they were both assigned to cook for a district cooperative of blacksmiths. Then, as always, in the presence of spies, he was able to have only one brief conversation with her, in which he expressed his sympathy over her son, who had been taken from her by Angka. Rosa (he still did not know her real name) lowered her head in acknowledgment. Smiling at him she said, ''I am patient. When your husband is gone and your child is taken away, there is nothing to do but wait for death so you can see them again.''

Pran pats the bullocks and talks to them softly. If they take fright and stampede, he is too weak to restrain them, yet sometimes the guards shoot in the air for fun and then punish the driver who has lost control. They are all waiting for death. Cambodia has become one enormous death camp. Rosa's patient endurance is the only dignified response they have left.

His animals prick up their ears at an unfamiliar sound. A guard lowers his rifle. In the paddy field, a young man is committing an act of madness: He is singing a song. Standing up straight and broad-shouldered, his arms by his side, he is singing in defiance of the spies, the soldiers, and the red flags flapping on the hill—a French song that Pran remembers well, a song taught in the classrooms of the old Cambodia.

> *Au clair de la lune*
> *Mon ami Pierrot*
> *Pretez-moi ta plume*
> *Pour écrire un mot*

Screaming, the guards wade into the paddy. The brave young voice is silenced with the butt of an AK-47. His mouth smashed and bleeding, he is led away toward the trees by two of the guards, his hands loosely tied behind his back. He cries out, "Welcome, Death! I am ready for you!" On the pretext of gathering firewood, Pran follows them at a distance. He needs to judge for himself the truth of the stories he has heard.

Picking up twigs as he goes, Pran leads the bullocks around the edge of the forest. Once the cart is out of sight of the guards on the paddy fields, he tethers the animals and heads deeper into the trees. He can hear the execution party ahead. The man—he must have been a student from the city—is still trying to sing through a broken mouth. The two guards are cursing and hitting him.

When Pran catches up with them, they have reached a site that must have been used many times before. There is a frying pan on the ground and the remains of a fire, which one of the Khmer Rouge soldiers is coaxing to light. They have bound the student to a tree, stripped off his shirt, and blindfolded him. Pran crouches in a rhododendron bush, taking care not to shake the branches. What he sees next will remain in his dreams for many nights to come.

One of the guards picks up a sharp knife and slices open the student's belly. The student screams in terrible pain, a naked, hysterical screaming, while blood pours out and white intestines protrude and sag over his thighs. The guard who has cut him laughs and says something—Pran catches the word *song*. With one hand he burrows behind the student's intestines until he locates the liver, which he proceeds to cut out with the knife. Still the man screams, the cries shuddering up as though they are no longer part of him. Not until the liver is almost cooked do his death throes subside.

After chewing and swallowing the liver to give them strength, the young soldiers take his body deeper into the forest for burial. Pran goes back to the cart and retches up what little there is in his stomach before leading the bullocks on. The bells around their necks make a hollow noise, like the bells which summon the dead. On his back he feels the weight of all the centuries it will take to expiate such sins as this.

Harvest time. Pran labors in the paddy, filling baskets with green rice and carrying them to the ox cart. Two and a half years of a starvation diet has reduced him to a walking skeleton. His pupils are the color of milk. To cross the knee-high embankments around the paddy fields he has to lower himself down on them and roll his body over to the other side. The only thing he has gained in all this time is information. He knows that the troops of Democratic Kampuchea are massed near the Vietnam border. He knows where their precious rice goes: It goes north to the Chinese, in exchange for guns.

An order from a cadre on the bank. Obediently, Pran collects a bucket of water from the paddy and carries it to the guards' shelter to pour into their cooking pot. He goes back for more water, on the way passing Nhiek Sann and taking care to avoid his eyes. When the cooking pot is full, he asks the cadre for matches. A PX cigarette lighter is handed to him. Lighting the wood underneath, he notices something gleaming in the mud—a razor blade. He conceals it and shuffles back to the paddy with head humbly bowed; the meal is not for him.

That night there is a special ceremony in the meeting place: (the meetinghouse on the hill cannot be used because no top official has yet arrived to open it). Pran sits closer and closer to the front as the rows of chairs behind him empty. The children beneath the platform are clapping and singing. One beats a wooden drum; another blows on a tin whistle. In the aisle, men and women stand in parallel lines. This is a marriage ceremony according to the rules of Angka.

Each person in line wears a number, which corresponds to a number worn by a member of the opposite sex. The cadre has paired them off apparently at random, although the younger women are donated to villagers who have done the cadre favors. Rosa is coupled with a man obscenely disfigured by scars from the war. Her face is calm, although her skin seems suddenly stretched tight across the bones. Pran gazes fearfully at Nhiek Sann, two rows in front. Nhiek Sann's face is a dusty white; his hands are white, clutching the chair in front of him. He half-rises, as if, in a torment of disgust and self-disgust, to put them both out of their misery—then catches the eye of the dwarf on the platform and sinks back into his chair. But his involuntary act has been noticed and filed away. Nothing escapes the agents of Angka. Pran reaches his hand to his rolled-up sleeve and feels the outline of the razor blade.

Around midnight there is rain and the crash of thunder. It is a good omen. Pran supports himself on his stick and staggers to the door. A light is still burning in the meeting place; the rest of the village is asleep. Treading carefully in his rubber sandals, he sets off down the track to the corral of bullocks near the river. He has to a make a long detour around the guardhouse. Thunder drowns a clatter of pebbles as he slips and nearly falls.

In the small corral, half a dozen bullocks are asleep on their feet. He creeps through them. With one hand he strokes gently at an animal's flank; with the other he uses the razor blade to cut a tiny incision in its neck. Putting his mouth to the cut he sucks deeply then draws away, blood and rain running down his throat.

Once again he sucks the blood, then moves on to the next bullock in line to repeat the procedure. This time it goes wrong. The animal tosses its head, the razor goes in deep. Within seconds the corral is a turmoil of panicking bulls.

Pran runs. Somebody is shouting. A light swings on the track. He tries to climb the corral fence; his legs collapse under him; he falls. The light dazzles over him and a face appears in it, the face of the Khmer Rouge soldier he saw cut open a man's belly with a knife. Hands clutch at his hair and arms. As they drag him back through the mud, his shouts come out as screams. "I do nothing wrong! I do nothing wrong!"

He is half-carried, half-dragged to the guards' house. Several of the cadre are there, including the stocky woman who is slicing a banana into a bowl of rice. Her mouth full, she issues an order. Pran is thrown to the ground outside the house. Within moments he is surrounded by Khmer Rouge with staves and axes and long-handled scythes used for cutting bamboo. He gets on all fours; an ax handle catches him in the stomach and knocks the breath out of him. A pole cracks into the back of his neck and flattens him into the mud.

"You steal from the collective! You are the enemy!"

They pound and beat him as he lies there. The stocky woman kicks him so hard, she spews a mouthful of rice over his head. *"Traitor! Traitor!"* Every moment he expects a scythe to swing down and chop off his head. But they haven't tired with him yet. They tie his hands behind his back and haul him, semi-conscious, into the woods behind the village. They dump him against a tree. This is

233

the end. He hears his voice coming from a long way away, a spirit calling from the dead. . . .

"I do nothing wrong!"

The stage was choked with pink carnations. Out in front were the tuxedos, the silks and organdies, the jewels taken from bank vaults. Schanberg waited in the wings while a man in a velvet bow tie read his citation as if he were announcing a variety act.

"Distinguished guests, ladies and gentlemen . . . for that brilliantly objective reporting, at great risk, in the most adverse conditions, the Foreign Press Award for an outstanding contribution to journalism goes to Mr. Sydney Schanberg of *The New York Times*! Sydney!"

Schanberg stepped forward through the carnations to loud and prolonged applause. In front of him, as he took the award, he saw all the familiar faces, wreathed in unfamiliar smiles. Winning was the name of the game. He leaned into the microphone.

"Anyone who knows my work will know that half of this belongs to Dith Pran. Without Pran, I wouldn't have been able to file half the stories that I did. It's nice to congratulate ourselves on occasions like this, but I can't stand here tonight without thinking of those innocent people Pran dedicated himself to helping me bring to the notice of the American public. As they pondered their options in the White House, the men who decided to bomb and then invade Cambodia concerned themselves with many things: great power conflicts and collapsing dominoes; looking tough and dangerous to the North Vietnamese; relieving pressure on the American troop withdrawal in the South. They had domestic concerns as well, which helps explain why they kept the bombing of Cambodia a secret for as long as they could. And they may be assumed not to have ignored self-interest in their own careers. What they specifically were not concerned with were the Cambodians themselves—not the people, not the society, not the country—except in the abstract as instruments of policy."

He paused. He could sense the unease of the audience. There was so much he could say—but not here, not now. These people didn't know; probably they could never understand.

"Dith Pran and I tried to record and bring home here the concrete consequences of those decisions to real people, to human beings, the people who were left out of the administration's plans but who paid the price and took the beating for them. I'm very pleased to accept this on behalf of Dith Pran and myself. I'm very honored. And I know that Pran would be very proud."

Applause carried him back into the wings, exactly the same level of enthusiastic, impersonal applause—the collective sound, it seemed to him, of people who had no convictions and a lot of heart. He didn't want to stay for the reception; he wanted to get a long way away. But his editor was here, and so was his sister. He couldn't leave her in this mob.

He wandered out into the main reception room. Clapping from the convention hall rattled like distant machine-gun fire on the outskirts of a city. Waiters were laying out the finger buffet: spiced sausage rolls; dimes of sliced olive on anchovy; curlicues of pink crab and pinker salmon on bite-size crackers; a guacamole dip with corn wafers; thin brown-bread sandwiches with a mock-caviar paste; nibbles of French cheese; a bunch of toothpicks in a liqueur glass.

He stood around, like a man who's come to the wrong

party. Under a mug shot of President Carter, a waiter bent with an urgent frown and plucked a crease out of the white tablecloth. People swarmed in, drifted up to him, and drifted away. A champagne glass was put into his hand.

"I don't want to stay long," he said to his sister.

"You're one of the stars, Syd."

More champagne. More handshakes. "Hey! Terrific. Good work. What's the news about . . . what's his name?"

"Pran. No news yet."

"No, well, terrific work. And I liked what you said just now, about collapsing dominoes and self-interest; that's exactly what they are. See you around, Sydney."

Knots of literary people talking politics. A roving TV crew with sun-guns, tracking the celebrities. In the dazzle, a senator's wife turned political columnist gave her views on Lebanon. Schanberg introduced his sister to Mike Wallace.

The sun-guns were getting closer. He was locked in an argument he hadn't intended, with a man from the *Partisan Review*. He said, "Our fault was keeping Sihanouk out and Lon Nol in."

"Lon Nol put himself in. And kept himself in."

"In Tam would have won the 1972 election and reformed the Cambodian army. That's a fact. Washington backed Lon Nol and let him corrupt the ballot."

The rimless glasses flashed. "You blame Nixon and Kissinger for everything, don't you, Mr. Schanberg? The United States fights Communism; it's as simple as that. To do that, you have to subordinate the parts to the whole, whether it's Southeast Asia, the Middle East, or Central America. If you don't have an overall strategy you louse up, like we're doing now. It's tough, but that's the way it is."

Schanberg looked at the man. "This grand strategy delivered the Khmer Rouge," he said. "They kill everyone with spectacles, you know. Even rimless ones. That's tough, too." He drained his glass. "Excuse me, I have to take a piss."

The washroom was unlike the one where they'd developed Pran's photograph. Schanberg made for the sinks and unwrapped an individualized cake of soap. A man came out of a toilet cubicle and straight across to shake his hand. He wanted an autograph—"For my son, he wants to be a writer." A pen was produced and a copy of the Foreign Press Awards program. Schanberg unwillingly signed his name.

Somebody was watching him. He turned. "Hello, Al," he said. "Were you out there? In the hall?"

He spoke uneasily, because there was a smile on Rockoff's washed and shaven face. It was wide, and it curved downward. Rockoff nodded and ran his hands under the tap, still smiling. "Very impressive," he said. "I was hoping you'd burst into song."

"C'mon, Al."

Rockoff stared at him. "Know what bothers me?"

"What?"

"It bothers me that you let Pran stay in Cambodia because you wanted to win that fuckin' award, and you know that you needed him. . . ."

"I didn't have any idea," Schanberg interrupted.

"The fuck you didn't! The fuck you didn't!" The intensity of Rockoff's rage was enhanced by the half-whisper with which he spoke.

Rockoff shook the water off his hands and flicked on the automatic hand dryer. Schanberg shook his head, at a loss for words. This was unfair; this was kicking a man when he was down. A couple of men barreled into the washroom, half-drunk and sharing a private joke. He felt vulnerable and betrayed.

"Anyway, nice to see you," said Rockoff. "I'm on my way to Florida—"

"I've done everything I possibly can!"

"I'm sure you have." The cynical smile was back. Rockoff put a comb through his hair.

"I'm *telling* you I have, for Christ's sake. There's nothing else I can do."

"Sorry again. I didn't realize you'd been out there and looked for him."

"Don't play games with me, Al. Don't play stupid games. Nobody can get in there, and if I thought I could, I would. I've sent hundreds of photographs. Every relief agency along the Thai-Kampuchean border's got a picture of him. If I got one *glimmer* of hope, I'd go. I'd go tonight. But life isn't a forties movie, Al. You can't just hop on a plane and make the whole world right. . . ."

He turned to face the photographer. Al had gone; Schanberg was talking to the mirrors. As he went out, he heard one of the drunks snicker at the basin. "If life was a forties movie, shit, I'd take Lauren Bacall."

His editor was waiting for him. So were the sun-guns. A pretty Japanese-American interviewer set the scene and pointed her microphone at the *New York Times* man. "First of all, Mr. Schanberg, congratulations on winning the Foreign Press Award."

"Thank you." He looked for a way out.

"You accepted it on behalf of"—she consulted a card—"Dith Pran and yourself. He was your assistant in Cambodia until the Communists won. Do you honestly think he's still alive?"

"I have never given up hope."

"What about Dith Pran's family over here in the States? Are you in contact with them?"

"Yes, I am." Taking his sister's arm, Schanberg edged away with a fixed smile. The camera and microphone circled around them; he was trapped.

"Just finally, Mr. Schanberg, what about the future? Will you be going out to cover the boat people?"

"No, I'm not. And I don't understand the purpose of that question."

The interviewer widened her eyes. "I'm sorry, Mr. Schanberg. I can understand your attitude—"

"Can you?" Schanberg's pent-up rage and guilt had found a target. "What can you understand? You've read three books and walked a banner around a campus. Now they send you out to make all the right noises while you snoop around for more juicy horror stories. Because Cambodia's gone stale, right? And your sponsor's getting worried about his sales. So come on, Mr. Schanberg, 'What about the fucking boat people?' "

He crossed to the door through a sea of silent faces. His sister hurried after him. He called a cab to send her home in it. "Tell them from me I loused up your day."

"What about you?"

"I'll walk home."

He walked eight blocks through a light rain and made a point of avoiding the doorman. His apartment was as he had left it—like a hotel room, clean, rectangular, and unwelcoming. The ashtrays were empty, the windowsills swept, the chair cushions uncrumpled, the clothes tidied away. His desk was a model of order. On the pad beside the telephone his pencils lay as neatly as bullets in a bandolier. A Tiffany lamp threw a discreet light on his new electric typewriter and the stack of virgin typing paper beside it. Close by, a pile of books about Cambodia, fattened with paper markers, lay in a perfectly adjusted pyramid, the widest at the bottom, the narrowest at the top. Newspaper cuttings in a Bulldog clip, a shelf of notebooks and videotapes on the wall, and a cork bulletin board pinned with photographs completed the impression of ultraefficiency.

Schanberg looked at his desk. He switched on the typewriter, inserted a sheet of paper, and typed the one word—*LIES*. It was all lies; all a sham. The awards were a sham. Objectivity was a sham. And the greatest sham of all, Sydney felt, was that he was a writer who couldn't write, a journalist who had lost faith in his ability to tell the truth.

That was why he was on his own. It wasn't so much that he'd spent all his time thinking about Cambodia—that would have been okay if he'd found an outlet and put his experience into a book. But he was blocked. He couldn't write. He was useless. And he'd taken out his frustration the only way he knew how.

He poured himself a large Scotch and wandered into the kitchen. The remains of a TV dinner from the night before congealed on the kitchen table next to more neat piles of cuttings and photographs. A cutting from *Time* magazine, entitled "Blood Like Water on the Grass," had a paragraph underlined in red ink: "Of the sixty or so executed, only about six were spared the bayonet. These were very

240

small children, too young to fully appreciate what was happening. In a killing frenzy now, the two executioners each grabbed a limb—one an arm, the other a leg—and tore the infants apart.'' Underneath, he had scrawled the lines from Orwell's *1984*: ''War is peace. Hatred is love. Freedom is slavery.''

Sipping the whiskey, he shuffled through the pictures as if they could tell him something new. There was one of Jon Swain in a pedicab; one of Sarun in the Telex office, massaging his shoulders to keep him awake; one of Al Rockoff in a baseball cap and shades at the Café Central, grinning in the sun. Then he came to one he hadn't found the courage to pin on the bulletin board. It was the one he took of Pran outside the Hotel Phnom on the day of the American evacuation. Smile! he'd called, minutes after Pran had said good-bye to his wife and family for the last time because Schanberg hadn't made him go with them. . . . What must he have been feeling in his heart?

You let Pran stay in Cambodia because you wanted to win that fuckin' award. Rockoff's voice hurt him physically, like something sharp he'd swallowed. It was something he hadn't openly admitted before, but something of which these books and cuttings and photographs spread through the apartment were a constant reminder—a way of punishing himself. He had used Pran, and by everything that was right and natural, Pran should have used him in turn to escape Cambodia with his family. Instead he'd stayed on and—what was unforgivable—he'd saved Schanberg's life.

He put the photograph aside, almost with hatred in his heart, and returned to the living room. He couldn't settle; there was nothing to settle to. He switched on the stereo;

"Nessun Dorma" was on the tape, a Puccini aria he'd played many times since he'd got back from the East. This time, it sounded like an accusation. What else should he have done? That was what it was like, being a journalist. You competed for stories; they didn't fall off trees. You reported on things you couldn't hope to change. You described them, as fairly as you could, and left it to other people to act on your dispatches. It was a tough life, and you didn't waste time pondering the finer points of morality. Pran knew that and accepted it. Maybe he was making too much of these guilt feelings. If he beat his breast much harder, he'd break a rib. As a journalist, knowledge was his only weapon, and right now he was weaponless. If only he knew something . . . if he knew that Pran was dead. It would confirm his worst feelings about himself. *It would free him to write.*

A flash of lightning. A figure slumped against the wire, which binds him to a tree. On the forest floor a razor-sharp palm leaf, the kind they draw swiftly and deep across the throat.

We kill him, the woman had said. Another cadre had spoken then.

Let us decide in the morning.

Steadily the rain falls, washing the blood off Pran's bruised and swollen body. All night he has prayed to Buddha. He has prayed in the name of his mother's milk and of all the things that Buddha might look favorably upon and grant him luck. He has dared to remind Buddha that he has not changed his name, which his mother and father dedicated to Buddha. He has promised to shave his head, if he survives, as a token of gratitude for his salvation. The hours have passed. Dawn has brought a matin of birdsong and sunlight slanting through the tall trees. Still he prays.

Footsteps approach. The birds grow shrill. Pran raises puffed and bloodshot eyes. Two cadre are standing over him—the dwarf whose cat he treated with penicillin and the teenage cadre with two pens in his pocket. Behind them, holding axes, wait a couple of soldiers. The moment has come: Pran greets it with resignation. His last thought is of what Rosa said. He will meet Ser Moeun and his children in the next world, and the time will not seem long. . . .

"Untie him," says the teenage cadre in Khmer. "The commune will conduct his self-criticism." He squats and looks hard at Pran, almost as if he has seen him somewhere before—perhaps years ago, perhaps as a little boy with an outsize helmet in Neak Luong given a shiny Mercedes badge by strangers. Whatever it is, it puzzles him; but to Pran the answer is simple and overwhelming. Buddha has listened and interceded.

Pran is paraded before the commune and denounced for his crime. He is made to promise that if he breaks the rules again, he will give his life to the cadre to do with as they please. In due course, he shaves his head, explaining to the cadre that it is to cure his headaches. He harvests and threshes the crop; he collects bamboo shoots from the jungle. Each day that passes, he feels his life is forfeit. The cadre are watching him now—especially the woman who spits orange peel, the one who tried to have him killed.

At the meeting place, twice a week, there are still fewer heads for the cadre to count. There is more food now—another hundred grams of rice a day—and not so many executions for routine "errors," such as falling asleep during lectures or being caught holding hands with one's wife. But the children are less in number. Few villagers and none of the people from the cities have been permitted to procreate, and all children from the age of ten are recruited by Angka for the war against Vietnam.

Political education is now directed less at imperialists and internal enemies, more against the "running dogs of the aggressor, expansionist, and annexationist Vietnamese." Pran has heard it all before. Vietnam as the great traditional enemy of the Khmer people was the theme of Lon Nol's speeches after he took power from Prince Sihanouk. It amuses him to hear the same phrases in the mouths of the Khmer Rouge. But there is no comedy about what takes place tonight. A ten-year-old girl with a face of stone is standing in the front row and pointing her finger at Nhiek Sann. He is being accused of meeting secretly with a woman of the village. Rosa.

Rosa's "husband," the man with disfiguring war scars, is brought up onto the platform. Nhiek Sann is hustled to the front. He is thinner and grayer than when he first reached Dam Dek. He seems to Pran to have aged ten years in as many months. Blinking shortsightedly, he makes his excuses. Rosa remains impassive, hiding her anguish. The cadre are looking at her, not him. Even when her new husband screeches his vitriolic denunciations, not a muscle in her face moves, not a glance strays in Nhiek Sann's direction.

It makes no difference. The husband is believed and silenced. An armed soldier escorts Nhiek Sann to the guards' house. Only now does Rosa look at him. In her gaze is all the longing and despair she has stored in her heart. She stands and announces in a firm voice to the cadre on the platform, "I have a confession to make."

Not a sandaled foot stirs in the meeting place. Pran sits frozen. Nhiek Sann and his guard stand still. In the gesture used by the little girl minutes earlier, Rosa raises her arms and points at the dwarf cadre on the platform. "He has been my lover," she declares. "This man you are taking away witnessed it. He has kept silent so as not to implicate me."

The woman cadre drops her orange. Curry Puff opens his mouth and shuts it again. Only the teenage cadre who spared Pran's life remains unmoved. He stands up, as if to bring the meeting to an end, patting the pens in his pocket.

"We shall investigate it," he said.

That night Pran lies awake on his rush matting. In the early hours of the morning, he hears steps on the track and sees through the wooden walls of his hut the flicker of a lantern. Very cautiously—since to be awake after midnight is still a capital offense—he puts his eye to a crack in the wall. His hands bound behind his back, the dwarf cadre whom the whole village hated is being led by armed soldiers into the forest. Behind him, their faces pale in the light of the resin torches, are Nhiek Sann and Rosa, their arms also bound. Three more soldiers and all the remaining village cadre accompany them.

Pran lies back on the matting. He wants to weep, but the tears will not come. The schoolteacher, Nhiek Sann's wife, has taken her revenge. She has sacrificed herself; but she has taken with her one of Dam Dek's greatest oppressors. Rosa, he knows, will be as resolute in her death as she has been in her life. She will welcome death because it will reunite her with her husband and her son. For Pran, left behind, it will be harder. A person of beauty and strength, the one reminder he has that life can be more than a conjunction of blind savagery and blind obedience, has been annihilated.

It is at this moment that Pran resolves to escape.

His opportunity comes sooner than he has prepared for. He is dredging mud into a basket at the edge of a paddy. It is late in the afternoon. Dragonflies are hovering, and yellow smoke from village cooking fires is drifting across the shallow water. Without warning, he is lifted into the air by a massive explosion. Eighty yards away, a jet of mud and water canopies in the air and comes crashing down in a debris of mud and stones and human limbs. Too big for a mine, it has to be a leftover five-hundred-pounder from a B-52.

Screams. Whistles blowing. The guards run into the paddy toward the badly injured. Pran, his head ringing, slithers over the paddy embankment and lies low. No guard shouts after him. Like a water snake, he twists on his stomach along the lee of the embankment and over the top of the next. Fifty yards more crawling and he is in the jungle; the shouting behind him grows distant.

America has come to his rescue after all.

He hides at the edge of the jungle until nightfall. When all is quiet and the last lights in the village across the valley have been extinguished, he finds a stick to support him and sets off along a track he knows. As he stumbles along, he prays to Buddha to protect him. There are other dangers in the forest beside the Khmer Rouge: panthers and buffalo, poisonous snakes and plants. The streams are full of leeches; each time he navigates one, testing ahead with his stick, he has to delay on the farther bank to pull the bloodsuckers off his legs.

The path climbs a low hill and descends sharply into the next valley. Twice Pran loses his footing and falls. The second time he loses his stick and has to grope around for it in the moonlight. Every sound stops him in his tracks. There is nothing friendly in the forest, he has learned that.

As Pran's legs begin to give out, the forest thins into scrub land. Wielding his stick, he pushes his way through high clumps of waving grass and towering bamboo. There is water here—he must be approaching paddy fields. Too dangerous to go on . . . too tired. He lies down for a moment in the shelter of the high grasses. Instantly, without even knowing it, he falls asleep.

It is the thin rasp of a jet fighter that wakes him. Looking up at the fluffy vapor trail in the blue sky, he thinks for a moment that he is with Sydney on the lawn of the guest house in Sihanoukville. But there is a sweet stench here that is making him gag. He looks down. A corpse lies beside him, staring with one eye socket and grinning with one side of its mouth. The other half is black with insects.

Pran jerks upright with a yell and staggers to his feet. He stumbles down the track beside the shallow water, slips, and is up to his waist in slime. Something nudges him, another corpse, the shirt buttons snapped on its ballooning stomach. Propped up beyond it is something too horrible to look at. He screams again and pulls himself back on the narrow path. He has heard about these places. These are the killing fields.

Prodding with his stick in front of him like a blind man, he stumbles through this land of the dead. He picks his way past corpses with flesh still on them; on their heads the paper bags that have been used to suffocate them. All around him lay skeletons half out of the muddy water, an entire graveyard risen from the rot and decay to show him the marks of their violent ends: children's skulls with pickaxe holes; rusty wire biting into bones; and over all, the fierce murmur of insects sucking out what the sun has not bleached dry. Tapping forward through this place of skulls, Pran prays to Buddha that he is not the only human being left alive.

Eventually he reaches higher ground; the path winds back into the trees. He struggles on upward without a look backward at the charnel valley. At noon, he finds a plover's nest with four eggs in it. He eats two and replaces the others under the mother bird with a repentant bow of the head. This hill is much higher; it is evening before he has crossed it and come down to the valley on the other side. In the distance is another village, smaller than Dam Dek.

He waits in the scrub until nightfall. The paddy fields are mirror-silver in the bright moonlight. He crosses them and is skirting the village when the figure in black comes forward with a rifle and bars his way.

Rocked, the bamboo crib squeaks like a starving baby. Inside it, a small boy sleeps, his thumb in his mouth. When his breathing is regular, Pran stills the crib and gets to his feet to pull down the mosquito net.

It is the largest house in Bat Dangkor. Almost luxurious by Khmer Rouge standards: a table and chairs; a small bedroom with a divan bed and alarm clock and a battered transistor radio. As Pran creeps away, barefoot on the rush matting, a man appears in the doorway, the same man who took Pran prisoner outside the village. In his late twenties, with a high forehead, he looks in the flickering candlelight as pale-skinned as a city dweller, not dark as the village peasants are.

Pran bows low. In Khmer he says, "The boy is asleep, Comrade Phat."

"Good." Phat opens the sack he is holding and takes out a mango. "Here. You may eat this." As Pran accepts it with every sign of gratitude and glides toward the door, Phat stops him. "Comrade, you tell me you drove a taxi in Phnom Penh before the liberation. . . ."

"Yes."

"What fare did you charge between Norodom Boulevard and the airport?"

Pran hesitates for a fraction of a second. "In the last months," he says, covering himself, "I was obliged to ask for five thousand riels."

Phat stares at him. His next question is very quiet. *"Est-ce que vous parlez français?"*

Pran feels a sliver of cold run down his spine. He remembers the last time he heard French sung in the paddy field, and what happened to the man who spoke it. And yet, a Phnom Penh taxi-driver . . . He grins and shakes his head.

Phat stares at him for a moment longer, then waves him away. With relief, Pran hurries down the steps to his wooden cabin between the stilts underneath the house. He tears at the mango with his nails and eats the peel after he has devoured the fruit. To Phat, the commune chief of Bat Dangkor, he owes his life. Phat has taken him on as his house servant and to look after his son; he is under Phat's protection. But the village cadre chief is not like the other

Khmer Rouge that Pran has met. He is intelligent and sophisticated and therefore dangerous. Pran will have to be more than ever on his guard.

As the days go by, his nervousness increases. Often at night he hears footsteps on the boards above his cabin, and hushed conversations, sometimes the faint undecipherable static of the radio. Phat himself is casual with him, as if deliberately trying to lull Pran into a false sense of security. Then there is the mystery of the MiG 19s. Not long ago, a pair of them rocketed out of the forest over Bat Dangkor at less than a hundred feet, sending the bullocks into a stampede and leaving in the air a sweet smell of kerosene.

Last week, while he was bathing the boy, Kim, at the river, he saw them again—four MiG 19s this time, heading west at about ten thousand feet. These are Vietnamese planes. Somewhere there must be a war. But how close? There are hardly any of the "new people" in Bat Dangkor. Almost all of them are the original peasant villagers. To find out, he will have to wait for an opportunity to listen to Phat's radio.

As he chops firewood in the garden and keeps a careful eye on Kim playing his three-year-old's games in the tobacco patch, Pran puzzles over the mystery. All day he has seen convoys of Chinese-made army trucks lumbering down the main road on the far side of the valley. There have been more vapor trails in the sky. All this military activity points to something serious. He had thought that yesterday, after the cadre had left, Phat was going to tell him what it was.

Two senior cadre had joined Phat for dinner, including one Pran hadn't seen before. Dutifully, he had cooked the meal of stewed green peppers and rice, holding out the serving bowl for each in turn to help himself. As always, though he kept his eyes lowered, he had felt himself to be under close scrutiny. Had the Dam Dek cadre circulated his description, as the police would have done for an escaped criminal? He had backed away from the table, his hands trembling.

Thirty minutes later, a heel banged on the floor. Pran had been licking grains of rice from the sides of the cooking pot; he crawled out of the cabin and ran into the house. The three cadre had finished; they were sitting in Phat's bamboo chairs smoking hand-rolled cigarettes. Pran began stacking the plates. The cadre he hadn't seen before took out a cigarette and flourished it in Pran's face.

"Avez-vous du feu?"

He wasn't going to be caught that easily. He mustered a humble smile and carried the plates away. When he got back, Phat was alone. He looked more drawn and sad than Pran had seen him. He spoke, half to himself, in Khmer.

"They destroy the Revolution."

"They—?"

"We made the revolution so that where the trees were, there also the fruit would be. So that the peasants who produce should not be the slaves of the townspeople who consume. . . . It is our Great Leap Forward to a better, more just society; like China. But unlike China we are small, almost defenseless. We have not enough guns, not enough planes, not enough tanks. So Vietnam attacks us, to destroy our Revolution. They betrayed us in 1972 and left us to fight on alone. Now they want to swallow us up. They know our Communist experiment is superior, and it puts them to shame."

The young commune chief said no more. Pran had

251

wanted to ask him about the progress of the war: Was it true that Angka was killing its own people and setting fire to the villages as it retreated? But to ask that would be to display curiosity and then confirm Phat's suspicions of him. He had bowed and retreated.

A cry comes from the tobacco patch. Kim has tumbled over and scratched himself. Pran picks him up and takes him into the house; it is time he went to sleep. He sponges the boy's face and hands, dries him, undresses him, and puts him into the big bamboo crib, whispering *"bon soir"* as he does every night to the child. Then he goes down to his cabin, picking up a cigarette stub on the way. Into his mind flashes a sudden, painful picture of happier times—of Sydney running a cigarette between his fingers and laughing.

The two of them were together in Battambang in 1974. Relaxing for once, they had had a good fish dinner with wine. Sydney was smoking pot, which was even cheaper in Battambang than in the capital, and had offered some to Pran. He had tried it and started giggling and smoked some more to stop and found himself suddenly as defenseless from his emotions as a baby, crying and laughing with Sydney through the streets of Battambang, past armed soldiers at checkpoints who stared at them in disbelief, past houses and shops and trees, until it seemed the only thing they could not leave behind them in their wild flight was the moon. . . .

And now Battambang is dead, the soldiers are dead, the world is changed utterly. Only the moon is constant. And his memories. In his mind, Pran composes a Telex that will never be sent:

MORE PLANES OVERHEAD TODAY: HAVE COUNTED SIXTEEN RPT SIXTEEN MIG 19S OF VIETNAM AIRFORCE: ALSO MUCH KR

GROUND TROOP MOVEMENT: REPORTS UNCONFIRMED THAT
KR IS KILLING ALL CIVILIANS IN THEIR PATH AS THEY RE-
TREAT BEFORE VIETNAMESE: AM FRIGHTENED THEY KILL EV-
ERYBODY AND LET CHINESE COME IN: THIS IS A TERRIBLE
LAND. THEY TAKE OUR RICE AWAY. MANY PEOPLE DYING:
EYE THINK OF YOU OFTEN SYDNEY: PLEASE SYDNEY LOOK
AFTER MY WIFE AND CHILDREN: END IT.

A week passes. The military traffic along the valley gets
heavier. Earlier in the afternoon a red Citroën 2CV bumped
along the track between the paddy fields to Bat Dangkor,
accompanied by motorcycle escorts. Khmer Rouge cadre
with three and even four pens in their pockets got out of
the Citroën to survey the landscape. They went into Phat's
house, perhaps to check on the movements of the villagers.

Pran has escaped to the river. He stands at one end of a
small, tethered boat, fishing with a net attached to a long
pole. Kim, whose fourth birthday is coming up, sits at the
other end of the boat, chattering and peering at his reflection in the water. Pran lunges for a fish, misses it, and
explodes with frustration. Kim giggles and applauds from
the back of the boat. Smiling, Pran shakes his head at him.
With his hands, he measures out a fish the size of a
thirty-pound pike. *"C'est très grand!"* The little boy dissolves in laughter.

After the Citroën and its outriders have departed, the
two of them bring their catch back to the house and build a
fire. Pran slices and guts the fish and impales them on long
sticks for smoking; Kim watches, fascinated. When his
father comes out and embraces him on his way to attend a
village meeting, the boy spreads his arm wide, in excitement.

"Tray gran! Tray gran!"

The meaning surely is unmistakable. Pran stares at Phat, the muscles of his face rigid, unable even to blink. Phat's smile has gone. He looks at Pran without expression and then at the dead fish sizzling over the flame. He turns and walks up the path.

When he is out of sight, Pran gathers up the child and runs indoors with him, as if to hide the evidence. After all his efforts at concealment, after the lessons he has learned from bitter experience—how could he have done it? How could he have been so foolish as to let himself be given away by an innocent child? It was not as if he needed to speak French to the boy. He had done it out of nostalgia and because it was a private language between them. Now he would suffer for it.

The boy seems to understand Pran's distractedness and goes to his bed without complaint. Pran walks around the room, trying to calm himself. He has to think what to do. It is no longer any good attempting to escape; the roads and tracks are full of soldiers. He is trapped. He stops by the crib and looks down at the child who has betrayed him. Kim is sleeping peacefully. His face is calm, untroubled. In a few months he will be taken to his first "education" classes to begin his long induction into hate, but for the moment he is free; he knows nothing of sadness or suffering, his world is the unbounded world of children his age everywhere . . . like Pran's own children not so long ago.

On the table is the radio. Pran lights the candles and stares at it. He has not dared touch it before . . . what does he have to lose? Everything. His life. But if he goes unpunished this time, there will be another. Buddha cannot protect him from his own mistakes. He puts out a hand and switches the knob. A fish eagle cries above the river; in a panic he jumps out of the chair. Silence descends again. He twiddles the knob, ear to the dial like a safecracker, and picks up the Voice of America. It drifts in and out like a spirit voice: "The Reverend Jim Jones . . . believed that upward of three hundred people . . ."

Phat and the two cadre walk in.

Nobody moves. The candlelight trembles on the wall.

". . . further unconfirmed reports say resistance in the countryside is minimal . . . New China Radio says Vietnam has penetrated more than sixty miles into the south of Kampuchea, capturing the important coastal town of Kompong Som without resistance. . . ."

Phat steps forward and switches off the radio. He says, *"Allez-vous en, Monsieur Pran."*

Pran stares. Phat is smiling at him. The two cadre are smiling. He flees.

A cold Christmas. Steam rose from the New York City manholes like the breath of subterranean dragons. Father and son stepped cautiously through the brown slush, both half-hidden behind grocery bags piled with food wrapped in crinkly cellophane. The shorter man, sprigs of white hair over a furrowed brow, spectacles pinching a thin nose, cleared his throat with a guttural rasp.

"It's been a long time," said Schanberg's father.

"I was over for Yom Kippur—"

"I mean you and your wife."

Sydney Schanberg shifted the weight of his grocery bag. "We keep in touch," he said.

"Is she still in L.A.? With her mother? What about the girls?"

"Same."

A train clattered past on the overhead railway. Schanberg had made this journey hundreds of times as a child, and nothing had changed. Only if you were born poor or very rich was the past left intact for you in America. He stopped to let his father go first and looked at the frail figure with affection as it clumped up the wooden steps to the peeling station.

The cold wind had brought tears to the old man's blue eyes. He said, "Your mother especially would have hated to see your marriage like this."

"Well, it has been difficult because I've seen so preoccupied with my work. Then, you know I have felt responsible for Ser Moeun and her family."

A train thundered in. They hefted the grocery bags and sat facing each other, opposite a couple of orthodox Jews in tall black hats who sat watching their hands folded in their laps. Down the station a group of Puerto Rican boys in wadded jackets listened to the Boomtown Rats. Schanberg gestured with his free hand, shouting to be heard.

"No one understands how difficult it is for Pran's family. There are four kids, she hardly speaks English, they're living in a couple of rooms next to a laundry—"

"Wait a minute." His father leaned forward and tapped him on the knee. "Let's stick with your own family for a moment."

"It's not as simple as that—"

"It is as simple as that. When it's a question of family, it is as simple as that. Take my word for it. Listen, you can see Brooklyn out the window anytime—your father's talking to you—your wife and children come second to no one. If you can get on a plane for Pran's family, you can get on a plane for your own. You know what I think? I think you got to get your priorities sorted out. What does your sister say? You've spoken to your sister?''

''About a week ago.''

''So what does she say?''

Schanberg sighed. There was no point even trying to get it across. To his father, a job of work was a job of work. It occupied your mind or your muscles, or maybe both, but your heart—your heart stayed with your family, like a keepsake you picked up when you got home at night. He sighed again and shook his head. ''Forget it, Dad, okay? Let's just forget it.''

He saw his father home, then set off on the once-familiar journey to Massachusetts. The Christmas traffic delayed him, and it was after dark by the time he reached the Goldrings' house. Close friends from way back—old man Goldring and Schanberg's father had started in the grocery business together—they maintained a standing invitation to Schanberg and his family to visit them over Christmas. It wasn't a festival Schanberg celebrated, but he needed to get out of New York. He needed to get away.

Coming here was like traveling back in time. He'd been raised in a town like this, full of peaceful, white clapboard houses with stoops leading down to quiet, treelined streets. He knocked on the door through a wreath of holly; Rachel Goldring opened it and kissed him on both cheeks. ''Come say hello to Father, why not? He's been asking me, why isn't Bernard coming, too? He thinks he's a young man, I don't know.''

Schanberg stamped off the snow and went into the warmth. The hallway smelled of furniture polish; there was laughter and chatter from the kitchen at the back of

257

the house. This was the first time in years he'd been here without his wife; it made him feel awkward, an overgrown schoolboy. He said, "Let me get myself straight, okay? I'll be right down."

It was the house that made him feel like a schoolboy; it was so like the home he'd known as a child. He went up the creaky stairs, along the passage, past what would have been his parents' bedroom and up another flight to the garret with its freshly made bed. This had been his old room, in another house, in another age. Out of habit, though it wasn't cold any longer, he switched on the bar heater and lay down on the narrow bed, his feet on his suitcase.

There would have been clothes spilling out of the cupboard. A table, in the corner there, with a record player that made the newest discs sound like crackly 78s. On the shelf, his high school debating cup had propped up a row of tattered paperbacks—Sartre, Camus, T.S. Eliot, Chekhov, Anouilh—the books he'd devoured in the days when he believed ideas could change the world, perhaps even make sense of it.

He got up and began unpacking. At the bottom of the case was a small, flat box wrapped in Christmas paper. The *Times* had forwarded it that morning from San Francisco. Opening it with dread, he found inside a bright green-and-yellow cotton tie and a color photo of Ser Moeun standing with her children in front of the TV. On the back of the photo, the eldest boy had printed, "Christmas Greetings From" in a neat hand, and they had all put their signatures underneath.

Schanberg folded the tie carefully. Looking up at the skylight, he saw that it had begun to snow again. In the semidarkness, the snowflakes came down solemnly and hugely, like ash from a burning landscape thousands of miles away.

He sat on the bed and put his head in his hands. After a minute, he lit a cigarette and switched on the radio on the bedside table. A bomb had exploded in Jerusalem, killing six people; Israel had retaliated with an attack on terrorist bases in the Lebanon. The latest round of SALT talks had broken up without agreement. Reports were still coming in of a major air crash in Sicily with many feared dead. Then came the news he'd been waiting for.

"The Communist government in Hanoi has confirmed reports that it has dispatched troops to Cambodia in support of rebel forces opposed to the regime of Pol Pot. According to New China Radio, heavily armed units of Vietnamese ground troops are pushing westward across Cambodia, renamed Kampuchea by its new rulers. A fierce battle is reported less than two miles east of Phnom Penh. . . ."

"Uncle Syd! Can I come in?"

"Door's open." Schanberg switched off the radio and managed a smile for Rachel's elder son, Neville. "How's business?"

The boy's eyes darted restlessly around the room. "Mom wants to know where you are."

"Tell her I'll be down when I've finished my cigarette."

"Can I have one?"

"No. I'll bet you smoke too much already."

"C'mon, Uncle Syd. Just a puff. It's Christmas."

Schanberg handed over the cigarette. The boy dragged on it and went into a fit of coughing. A red flush spread over his pale face. Schanberg beckoned for the cigarette. "Tell Rachel I'll be down in a moment, okay?"

"Okay. Where's Auntie J? Why doesn't she come?"

"She's in Los Angeles."

"Have you stopped being married?"

"You could put it like that." Schanberg opened the suitcase. "Here, take these presents down to the tree."

Neville squinted at the yellow-and-green tie draped over the bedpost. "Is that for real?"

"It's a Christmas present. From Dith Pran's family in San Francisco; I told you about them, remember?"

"The refugees." Neville rested his chin on the parcels he was carrying. "Is there a present for me?"

"Depends on if you drop any."

Alone, Schanberg changed into a clean shirt and tied on Ser Moeun's tie. He lit another cigarette and went downstairs.

> Tidings of co-omfort and joy, comf't n' joy,
> Oh-oh ti-idings of co-omfort and joy!

"Turn the radio off, please, Neville. Your grandad's going to carve. Sydney, would you mind opening the wine? No, Jonathan, your uncle will do it, your uncle'll open the wine. Eddie, will you make Jonathan sit down, please? Neville, you on the other side, next to Mr. Pisk. Afterward Neville, I know it's a nice present, just take the pictures afterward, we've got the plates on the table now. Eddie, please don't eat the potato chips, you know it sets the children a bad example. Pass the plates up to your grandad, Jonathan—Jonathan! If you blow that whistle, you're going straight out of the room. No more wine for me, Sydney, I've got enough to do. . . ."

Schanberg sat down opposite Arthur Pisk, the neighbor who'd been coming in for Christmas dinner as long as the Goldrings had lived here. It was always best to leave things to Rachel on family occasions; she resented it if you tried to take some of the burden off her shoulders. Dutifully, he passed up his plate of turkey breast to be heaped with peas, diced carrots, chestnut stuffing, and cranberry sauce.

The dining room was its usual bizarre mixture of Jewish tradition and Christian festivity. On the big mahogany sideboard stood a brass menorah surrounded by Christmas cards. Rachel had stuck more cards around the frame of the mirror over the mantelpiece and on the side table beside the tasseled armchair. Most of them were addressed to her and her husband Eddie, but Christmas was wherever Rachel found herself.

They toasted the turkey. They toasted Rachel for cooking it so well. They toasted Eddie for getting the floor manager's job. They toasted Mr. Pisk for no reason anybody could think of. Neville told a turkey joke; Jonathan had heard it. They toasted Schanberg, although he could see Rachel look askance at the way he was picking at his food. They toasted Norman's near-blind sister who was with her own children's family in Buffalo. Rachel proposed a toast to President Carter, but Norman said it would stick in his throat. That was the end of the toasts.

"Sydney, is there something wrong?"

"No."

"You don't like my turkey? It's too crumbly? It's too crumbly, I should have taken it out ten minutes earlier, it's the stove in there. Eddie I'm telling you, we can't go on with that stove. Why don't I just go out and buy a new stove?"

"The turkey's good, Rachel. It's really good. I think I'm just not very hungry at this moment."

Mr. Pisk broke the difficult silence. "Who gave you the camera, Neville?"

"Uncle Syd. It's a Polaroid." Neville sneered. "He gave Jonathan a Donald Duck computer game."

"So what! Grandad gave me a gun!"

"A toy gun!"

"It is not!"

Eddie lifted his face from the turkey. "Shut up, children," he said dismally, and fell to eating again.

"What about that tie, Sydney?" asked Mr. Pisk, exhibiting symptoms of festive spirit. "Was that a present?"

"It's from a family of Cambodians in San Francisco."

"Have some more wine, Arthur," said Norman. Mr. Pisk was not to be deflected.

"It's a bit of a showstopper, Sydney."

"People on welfare," young Jonathan announced, "shouldn't buy presents."

This time the silence was as deep as the snow outside. It lay in drifts, and it froze. In a calm voice Schanberg said, "A tie?"

"That's not what I said, Sydney." Norman Goldring was flushed. "That's very bad of him to repeat things like that. And that's a very bad thing for you to say, Jonathan."

Jonathan's lower lip was stuck out. Tears were glistening, ready to fall. "You *did* say it!"

"I did not say it!"

"C'mon, Dad." Rachel patted his hand. "Calm down. Eat your dinner."

"I was talking in general terms. Nothing to do with Syd's people." Norman pushed his paper hat up past his forehead. "I happened to say—and Sydney knows my feelings on this subject—I said, the United States is carrying a big burden. I said this country is practically bankrupt, and it's having to support half the people of the world. That's what I said. I said that this country doesn't have the money."

"Money!" Schanberg stared at his father's friend. "We spent seven *billion* dollars bombing what you call 'Syd's people.' We dropped so much shit on what you call 'Syd's people' in '73 that the bombers had to be stacked as they got back to base. All my life I've been told it was the Jewish people who suffered because not so long ago it was they who became 'nonpeople' in Germany. Death was different for them, or so the authorities made out. They didn't *feel* it like other people . . . it was less important, like killing insects. Because before exterminating anything you've got to convince yourself it's less of a human than you. I would have thought, of all people, you would have understood that, Norman."

Schanberg stood up. There was nothing else to say. Nothing else to do but leave. He walked into the empty hallway and went up to his room.

He had his suitcase open on the bed when Rachel came in.

"Don't ask me," he said before she could speak. "I don't know why." He sat on the bed, looking at his hands. "I must have written five hundred letters," he said in a low voice. "I've written to the U.N., the International Red Cross, The World Health Organization, people in Thailand—"

"I know you did, Sydney. You told me."

"I don't know who I haven't written to. . . . It makes me smile, you know?"

She sat beside him on the bed. "What does?"

"All my life I wanted my father to feel proud of me—and now that he's proud of me, I can't feel proud of myself; in fact, I hate myself. Isn't that a joke?"

"No, it's not. You've got to stop this, Sydney! You've got to stop doing this to yourself—"

"I never really gave Pran a chance, you know? Only time he ever mentioned leaving I screamed in his face. I discussed it with Swain and Rockoff; I even discussed it with idiots in the embassy, but I avoided it with Pran. He stayed because I stayed. And I stayed, because . . ."

He shook his head, close to tears. Rachel put her hand on his shoulder and rested her head on it. He saw the streaks of gray in the thick black tresses.

"Come, eat," she said. "You've got your friends. I've made your favorite cake."

"I've got to go, Rachel. I can't stay here." His mind was made up. He'd take a cab to the airport and await the next flight to San Francisco.

It was not snowing in San Francisco, but the wind off the Pacific was like spears of shrapnel. It blew bits of garbage across the street; the cabdriver cursed and swerved. Schanberg, in the back, looked out at a vista of peeling frame houses, empty lots, and squat apartment blocks streaked with damp—an area of San Francisco that didn't get on the postcards even when the sun was out.

So far, on the journey, the only sign of Christmas had been the glimpse of a red hood and white beard in the backseat of a passing police car. A group of Vietnamese-looking children, muffled in thick coats, hung about at an intersection watching the few cars go by. The cab pulled up just past the Glad Boy Soy-Joy factory; Schanberg paid and got out with his suitcase, trying not to feel like a social worker. Ser Moeun's apartment block was opposite, between the street and some railroad tracks. The first time he'd been here, Ser Moeun had fled weeping into the other room. When he'd eventually gotten her to talk about it, she'd said something he'd never forgotten: "I thought when you come, you bring Pran with you." He crossed a concrete playground and climbed, heavy-hearted, the flights of iron stairs.

Ser Moeun met him at the door. He shook his head. Her smile faltered, but was back for the children when she turned and clapped her hands. They sprang up from the television and clustered around him—the youngest boy in a John Lennon T-shirt, the oldest proudly showing off the baseball glove he'd gotten as a Christmas present. Schanberg opened his suitcase and took out the gifts he'd bought and had wrapped at the airport. Along with his tie, they were the brightest things in the room.

Ser Moeun made the coffee. Schanberg sat in the one armchair, trying to think of things to say. He talked about baseball and the New York Yankees and looked at the big photograph of Pran on the wall. An electric convector heater spilled red on the carpet. Outside, freight cars rattled by on the tracks, and the windows misted. He said to Ser Moeun when she came back, "You must go on being patient. I'm sure he's okay."

The eldest boy, a star pupil at school, translated. Ser Moeun said in English, haltingly, "You have news?"

"No. But you know that things are changing. The

Vietnamese are overrunning Cambodia. They are nearly in Phnom Penh. Everything is in confusion. That will make it easier for Pran to get away.''

He waited for the translation. Ser Moeun bit her lip. He started again, covering the same ground, the words beginning to sound hollow in his ears. ''Pran is very, very resourceful. I know it's been a long time. But now things are changing. Your husband is very cautious, very clever. He will wait until the time is exactly right, then he'll cross the border into Thailand. You'll see. . . .''

Ser Moeun had her back to him. Schanberg gripped the coffee mug tightly. On the TV, a rich voice was dreaming of a white Christmas, and Danny Kaye was in a giant toboggan with the children of the world. Pran was a survivor: He had to go on believing that. Ser Moeun was muttering; he asked, ''What's that?''

''She says,'' the boy gulped, ''our father is dead.''

''No, no. That's not true. Tell her absolutely that's not true.''

''She says in Phnom Penh, the day before the Americans left, a picture of our father fell off the wall. The glass broke in the frame. She says this is very bad luck.''

Schanberg paused. He remembered the bats Pran had seen in the French Embassy. There was no answer to superstitions. ''I know he'll survive,'' he said lamely, fingering his tie. He watched as Ser Moeun said something more to her eldest son and then left the room, holding back her tears. He got to his feet. The boy came over, with a shy grin.

''She says to thank you very much for the monthly checks,'' he said.

Another train went past. Schanberg embraced the children and said good-bye and Happy Christmas.

As he left, his presents sparkled, unopened, on the floor.

Pran crouches in his cabin. Above him in the house, cadre are arguing as they have been arguing all day. A steady thunder rumbles on the horizon, the sound of Vietnamese artillery. All is confusion.

In the twelve days since he was caught listening to the radio, Pran has been tormented by doubts and questions. The signs are that the Vietnamese, presumably Soviet-backed, have mounted a full-scale invasion of Cambodia. This does not surprise him: The Vietnamese are long-standing enemies of the Khmers, uniting only to fight off common aggressors such as the Americans and the French at Dien Bien Phu. What is more uncertain is the attitude of the Khmer Rouge. Some, like the cadre in Bat Dangkor, seem prepared to submit themselves to the will of the people when the Vietnamese arrive. Others, from what Pran has heard, are obeying the orders of Angka—razing the crops and staging mass executions of villagers. Earlier this morning, the red Citroën 2CV returned to Bat Dangkor, and senior regional cadre came into Phat's house to talk to him. That was when Pran took shelter underneath.

A noise of footsteps and scraping chairs. Rubber sandals slap down the steps; the Citroën starts up and turns away down the village track to the main road. A stick bangs on the floor; Pran worms his way out of the cabin. Phat stands at the top of the steps, his face masklike. "Burn the tobacco," he tells Pran in harsh tones. "Dig up all the garden. Bring me the potatoes, destroy the rest. Nothing must be left to the enemy.''

Pran obeys without a word. A work detail is coming back from the rice fields under armed supervision; one of the guards stays behind to keep watch on Pran. Across the valley, when he looks up from his digging, he can see the main road filling up with retreating columns of Khmer Rouge troops and APCs. If the Vietnamese are moving at a quarter of this speed, they must be advancing at the rate of at least one mile an hour. The gunfire is close enough now to be able to distinguish the weapons—mortars and machine guns laying down a steady barrage.

First testing the wind, Pran sets fire to the tobacco crop and drags a sack of the potatoes he's dug into Phat's house. The young commune chief is playing with his son. The face he turns up to Pran is full of sadness.

''I have failed Angka,'' he says.

''Why?''

''I have not ordered enough killings. I have not liquidated enough enemies.''

Pran puts down the sack on the floor. After a moment, he says with a deliberate emphasis, ''We are not your enemies.''

Phat appears not to have heard him. He kisses Kim and ruffles his hair. Outside, Pran hears shouts and firing and the sound of running feet. Phat stands up and gives the child into Pran's arms. *''Je vous prie d'avoir soin,''* he appeals in a low voice. Pran gets to the door just as a truckload of Khmer Rouge soldiers crosses the bridge over the river into Bat Dangkor.

Phat has concealed something in the boy's clothes. Crouching in the cabin under the house, Pran takes out a small package and opens it. Three hundred dollars and a hand-drawn map on a square of white cotton. Fearful, he glances over his shoulder and conceals the package in a hiding place in the floorboards above his head. "It is a secret!" he whispers to Kim in Khmer.

Two photographs have fallen on to the matting. As the shouting outside gets louder, Pran picks them up in trembling fingers. One of them is a picture of Phat and Kim's mother on their wedding day—both very young, smiling, very happy. The other shows Phat surrounded by youths of his own age who are making faces at the camera. He is wearing Ho Chi Minh sandals, which were a fashionable symbol of dissidence among the more radical students before the war began. In the background, Pran recognizes the University of Phnom Penh.

With Kim on his knee, Pran studies the photographs. Phat must have had contacts with the Khmer Rouge— perhaps a relative—and got out to them in the early years of the war, '71 or '72. His wife, so obviously Kim's mother, must have survived another three or four years in the jungle. Was it after her death that the young student rebel, intoxicated with Marx and Mao and theories of permanent revolution, had begun the long slide into disillusionment? Certainly he had been too clever to let it show. Angka had trusted him, made him a village administrator. But Phat's education had caught up with him in the end. It had given him a respect for human life and civilized values that younger Khmer Rouge cadre had never had the chance to learn. *I have not ordered enough killings.* . . . It was a weakness that Angka would one day punish by ordering his own.

A jet shrieks overhead. Explosions shake the ground.

Stuffing the two photographs in the hiding place, Pran scoops up the boy and worms his way out of the cabin to crouch by Phat's steps. A house down the track is a bonfire of blazing logs and thatch. Three bullocks gallop past it, tossing their heads, and plunge down toward the river. Another jet screams down the valley, shooting up Khmer Rouge troops on the main road. The soldiers, and most of the Bat Dangkor villagers, pay almost no attention. They've had five years of this, Pran realizes. American markings or Vietnamese markings, on the ground it felt the same.

The Citroën is back. Under the eyes of the senior cadre, villagers have been brought in from the paddy fields and are being herded into groups—four groups of about thirty men each. Phat is there, watching silently as the soldiers wave their guns and warn away the women and children.

Pran crouches deep in the shadows, absolutely still. But Kim has no conception of terror. Recognizing his father, he waves to him. A soldier, seeing the small movement, runs over and muzzle-gestures them out of hiding. The officer in charge shouts an order that Phat immediately appears to countermand. Seizing his chance, Pran swiftly carries the boy into the house.

He watches from the window as another MiG screams overhead. Phat has suddenly come to life. He is arguing with the officer, asserting his authority. The officer pays no attention; he yells through a megaphone, urging the roundup to be completed—the villagers are being trucked away for "further education." Phat appeals to the senior cadre. They stare back at him with expressionless faces. Another soldier is dispatched to collect Pran and the child.

Pran cannot move. He hugs the boy close, paralyzed

with fear. Phat is shouting now. The officer raises his rifle until it points at Phat's chest. Still the senior cadre stares. Phat puts out his arm as if to demand the rifle. It is a bullet he gets instead, a bullet in the heart; he crumples on the ground.

Pran presses Kim's face against his shirt and gazes around wildly. The soldier is at the foot of the steps; he has nobody now to protect him, nowhere to hide. He begins to pray to Buddha; but it is the enemy who saves him. The MiG comes back over the village at two hundred feet, guns and rockets blazing. One of the cadre, four soldiers, and twice that number of villagers go down in a hail of bullets. The Citroën is on fire; so are three of the village huts. Before Pran's eyes, Angka's implacable order ceases to exist. The villagers run, the soldiers run, the cadre run. Still holding the boy, Pran races down to the cabin under the house. He pulls a heap of sacks over them both and lies there, his heart pounding, the child's muffled tears making a soft wetness on his shirt.

Together they wait for the dark. There is no longer any sound from the village and no movement except for the smoke of burning thatch and engine oil drifting up the track. As dusk falls, the frogs start croaking from the river. A bullock wanders past, starting at shadows, disturbed by its unaccustomed freedom. Birds settle around something just out of sight, perhaps the body of the soldier sent to get Pran.

Then new sounds—tank treads and a deep-throttled engine. Leaving Kim asleep under the sacks, Pran creeps forward on his belly to the edge of the stilts. A light infantry tank is rolling slowly down the main street of Bat Dangkor. It stops about a hundred yards away; its gun turret makes a three-hundred-sixty-degree turn, as if challenging some invisible enemy to show itself. Nothing moves. With a roar from its exhaust, the tank's diesels shut down. The silence lasts for a minute or more.

Then, with a snapping of locks, the turret opens. A dead leaf appears, hanging from a twig, then the mud-stained helmet into which it was stuck as camouflage. Under the helmet is one of the daftest faces Pran has ever seen— about sixteen years old, with round, squinting eyes and a vacant mouth with three teeth stuck in like fence palings, wide gaps between them. The face swivels from side to side. Seeing nothing, it squints up at what remains of its camouflage and splits into a grin.

The Vietnamese have come to town.

Pran has seen the smiles on the faces of "liberators" before. He has heard their promises before. It is mid-morning of the following day before the miraculous, unfamiliar smell of cooked meat tempts him out into the open with the boy. About thirty Vietnamese soldiers have set up tents in the main street and built cooking fires. Over one of them a whole pig is being roasted—a spectacle rare enough in the old days; unheard of under the Khmer Rouge. One by one the villagers have come out of their hiding places. Now they stand around, men on one side, women on the other, in reverent silence, observing the phenomenon of pork.

A Vietnamese officer arrives with a trailer loaded with sacks of rice, plainly liberated from the communal depot of stores intended for Peking. A sackful gets poured into a cauldron over the second cooking fire, and the officer, speaking in Khmer, asks for volunteers to help prepare the food. Nobody answers him; every face displays fear and confusion. Angka's "requests" were always veiled orders. The very word for request in Khmer—*snoeur*—had developed a new meaning in the villages: "to take away and kill."

The officer repeats his question. A man steps forward. A woman calls out to him, his wife or his sister, and walks forward to face him. As one, the village holds its breath. Nobody is shouting at them, no Khmer Rouge guard is beating them away. The woman bursts into tears; she embraces the man she has loved and been kept apart from all these years. Other men and women, some holding children by the hand, step forward, hesitantly at first, then run forward and embrace each other and weep, until the main street of Bat Dangkor is a confluence of hugging, crying, laughing people—a scene of such joy and pity that Pran sees the Vietnamese soldiers turn their faces away to hide their own tears.

Pran picks up Phat's son and kisses him and holds him tight. On this side of the world Kim is all he has left to love. Kim is his family now. He thinks of Rosa and Nhiek Sann in Dam Dek, sacrificing their lives to assert the dignity and self-respect the Khmer Rouge were denying them; he thinks of his brothers and his sister arbitrarily executed, and his father dying of starvation. For reasons that only Buddha knows, he, Pran, has been allowed to live. Whatever happens now, even if he dies trying to reach the border, he has seen the worst. Uttering up a prayer of thanks, he walks forward, holding Kim by the hand.

*   *   *

273

So many gray hairs . . . Schanberg lowered the razor and leaned into the mirror, studying himself. Half-shaved, half-daubed in shaving cream, he looked like Janus presenting two faces to the world—one side honesty, the other hypocrisy. The eyes, bloodshot, didn't find this funny; the mouth wasn't laughing, either. No sense of humor these days, his face.

The phone rang. He picked it up in the living room. A voice he didn't recognize.

"Sydney? Sydney Schanberg?"

"Yes."

"Andreas Freund. Paris bureau. Ever heard of Gerhard Leo?"

"No."

"East German. He works for Neues Deutschland here in Paris. He's asked me to pass on a message from someone, said you'd appreciate it. It reads, 'Dith Pran survivor, living in Siem Reap, Angkor.' "

Schanberg sat down. "Give it to me again." He listened. "I don't believe it!" The whoop of joy blew shaving cream in all directions. "Andreas," he declared when the Paris correspondent was through, "did you ever realize how easy it was to make a friend for life?"

He got a line and dialed Gerhard Leo directly. The early-morning sun through the window was so bright, the whole apartment shone. Through a mouthpiece white with soap, he choked out his gratitude. Leo gave him the details he'd waited four years to hear.

"This was two months ago. February. I would have informed you at an earlier time, but I am sent on to Vietnam to cover the Chinese invasion."

"But you saw Pran! You met him!"

"Near Angkor, yes. Siem Reap. I was with a party of . . . of friendly journalists invited by the Vietnamese. He came up to me, I was alone, he gave me this message. He said, 'It will make him happy.' Also, he asked me to take his photograph, which I have sent to you at *The New York Times*—"

"Was he okay? How did he look?"

"I should say, in relatively good health, Mr. Schanberg. But I am concerned for him. I came back via Angkor Wat last week, to complete a story. Pran was not any more in Siem Reap. They thought he might try to cross the frontier, very foolish. . . ."

"Don't worry. Pran's a survivor. If he's got this far, he's going to be all right!" Schanberg thanked the East German and put the phone down, blinking back the tears that had started after Freund's call. Pran was a survivor, all right—"in the Darwinian sense," as Henri Savarin had written to him after they'd gotten back. This was it. This was what he'd waited to hear.

He toweled off the shaving cream and threw on the first clothes that came to hand—who gave a shit! His sentence of guilt lifted, energy filled him like sap in a leafless tree. He stood by the window and gazed over the morning skyline, drawing the deep breaths of a pardoned criminal, an accessory to a murder that never happened.

He phoned Ser Moeun in San Francisco and heard the joy on the other end of the line as if it were his own the first time. Ser Moeun wanted to know, if the news was this good, why wasn't Pran out already? He probably was, Schanberg assured her. If not, it was just a matter of days. He would go out himself today and bring him home!

But first give him time, just an hour or two, to celebrate.

He raced downstairs, caught a cab to the *Times*, and bought some daffodils, in what order he couldn't remember afterward. He phoned his wife. He left a message for Al Rockoff. He sent his secretary for paper cups. He raided the editor's office for a bottle of champagne, found whiskey, and poured that around instead. Daffodils on the keyboards, daffodils on the floor. . . .

"A toast! I'd like to propose a toast! To the most wonderful East German living. And to any Vietnamese who keeps Pran safe till I get there!"

The Scotch settled on Schanberg's empty stomach like Pentecostal fire. There was so much to say, so much to write! Nothing could keep him back any longer. Picking up a daffodil, he threw it on his secretary's desk. He said, "Book me on the first flight to Bangkok."

The creaking comes nearer. Pran blows out the candle. In the darkness, his five companions are as still as gravestones. He can smell their fear without being able to see it on their faces.

They crouch in the rubble of the ruined house until the stranger on the bicycle is long out of hearing. Perhaps a villager, perhaps a Vietnamese—it makes no difference when you're on the run. Keo, one of Phat's old colleagues in the Bat Dangkor cadre, relights the candle with one of their precious matches. Pran holds it up to the wicker basket to check that Kim is still asleep. Then the six faces bend together over the cotton square of Phat's map. With a broken fingernail, Pran traces the route north through farmland and jungle into the mountains of Odder Mean Chey. Beyond the mountains—Thailand.

This is the journey Pran began in Dam Dek almost a

year ago. As soon as the Vietnamese had given permission for Cambodians to return to their home villages, he left Bat Dangkor and traveled west to Siem Reap to locate what was left of his family. There, he saw the East German, and took the gamble of giving him a message for Sydney.

In Bat Dangkor, he might have gotten away with it. But in Siem Reap, his hometown, there were those who knew him and who envied his survival. One of them informed on him to the Vietnamese governor of Siem Reap. Pran was called in for interrogation.

It was then that he saw there could be no future for his native land. Standing with bowed head as the governor banged his fist on the table and accused him of being politically unclean, tainted with unrevolutionary thoughts, Pran had realized that Cambodia had merely exchanged one despotism for another—milder, for sure, but still ruled by an unbending ideology. Sent away in disgrace, he gave the Vietnamese no time to contemplate a suitable punishment. That same night he made his escape, together with the five people who had planned it with him and the child Phat had left in his care.

They have been on the road three days, taking turns to push the bicycles and carry the boy. At first it was easy: they could mingle with the refugees returning to their homes. But the roads have gotten emptier as they'd pushed on westward. Now there is no traffic on the crumbling roads except for the occasional bicycle or Vietnamese army truck. It is as though they have entered a prohibited zone.

A new-moon night, too dark to risk journeying farther. Pran sleeps fitfully in a roofless corridor. In the morning, he feeds Kim a mash of banana in milk, and they set out again toward the purple rim of mountains in the far distance. The road winds through a burned-out landscape, gouged with bomb craters, spiked with charred trees, lined with the rusting hulks of the tanks, jeeps, and APCs, whose drivers created the wasteland before becoming part of the scrap. Kim stares openmouthed at the jagged, intricate shapes of torn metal and scorched wood: It is a playground of a sort he has never seen before.

Toward midday they come to a town to which only plant life has returned. Half the houses have been leveled; most of the rest are inhabited by vegetation. Roots buckle the pavements and fracture the walls. A banana tree has sprouted in the middle of the road. A shutter bangs, but it is only a gust of wind. Nobody has lived here for five years. Even the dogs and rats have deserted the town—or else been eaten. They walk down the main street in silence, past empty shops with tattered awnings and wreckage of television sets, café tables, washing machines, and an old Renault with wild tapioca growing through its shattered windshield. A gas station has been dynamited and burned to the ground, leaving a rusting Esso sign lodged in a tree. Khmer Rouge graffiti urging evacuation fade on the whitewashed walls of a dynamited hospital. The messages mean nothing any longer. The town is a junkyard trapped in undergrowth—it will never come back to life.

Only once that day are they forced to abandon the road, when a Russian T-62 tank roars past in a cloud of red dust, the flag of the People's Republic of Vietnam flying from its turret. In the early evening, the clouds that have been building all day over the mountains move overhead and release a drenching rain. Pran struggles on, holding a polyethylene sheet over the child on his back. The going gets rougher as the road dwindles into a cart track and begins to wind uphill between eucalyptus trees. Near the top of the hill, they come to a ruined pagoda. Keo enters first, checking for booby traps. The others follow him: it will be their shelter for the night.

The Khmer Rouge have paid this pagoda their usual respect. Half the roof has been shot away. The giant statue of Buddha against the far wall is headless, its torso and squatting legs chipped where the soldiers have used it for target practice. At some time in the past the pagoda has been used as a pigsty—straw and pig's dung litter the floor amid the shards of blue tiles that have fallen from the roof. But the pigs must have been eaten long ago. Birds and bats inhabit the temple now, and the forest has broken in.

Kim has a persistent cough. His forehead is sweating, and his eyes are very dry and bright. Pran wraps the boy in a blanket and lays him in the wicker basket. Quickly they get a fire going with sticks and straw and dried guano. They boil up rice in a cooking pot and chop into it the last of the dried fish brought from Siem Reap. Kim eats a little of it but cannot keep it down. Pran rocks him in his arms and sings him a lullaby. They still have a long way to go, and the trail gets harder.

The others are as tired and drained as he is. Keo, the oldest of them, is probably the most alert. He sits tending the fire, looking into it with hooded eyes. Rong and his wife are snuggled together against the pagoda wall, eyes shut, in attitudes of exhaustion. Rong was at school with Pran near Siem Reap. He married his wife early in 1975, a matter of days before Lon Nol's troops laid down their arms or fled before the Khmer Rouge. Until the arrival of the Vietnamese, Angka had kept them apart. Rong has told him nothing, but Pran suspects that this ardous journey has an unseen purpose—that Rong's wife is pregnant and they want the baby to be born in freedom.

Gently, Pran rocks the boy and watches the huge shadows of Buddha thrown up by the flickering fire. When he crosses the border into Thailand, he will register Kim as his son. In due course he will take him over the sea to America, and Kim will become one of the family, growing up with his own sons and learning to speak English . . . not forgetting his Khmer so that he can go on saying his prayers to the Blessed One. This is the most important . . . but Pran is too tired to finish the thought. He closes his eyes and sleeps, the boy still cradled in his arms.

They are awakened at dawn by the sound of vehicles. Pran hands the child to Keo and creeps out to investigate. Two half-tracks and a convoy of Vietnamese trucks are heading west along the valley road. More anxious discussions over Phat's map, and they decide to make a detour northward to avoid them. Either way it is now a steep and rugged trail, under a blazing sun. Rong's wife is pale, but she refuses assistance. Pran goes in front of her with Kim on his back. Rong and Keo maneuver the bicycles up the narrow path. As they trudge up to a crest in the foothills, they see puffs of smoke on the hill flank opposite, followed by the dull thud of exploding mortars. Evidently, Khmer Rouge resistance fighters are using the last of the dry season to mount a guerrilla attack on the Vietnamese.

It means another change of plans. After a silent meal of coconut milk, cold rice, and the tiny yellow fruit of wild banana trees, they strike out due west across the valley floor. Bicycles are useless in this stifling undergrowth of ferns and marsh plants and tangling lianas—they abandon them and struggle on as best they can. At each place of running water, they stop and salt the leeches off their legs before plunging on.

As they reach higher ground, Keo warns them to be vigilant. Warfare in these frontier mountains is made not with bombs and bullets but with traps and snares. Every step has to be taken with elaborate caution. For another two hours they walk, climbing steadily. Every elevation brings a new one into view ahead. Once they hear the voices of a Khmer Rouge patrol and crouch in the dark green shadows until the danger has passed.

Pran has handed Kim to Rong and taken the lead. A vague darkening of the path at his feet brings him to a sudden stop. With his staff, he knocks the leaves and vegetation away to expose a Punji trap, the oldest and cruelest of the traps in these mountains—a deep hole dug in the path with eighteen-inch sharpened bamboo stakes protruding out of the flooded base to provide an agonizing death for the unwary. Grasping Pran's staff, Keo prods in the bushes until he discovers a safe path around the trap. Rong follows him, Pran goes third, the boy back on his shoulders.

Five yards up the path, he sees the wire as Rong steps on it and screams a warning. Keo and Rong stand motionless for a split second as birds rise slowly into the sky. Then the blast. A screech of monkeys. Rong and Keo dead; Pran falling to his knees with a shrill cry, blood running through his fingers from the shrapnel wound in his side.

The screams go on around him, the blood is on his fingers, he is in Dam Dek with the staves descending.

Dazed and terrified, he clutches Kim and runs into the undergrowth, anywhere, away from the Khmer Rouge. The wire two inches above the ground, the two grenades in tin cans either side of the path . . . it is one of the traps Keo warned them of; now Keo is dead. In shock, crying with the pain in his side, he runs until he can run no farther. None of the group has followed him. He and Kim are alone. Hugging the boy to him he sinks down. . . .

The boy is dead.

This is not something Pran can understand. He lays Kim on the ground and sees where the splinter of shrapnel drove into his neck. But he is confused. He picks the child up and holds him to his bloodstained shirt. Kim's eyes are open, but there is no fear in them. His face is as calm as when he is sleeping in Pran's arms, his father's arms. He must have died instantly. Kim is dead.

Pran kisses him on the forehead and lays him down. Moving painfully, the wound in his side throbbing, he builds a pyre of dry sticks and branches. The sun has gone down by the time he has raised the pyre to waist height. Very tenderly, he lifts the body of his adopted son on top of it and lights the wood with the last of the matches. Only then, as the white smoke rises up through the trees into the dark sky, does Pran give way to tears, the first tears he has shed in all this bitter time. Raising his hands together, he bows his head in farewell.

All night, careless of what enemies will be led to him by the smoke, he stays by the smoldering pyre, offering up prayers to the Lord Buddha for the boy's *karma*, which would some day reexist. In the night wind, the bamboo around him creaks and wails. Shortly after dawn, when the sun has warmed his stiffening side, he starts walking up toward the ridge.

Don't worry. Pran's a survivor. If he's gotten this far . . . But Schanberg was beginning to regret the optimism he had brought duty-free to Bangkok. Each day for a week a taxi had picked him up before dawn from the Hotel Oriental and taken him to one of the refugee camps huddled on this side of the mountain frontier with Kampuchea. Each day it had delivered him back empty-handed, with the same answer from officials and relief agency workers: "We've had no one through from Siem Reap."

He yawned and looked with bleary eyes out of the taxi window. In the early-morning light it might have been the Phom Penh road to Battambang. White clouds streaked with yellow scudded across a huge sky. On either side of the banked-up road, shoots of green rice speared through the still water. Maybe he should have waited in New York for confirmation that Pran was out. . . .

But he'd had to come, he'd had to make his presence known along the border. The Thais disliked the Khmers at the best of times—in particular, they disliked Khmer refugees. If Pran arrived alone, without contacts in the camps to get him legally registered, he would probably join the thousands of refugees whom the Thai government had recently pushed back over the frontier into Khmer Rouge–occupied Kampuchea. One way or another, Schanberg had to be here. At the very least, he had to find a refugee from Siem Reap who might be able to tell him if Pran was alive or dead.

The mirror-flat landscape began to swell with high ridges as the hills approached. Surin, he had been told, was one of the bigger camps, more established than some of the wretched places he'd visited this week—single-roomed bamboo hovels on low stilts around a narrow track axle-deep in mud.

These were the camps in which a hundred or more people died every day from malaria and malnutrition and were buried in common graves. The Khmer Rouge "resistance forces" plundered them at will, coming down from their mountain enclaves to steal the food provided by the relief agencies, buy new weaponry from Thai arms dealers, and kidnap young refugee boys for guerrilla training. Nobody stopped them. Pol Pot's murderers were recognized— were they not?—by the United States and England as the legitimate government of Kampuchea. The red flag of the Khmer Rouge flew over the United Nations building in New York as it had flown over the death camps of its own people.

The road had started to snake upward through boulder-strewn, thinly wooded hills. Sunlight sparkled on the strip of gold foil at the top of the taxi's windshield; Schanberg remembered Pran telling him how the Buddhist taxi drivers took their new cabs to be blessed by the temple priest who draped flowers on the front bumper and provided the foil to ward off evil spirits. That custom would have been killed off in Kampuchea, along with half the population. He had brought with him to Thailand details of the 1979 census released by the Vietnamese: out of 11,000 students, 450 left alive after the Khmer Rouge terror; 207 secondary school teachers out of 2,300; 5,300 of their pupils out of more than 100,000 before April 1975 . . . and just five journalists left alive in the whole country. The figures could be dismissed as Vietnamese propaganda if indepen-

284

dent reports from the refugees hadn't confirmed the almost impossible scale of the catastrophe.

Clouds were beginning to mass over the distant mountains. Schanberg sat forward. The taxi clambered over a ridge and started its descent into a wide green valley that nosed deep into the hills. At the far end, Surin Refugee Camp sprawled in an untidy confusion of alleys and longhouses, the sun glinting off corrugated iron roofs daubed with the markings of UNICEF and the International Red Cross. Outside the barbed-wire fences were neat rows of gardens. Schanberg's spirits lifted slightly: only in Khao-I-Dang, the four-star Red Cross transit camp, had he seen more prosperous surroundings. Nervously, he got out his identification document with its photograph stamped SURIN. The relief worker who had made it out for him last night in Bangkok had smiled and shrugged. "No harm in trying," she'd said, "but we've heard there are bodies every half-mile on that route out over the border."

A coach went past them from the camp, then a heavy refrigerated truck blinding the road with dust. There could be up to forty thousand people penned behind the Surin wire. As usual, at the military checkpoint, a Thai officer checked his ID before raising the barrier and waving them through to the administration block. As usual, Schanberg felt his stomach contract and the sweat break out on his temples as he went up the steps into a cool, whitewashed room. The girl was busy; he lit a cigarette and stared at the travel posters on the walls. Singapore . . . New York . . . Paris . . . destinations that to most of the inhabitants of Surin would be no more than a taunting dream. Even in the transit camp of Khao-I-Dang, physically rehabilitated and ready to move on, many of the refugees had already spent four years of their lives and would spend many more. If ever he came to publish the story of all this, places like Surin and Khao-I-Dang would still hold more refugees than all the words he could put on paper.

"Mr. Schanberg?" The girl at the desk looked Thai, but her accent was pure New Yorker.

"Yes." His throat was dry. "I've come a long way. I hope you can help me. I'm looking for a Cambodian refugee. His name is Dith Pran."

The girl consulted a card index. She shook her head. "I'm sorry. We've no record of a Dith Pran. When did he cross the border?"

Schanberg hardly heard her question. For the first time, he began to admit to himself what all along he had refused to believe—that Pran might not have made it. "Don't know," he mumbled. "Maybe a week or two."

She shrugged. "We have a few recent arrivals without clearance papers, waiting to be sent back over the frontier. That's D Section. House numbers 14 to 18."

"Okay. Thank you for your help."

She saw the way Schanberg looked and accompanied him to the door with the sympathetic touch of a doctor consoling the bereaved. Outside, a swarm of young children, attracted by the Bangkok taxicab, held up wooden knick-knacks for him to buy: a three-legged stool; a dumpy bird on a perch. Some, grinning hopefully, just held out their hands. The New York girl began to speak; Schanberg stopped her.

"I know what you're going to tell me," he said tiredly. "To not encourage them to think I'm going to take them home."

He got into the taxi. The children scampered after him

for a few yards, then fell away. They drove through some gates in an inner fence, down one street and then another, stopping to ask directions. Each time children pressed up to the car, some hobbling on crutches, while the adults, a few still in black pajamas, sat on their doorsteps and stared out with lifeless faces. A line he'd read somewhere came back to him: *"The struggle of men against tyranny is the struggle of memory against pain."* For these lined faces, the pain was too terrible to bear remembering; they had blanked out the past and, in doing so, had blanked out any expectation of a future that could be better than this living death.

The question. How did you raise a people from the dead?

More directions. They came at last to a narrow street where there were no children. A water tower reared like a guardpost at the far end. Schanberg got out of the car and had the taxi driver speak to an old man sitting at a bamboo table.

Somebody came out of the longhouse opposite and hobbled across the road—an odd-looking figure in tattered blue trousers and a bloodstained shirt. The figure stopped. Schanberg looked at him and looked again. He opened wide his arms, and the man reached into them, his head pressed into Schanberg's shoulder, his frail body shaking with sobs. Schanberg clasped him, not quite believing, pressing him closer, tears of joy running down his face.

"I'm so sorry," Schanberg said.

"It's okay. You came," said Dith Pran. "Sydney, you came."